Coming Home Again

T.I. LOWE

ISBN -10: 1511641401
ISBN-13: 978-1511641401

DEDICATION

I dedicate this book to anyone who has lost himself or herself. Hoping you will be found soon.

In memory of those who were unable to be found.

17.7 million American women have been victims of attempted or completed rape.

—National Institute of Justice and Centers for Disease Control and Prevention

33% of rape victims have suicidal thoughts.

13% of rape victims will attempt suicide.

—2002 National Crime Victimization Survey

BOOKS BY T.I. LOWE

Lulu's Café

Goodbyes & Second Chances

A Bleu Streak Christmas

A Bleu Streak Summer

Julia's Journey

A Discovery of Hope

Orange Blossom Café

Orange Blossom Bride

The Reversal

Until I Do

Until I Don't

ACKNOWLEDGMENTS

Always a big thank you to my readers. Without your enthusiastic cheering, I may not continue to be brave enough. You make me brave.

My Lowe and Stevens Bunch for putting up with my daydreaming. Love you all.

To my author sister, Christina Coryell, thanks for being so supportive and generous with your abundant advice.

My beta readers—Sally Anderson, Trina Cooke, Lynn Edge, and Jennifer Strickland. Thanks for having this ole girl's back. Your input and support are beyond appreciated.

My heavenly Father, you get all the credit for these stories. Thank you for allowing me to share you and your incredible love through these stories.

Dancing With the Devil

I lost myself. Where did I go? Can I find myself? I just don't know…

This is the most perfect evening, on a perfect seashore, with a perfect man. Everything. Is. Perfect.

The gentle lull of the ocean, complemented by the velvety white beach, emits a natural calming effect, and I greedily breathe in the peace. Tilting my head slightly, I regard the tranquil ribbons of silver moonlight, showering over us in spectacular bands, in awe. A delicious shiver evoked by the cool night air caresses my body and dances with the soft, gauzy layers of my evening gown to its own melody. I feel beautiful and feminine with my hair spilling in indulgent curls down my open back.

Loved… I am loved.

Contentment settles over me as I admire this stunning being accompanying me tonight. Sultry, clear eyes watch me possessively in the cascading moonlight—observing my every movement. His unbuttoned white shirt undulates in the light breeze, beckoning my attention to the exposed, well-built form of his chest and the marvelous flat plains of his abdomen. My focus trails all the way down to the dangerously low-riding black tuxedo pants, which seem to be grasping just barely to the V of his lean hips. He is exotic, and I am unable to do anything but openly appreciate him. The heat of his stare engulfs me as my gaze begins a long, slow journey back to that beautifully sculpted face, where I see approval in his eyes. He relishes in being admired, and I want nothing more than to do just that. My hands sweep through his thick, dark hair, testing the silkiness of the texture as our bare feet leisurely kick up the powdery sand while we dance. I feel safe, cherished, and completely desired.

An addictive tingle ripples through me in sheer delight when he finally wraps his arms around me and pulls our bodies closer. Resting my head on his strong chest during this unending dance, I listen to the even and restful beat of his heart. The sound of it is like a perfectly orchestrated lullaby, and I am spellbound by it.

As the enchanting lullaby plays on, this magnificent man tilts my head with his gentle hand and studies my every feature. He slowly leans down and warms the sensitive skin along my neck with his soft lips. He whispers praises of how perfect I am, how he desires only me, how I am the most perfect rose he has ever seen. Then, when I feel that my heart can't take any more anticipation, he rewards me with a kiss that I have longed for all night. The kiss begins as light as a faint whisper fluttering over my lips—gradually building as he gently nips at my bottom lip, teasingly. He presents his lips to mine for a kiss so full of desire and urgency that it reflects the passion along my body in flickers of warmth.

We continue to dance and to love for a long, beautiful spell. The intensity grows until it is overbearing and I start to feel curiously odd, as if some alarm demands me to protect myself. But I can't grasp how or why to do that.

His taste grows from sinfully sweet to bitterly sour, causing me to gag against his mouth. Panic ricochets violently over me as I push away, but his gentle hands have become uncomfortably tight. I find myself trapped in his grasp. Sharp stings attack my back as his nails penetrate. I try to cry out in pain and terror but I am being suffocated from his lips overwhelming my own. My lungs burn and squeeze as I fight against the attack until he abruptly ceases the torture. Confusion blurs my understanding and I try unsuccessfully to blink it away. As I look up to question why this majestic man would do such a thing, a piercing fear slices through me. My companion is gone, and an ugly beast has taken his place.

Terror engulfs me from the vulgar transformation. His glowing skin is now tarnished with sickly, rough, brown patches and is scored with unhealed scars oozing grotesquely. Those delicate hands that caressed me tenderly just mere minutes ago have now turned into hideous claws. His scaly talons strike out and tear my beautiful gown savagely into shreds. I am frozen in the sand by fear and cannot escape or protect myself. Violent tremors are the only movement evoked from my body.

Suddenly, he begins pushing and pulling at me in some type of horrendous dance. Every touch riddles my body with searing burns and throbbing blisters. A muted sob vibrates from my throat as I take in the thick blood slowly seeping down my bare thighs in wet streams. More confusion riddles me at the sight of my long brown curls scattering over the sand. Panicking, my hand flies to my head and I can only feel scaly, bald patches.

Hated... I am hated.

I scream out in anguish, but no sound arises from my mouth. I have no voice.

Defeated awareness cinches my stomach, causing rancorous acid to scorch my throat as I realize dancing with this beast will have a deadly consequence. His clear eyes have spun to a vicious red and now he watches me in a revolting way—making me feel dirty and repulsive. He is growling out with laughter at me. Mocking me.

I tear my gaze away from his revolting form to search for help but only discover the moon bleeding a scornful shade of scarlet and the inky-black ocean crashing against the shore in a bitter attack, wave after wave. Even the powdery sand has turned on me and is now pricking and tearing the soles my bare feet. I study it in bafflement and find it to be shards of glass.

Angry... Everything is angry.

Lightening slashes hatefully through the sky and thunder screams in aggravation as I mutely beg for help. *Please someone. Please save me. Please...*

I'm trying to pull my arm out of his grasp when I realize it has withered to resemble a dead vine. More attempted screaming. Still no voice. I'm in agony, and my heart is beating in an erratic pattern so intense it pounds harshly in my ears. Surely, I will die in this beast's arms. I even beg death to claim me. I need relief. I need this to stop. Now! I've danced a dance with death, yet only excruciating pain claims me. I can find no relief.

I continue my attempted screams in agony, voiceless, until finally the volume begins slowly rising in my vocal chords as I'm released from the nightmare. Suddenly awake, I bolt up in a sitting position in my bed, shaking in a cold sweat. I hold myself tightly to discourage my trembling and rock back and forth.

It was only a dream… It's okay... He is dead... He can't hurt you anymore… It was only a dream... He's dead… He can't hurt you anymore… It was only a dream…

Chapter One

Dear Friends,
It would be an honor for you to join us for a
Night of Fabulous Food
And a Celebration of Friendship
On the Evening of…

Dear Friends,
I would like to apologize for not being able to carry on.
Please forgive…

The Evening's Menu
Smoked Gouda Canapés
Watercress and Endive Salad
Lobster Stuffed…

My earthly possessions are few but should belong to…

Dessert Menu

Fresh Strawberries and Dark Chocolate Mousse…

I cannot fight the demons any longer…

With the ghosts of failures past and the demons of my history dancing nonstop today, nothing feels right. My mind is such a terribly confused place. All I want is some peace, and offing myself seems to be the only way to obtain it. I beg the demons to hush up! *Focus, Savannah.* Reluctantly, I pull the dinner invitation back on the screen, hiding the suicide note underneath so I can try once again to focus on the planning.

Tucked away in the den of my beachfront condo, I slouch at the desk with my eyes continuously sweeping from my laptop screen to the dreamy views of the Atlantic Ocean outside my window. It's early, and the sun has just begun its morning meeting with the sky. Warm rays are glistening off the ocean waves so serenely. This is the same ocean I grew up loving, but it is a great deal farther north from the beaches of South Carolina. Rhode Island's coastal water never seems to warm enough for leisure hours in the surf for my southern blood except for only a short window of time each summer. It's satisfying enough for me to just be able to see the beauty of the majestic creation anytime I see fit. I give the view a little bit more of my attention, but with a sigh, I place my focus back to the computer screen. *Focus, Savannah.*

Another dinner party should be a breeze for me by now. I should be excited, right? This is what successful CEO wives pride themselves on accomplishing with perfection. Right?

I don't mean to sound so bratty, nor do I want to be difficult. But honestly, a fancy dinner party hostess I am not. I'd rather have a tooth pulled over getting all fancied up and serving fancy food. Glancing down at my comfortable loose-fit jeans and long-sleeve T-shirt, I cannot help but chuckle. Sure, I have a closet full of fancies, but they are not me.

Who am I, exactly? It's a question I have to ask myself a little too often. Today, my answer would be a resounding, "I haven't the earthliest idea." I've lost myself at some vague point along the way and am having the hardest time tracking down that elusive being.

If you ask my mother, she would gladly tell you that I am a stubborn, smart-mouthed procrastinator who rarely follows through with anything.

Don't listen to her!

Well…she may be right, just a little. The only thing I am sure about is God made a mistake. Yes, He did! I was a mistake, and my mother would agree. I'll explain later. Maybe… I'll try to get around to it. You might need to remind me, though.

The broken record of *I'm lost…I'm bored…I'm worthless…I'm confused…*is on a repeat and won't leave me the heck alone. I'm at my wits' end with myself, and that is why I'm wrestling with the decision to just autopilot another stupid smile-until-it-hurts dinner party. Or, should I just bite the proverbial bullet and write the dang suicide note already?

Overwhelmed. *I'm so overwhelmed...*

As I rise from the desk, my anxious legs drag my body in a nervous pace around the den. I skim my hand along the back of the plush couch as I pass it while thoughts of a nap flicker. I don't sleep well, no matter if it's day or night. I abandon the nap idea by the couch and pace some more. As I take a deep, cleansing breath, the rich aroma of coffee assails me. I glance towards the kitchen. *Maybe a third cup*. No. This idea is dismissed as well. My insides are already jumping and hopping in a restless torment, and more caffeine will only make it worse. I wring my hands to smooth the trembles out. It ain't working.

"Argh!" I yell, trying to relieve some of the built-up frustration. I wish I could take a break from myself. *I could really use a break…*

With this thought, my eyes glance back over to the computer where the hidden document calls out to me. *Just hit print. You can do it…*

I sort of have the suicide planned out. I should probably keep this to myself… Yes… No… Okay. I've gone as far as to purchase three bottles of sleeping pills. They are tucked away in the back of my vanity, waiting patiently. I don't sleep well, so I thought this would be the perfect way to go. A nice, deep sleep sounds heavenly. My eyes grow heavy and my mouth waters for a pill right this very moment. Fatigue weighs down on me so heavily; I have to plop on the couch. My eyes drift shut but too many demons attack in the darkness of it, so I have to pry them back open.

I demand my focus to shift toward the silver picture frames littering the coffee table with hopes of pulling up a good memory, but my eyes land on a poor choice. It's us in our small aluminum boat. It's the very same boat I plan on taking out as far as I can in the ocean before popping the pills. I don't want to stain our home with the memory of my death. Lucas doesn't deserve that. My sweet husband deserves better than me. Most days, I can almost talk myself into taking that boat ride but, of course, I'm a procrastinator and keep putting it off.

With all this nonsense whirling around in my confused mind, I'm thinking a quick walk down the coast is in order. I just want the demons to stop dancing for a while. Maybe I can outrun them for a spell.

Easing back over to the computer, I hesitantly delete the suicide note and save the invitation instead. I feel good about this decision for now. As I power down my laptop, the phone begins to taunt me with its annoying ring. I'm not much of a phone person. Chitchat isn't my thing. As I glance at the hour on the wall clock curiously, I have no idea who would be bothering me this early in the day. It's not quite seven in the morning. I catch a glimpse at the number displayed on the phone and it nearly sends me right back to composing my suicide note.

Caller ID can do that, as I'm sure you know.

The area code is from a region located about five states south of me and has sent my will to live crashing down. Talk about perfect timing.

~ ~ ~

Forcing myself to head towards the one place I have avoided for the past several years, all I can think about is how it's going to feel to come home again. Home is the wrong word. Personal hell is a better description. Why would someone willingly go back to a place such as this? No other way around it, I suppose.

Home is Bay Creek. It is a small touristy town located on the eastern coast of South Carolina. You have the indulgence of the warm, sandy beaches and the unending view of a vigorous ocean. The appeal of nearby farmland and the sleepy little beach town makes for many an ideal place to settle down and raise a family. Not for me. It holds too many nightmares. As soon as the opportunity presented itself, I escaped with not so much as one glance back. But look at me now—Savannah Monroe, a terrified twenty-eight-year-old girl heading home again.

Before I can wrap my mind around what's happened, I have packed my bag and am heading towards the most colossal challenge of my life. Sliding into my car, I poise the keys towards the ignition. "Come on Savannah. You *have* to do this." Before I can change my mind, I cram the keys into their slot and twist the car to life. Taking a deep breath, I put the car in drive. With trembling hands, I pull out into traffic with a churning combination of determination and trepidation to begin my unexpected trek home.

I hope you don't mind too terribly that I'm sharing my story with you. You seem like such a polite listener, and honestly, I think it's time. Well, I guess we best be on with it.

Chapter Two

As the miles pass by, the interstate becomes a haze of memories, and memories are such a tricky thing. You can try to distort them and even try to completely forget about them, but it's hopeless. They are what they are, and you just can't get rid of the dang things. Sometimes I find myself drifting back in time and have to slam the door on it quickly. Nothing is ever accomplished digging around in the buried past. That's what my grandmother always said. She said it could only cause more hurt, and I can assure you I have had my fill of that mess.

Unfortunately, there is no holding the past back on this day. So much is awaiting my arrival, and my heart keeps urging me to prepare. Panic starts to creep up on me with the first signs of sweaty palms and fluttering heartbeat. I begin taking long, deep breaths to try to push the unease away. I ain't got time for this today. Before I can totally lose it, my phone comes to life and snaps me out of the attack. Tamping down the anxiety, I reach for my phone. *Please, don't be any more bad news.*

Checking the Caller ID, I find this number not so scary, and my finger easily presses ACCEPT. "Hey. Don't be mad." Guilt of leaving abruptly washes over me. "I don't have any other choice."

"You always have another choice, love. You know I would have gone with you." The pity is clear in Lucas's voice. It's a quiet voice that is incredibly strong. "I love you."

"I love you too. I'm gonna have to call you back later. Right now I need to focus on driving forward." I don't wait for a response. I hit END on the keypad and toss my phone onto the passenger seat. All he would have had to say is *come back to me,* and I have no doubt I would have obeyed. Today, that cannot be an option.

Maybe one would think I'm overreacting to my past. Maybe I am. I'll probably share more of the past later, so you can be the judge. I mean, who really thinks happy thoughts about their past? Heartache, embarrassment, regrets—these are part of a past's makeup, right? This is what I've told myself many times, but I don't believe it for one minute. Do I blame the usual suspect? Absolutely! I blame my mother. Jean is at fault, and there is no changing my mind on the matter. So please don't even try.

I suppose you want to know a bit more about her. I guess you deserve that, but please don't expect too much. Most of what I know about my mother is hearsay. And I'm only going to tell it once, so take note.

The sneer she always had, special just for me, flickers through my mind and I cannot control the grimace that creeps over my face. My mother is an absolute knockout with silky blonde hair and bright blue eyes, but those exquisite eyes never held an ounce of kindness for me. The aging hands of time seem to have no effect on her, no matter that too many cocktails and cigarettes have been her main diet staples. I've not laid eyes on her in quite some time, but I guarantee she still looks the same. We shall see shortly. Ugh. Thinking about seeing that woman again sends pure dread to the pit of my stomach. My left hand releases the steering wheel and clutches my stomach as I hope to push the pangs of uneasiness away. *Hold it together, Savannah.*

My mother was sixteen years old the first time my father laid eyes on her, and he has never seen anything else out of those eyes since. John Paul

Thorton II was smitten immediately that summer when a young Jean entered his family-owned restaurant, The Thorton Seafood House. He was busing tables and nearly dropped the dish bin as he spotted her—his words, not mine.

He used to proudly recount how he had walked up to her table, where she was dining on fresh broiled shrimp with her parents, and welcomed them to Bay Creek. He would often tease my mother on how she wouldn't even acknowledge the charming busboy. That didn't deter him. No. He was adamant about meeting the most beautiful woman to ever step foot in Bay Creek. I've seen plenty of photos of Jean to know he wasn't exaggerating. My mother's beauty is the type to spawn jealousy in the most self-secure of females. It's really not fair.

It only took Jean until the next day to find out the goods on John. While sunbathing on the beach, a group of teenage girls filled her in on the fact that John was an only child and his parents not only owned The Thorton Seafood House, but also owned The Thorton Seafood Market next door to it.

Thus, the epic love story of my parents began. Jean agreed to marry my father right after she graduated high school, thinking life with a successful businessman would be a piece of cake.

Married life was nothing like Jean expected, and

she had no qualms on sharing her disappointment over the years. She never could figure out exactly what she needed to make herself happy and always looked to her husband to figure it out for her. Of course, he failed miserably.

My father simply wanted them to be a team, with Jean working alongside him in the family-owned businesses. She had other plans, and he gladly let her do as she pleased. He only wanted her happy, no matter what it took.

My mother's only redeeming quality is she is an absolute culinary genius. Give her a few ingredients and she can produce a masterpiece. Her creations dominate the menu at the restaurant. Her famous spicy shrimp and grits dish is the bestseller to this day. I'm rolling my eyes because, honestly, complimenting my mother leaves a bad taste in my mouth. It's something I don't take too kindly to doing.

Jean eventually decided that maybe a baby would make her happy. This delighted my father to no end. He had tried to talk her into it from the start of their marriage, but she had her reservations.

Almost nine months after her decision, a beautiful baby girl named Julia Rose Thorton was born. She looked just like Jean, with bright blue eyes and curly blonde hair.

The fairytale of motherhood ended as soon as the first not-so-beautiful diaper occurred. This had my father scurrying to find a nanny.

A year after Julia's birth, Jean became pregnant again. She had promised my father a son, and she wanted the whole "growing a family" business behind her as soon as possible.

John Paul Thorton III was born with the exact blue eyes and nearly white-blond hair as my mother and sister. My parents had the perfect family. With a nanny by her side, Jean spent most of the family's time between the beach and the family businesses. Life was good for them for nearly three solid years until the unfortunate mistake happened.

Jean was devastated when she discovered she was pregnant for the third time. My parents were content with two children and had decided that was enough. *I'm* smart enough to know what it takes to prevent more children. I guess they were a bit naïve. That's what they get, if you ask me.

My mother has told this story more than once over the years. Cue the violins. She stayed utterly miserable for the entire sentence of the pregnancy. I weighed in at birth over a pound more than my siblings weighed and have never lived that one down either. She says I caused her hideous stretch marks that ruined her perfect abdomen. Well, let me just say for the record, I have seen that abdomen in a bikini over the years, and it looks flawless to me.

"You were already giving me a hard time before you were even born." She would complain on and on about this in her whiny drawl. Scarlett O'Hara has nothing on my mother. "I stayed sick the entire time. On top of that, you decided to be a week late. No surprise with your procrastinating self."

I was born a procrastinator and really haven't ever been motivated to get over it. So I like to take my time. What's the big deal? I've been witness to poor choices being made in haste over the years and really want no part in that.

Jean never really shared much with me about her life, but she had no trouble articulating her disappointment in me. Never letting me forget. Never forgiving me.

To emphasize the mistake point, I also look nothing like my perfect family. I take after my father's side, with grey eyes and dark brown hair. I have the height and dark complexion, but that is where the similarities end. I guess that deemed me unfit for a "J" name, so I have an "S" name. Who knows what the symbolism of that is? I could guess a few reasons, but what's the point? I really don't care enough to figure that one out.

Brushing my rebellious hair behind my ear, I scan

the congested interstate. Summer is not the time to have to head down south on the fly. It's full-blown vacation season… Ugh… Another memory reaches over and pokes me harshly in the side, feeling like a thorn pricking me. I actually jolt with the pain of it.

I took too much out of my mother with my unwelcomed presence. So before I turned nine months old, she took her first of many extended *vacations*. She was gone nearly a month before my father tracked her down in Virginia. He had to plead with her to come home, promising to hire a housekeeper as well. She hesitantly agreed to come back. This is when a bottle of wine and a pack of cigarettes were what it took to get Jean through the day. I've had a few heart-to-heart conversations with some of the staff at my dad's two businesses. They seem to find some satisfaction in sharing unpleasant things about Jean. I'm not the only one she rubs wrong.

I've not needed anyone to fill me in on some things, though. I have known from the get-go that I was a mistake. Maybe God had an off day or something. All I know is He made a mistake. Sadly, I wasn't the only one.

Only a few years into my mistake of a life, another tragedy hit our family. Jean's cousin, Rena died of a drug overdose. Rena was the black sheep of my mother's family, so her son had to wear the scarlet letter as well. Sadly, a five-year-old Bradley was found lying next to his dead mother. People say he sat beside her lifeless body for two days before a neighbor found them. My heart squeezes too tight at this thought, and I have to rub my chest to loosen the pain's grip.

Bradley was only a few months older than my brother John Paul, so family members encouraged my parents to take the poor boy in. They all thought he would adjust better with us. Reluctantly, my parents agreed. My dad was quick to get the adoption complete, even though Jean bickered about the senselessness of it. My dad took pride in making Bradley a Thorton.

Bradley and I had a few things in common. We seemed to both be unwanted guests in Jean Thorton's household. He didn't too much fit in either, with his unruly red hair and green eyes. His fair skin took a beating with our many beach excursions. Jean always had a hard time remembering sunscreen. Her excuse was that it was all she could do to keep herself straight with having to raise four rowdy children. Whatever. Eyes are rolling, because I remember the presence of maids and babysitters much more than I remember Jean's presence. The word *babysitter* inflicts its own unique pain, and I recoil away from it before it can leave another mark.

In the years that followed Bradley joining our family, our house was filled with too much noise, too little love, and too many vacations for Jean.

Enough with the thorny Thorton family tree. I'm sick of the dang thing poking me. It's on the verge of drawing blood. I don't want to think about that anymore, and I'm sure you've heard enough. I need to focus on the demons dancing and try to figure out a way to get them to stop once and for all.

Chapter Three

After several hours driving down this unwelcoming paved path, I am completely over the idea of going back home. It's late in the afternoon, and I'm sick of being trapped in the confines of this blame car. I start scanning the green signs for an appealing exit, and it only takes another half hour to find one. It's a beach exit, and I can hardly wait to bury my feet in the warm sand. I ease my car into a public beach access lot, and my lungs are already craving the savory Atlantic air. After killing the engine, I slip off my shoes, grab my phone, and take off towards the beckoning waves that call me in whooshes and muted rumbles. As my feet find the sizzling beach surface, I shoot Julia a text. *Where r u? R u on ur way?* I wait a few moments for a reply. As always, it goes unanswered. I send Lucas one next, letting him know I am okay and taking a rest stop.

I walk down the coast for a good stretch, trying to work out the kinks in my back and legs from traveling in the cramped car. I take several deep breaths of the warm, salty air as I check out the beach scene. It's pretty packed with vacationers. Virginia has gorgeous beaches, and this one is lined with a welcoming boardwalk, unlike the beach back home in South Carolina. My home beach is lined with beach houses and condos. The breeze is quite warm and whips my long hair in my face. I shuck off the lightweight hoodie I had to put on before leaving Rhode Island and twist my hair into a knot. Relief is instant with alleviating the stifling hair off my neck. The breeze scoots back by and tickles the newly exposed skin, allowing me a contented sigh.

My body is overheating almost immediately. I have an overwhelming desire to shuck my clothes and dive in, but restrain from doing so. Instead, I yank up my sleeves and roll my pants legs up before strolling over to the shore to test the temperature of the ocean. It's heavenly and refreshing on my scorched feet. I love the texture of the squishy wet sand as the tide washes it between my toes. I stand here until I've sunk enough that my feet are now hidden and probably intruding on some hermit crab's home.

If I ever felt like I belonged anywhere, it has to be on a sandy beach or in the saltwater. I'm an average surfer. Or I was the last time I rode a wave, and that was well over five years ago, closer to six, I think. Maybe I'm considered an ex-surfer now, but I still feel the want running through my veins though. I was never as good as my brother or Bradley, but I could hold my own. In my defense, they had a better teacher than I did. I was self-taught. The brief thought of their teacher stings and sends an ache through my stomach.

Weakness subdues me all of a sudden. I push my way out of the water and plop down in a dry vacant spot on the sand to stare at the ocean. Looking out over the crashing waves, I notice the ocean seems right agitated today. It keeps growling at me, and after a while, I growl back. The foul mood is in the air, I do believe. I stand my ground and glare back at the moody tempest of the Atlantic Ocean. Farther out, the sky is bruised with deep purples and black. Although that storm is far away, I can see its effect on the sunny beach. People around me are taking notice and seem to be hesitant on their next move. Stay or go? Be cautious or pay no mind to it?

I'm wrestling with my own storm. Stay? Or go? Be cautious? Or pay no mind to it? Memories tap me on the shoulder and whisper in the breeze. *Remember me? I've not gone anywhere. Remember?*

A car crash or a fatal heart attack is an instant mind-numbing catastrophe. Immediate and sharp is the pain, and your mind refuses any comprehension of it. Sometimes a tragedy slips in unnoticed for an unmeasured period. By the time you give notice to this devious disaster, it has already done its irreversible damage. Like a disease, it's relentless and selfish as it snakes its poison in hidden crevices until everything is infected.

Evan Grey was an invisible tragedy. He brought so much light into our dysfunctional family, and that light consumed everyone. They were so fascinated by the wonder of it that the darkness seeped right in without detection.

It's easy to be so starved for attention to the point of becoming addicted to it, if ever given the opportunity. Dad had no attention to spare between Jean and the businesses, and Jean used all of her attention on herself. Her family would describe her as spoiled. I would just say she's rotten.

Evan walked into our family one afternoon with an abundant supply of attention and gave to each one of us children generously. He spent hours upon hours showing the boys how to throw a curveball, bait a fishing hook, and how to ride the perfect wave. To us girls, he gave us a listening ear and unwavering affection.

How did this young man enter our lives? I blame it all on Jean, of course.

~ ~ ~

"Children! Come meet our new friend," Jean shouted from downstairs.

Julia and I were sorting our cassette tapes, arguing over who was the true pop queen. I believed it to be none other than Cyndi Lauper, and Julia insisted that Madonna should hold the title. I could hear the boys down the hall, sounding like they were about to come through the wall. Sounds reminiscent of a demolition site came from their direction, which was nothing unusual.

We convened in the hallway and headed downstairs to meet whomever our mother had dragged home this time. Standing at the foot of the stairs was none other than Adonis in the flesh. This god of beauty and desire had golden-brown hair and ice blue eyes that seemed almost clear. His skin seemed to glow with a bronzed tone.

Jean waved her perfectly manicured hand in his direction. "This is Evan. He will be keeping an eye on you every now and then, so I can run errands," she said with her southern drawl a bit thicker, as usual, when in the company of a man. Errands to Jean meant beauty appointments and lunch dates with her girlfriends. She didn't have any of us fooled.

"Momma, I think we can keep an eye on ourselves." John Paul bucked up, trying to sound gown-up in front of our new guest. Bradley stood a bit taller, mimicking our brother.

"I agree. Talking your father into that is another story," Jean said. For some reason, our father was always adamant on not letting us stay home unattended. He said too many mindless accidents happened when children were left alone. *He had no idea.*

Evan didn't seem bothered by our disappointment. He simply smiled as he gave the boys a manly handshake and slap on the back, using what reminded me of a coach-like gesture with his players. The boys told him their names and then shot back upstairs to continue to do who knows what in their room. I stood listening to the banging and hoped I could escape soon, too.

Evan approached us girls next while our mother introduced us. The gentle hug he gave Julia caused a girly giggle to slip from her prissy lips. "It's nice to meet you ladies."

Evan then turned towards me, but I dodged the

hug with a quick side step out of his reach. Physical contact was not something I had much experience with and had no desire to receive it from a stranger. Even before the disease of things to come began festering, I was already adverse to people intruding in my personal space. Sure, Dad would give us the one-armed side hug every now and then, but that was very rare. When Jean was around, she required and obtained all of his attention.

"Now Miss Savannah, that was terribly rude," Jean snapped. She turned her attention to Evan. "She's my youngest and a bit feistier than the others."

She cut her eyes towards me to make sure I was listening.

"She is what you would call an unplanned surprise."

She said this like the words tasted sour on her tongue. My mother always felt the need to share that tidbit with every new person that came along. It was like she always wanted everyone to know the burden I was on her. I guess she didn't want me to forget it either. Trust me. I never have.

I rolled my eyes in my older sister's direction, and she returned the gesture to me. She was on my side back then. My throat thickens as I wish that were still true.

"Oh, I enjoy feisty." Evan laughed. "That will

keep me on my toes."

He winked in my direction, making my face flash heatedly in a blush. Yep. He was definitely Adonis.

Evan had recently moved to Bay Creek to attend his senior year of college and to be close to the beach. He was an avid surfer and would have been on the west coast but his grades weren't up to par and, as punishment, his dad would not send him. Bay Creek was their compromise. When asked what his major was, he would reply with a smirk that *Fun* was his major. He didn't take school seriously, hence the poor grades. He came from old money that came cushioned with a trust fund, so he had no worries in the financial department.

Evan would normally hang out with us once or twice a week after Jean dragged him in our lives that naïve day. The boys took up most of his time in the beginning. Most days, they would disappear to the beach, the batting cages, or to the pier. I enjoyed all those activities, but Julia and I were always stuck at home doing an endless list of chores.

He would abandon the boys every now and then to help us out. It was great. He would let us watch all of the MTV we wanted, and we would spend afternoons dancing around the living room to the latest jams.

Things were great in the beginning, as most

things are. It only took a few months for the darkness to become evident. The disease would be irreparable, leaving lifelong side effects that would be debilitating at times or a nagging, festering sore so easily aggravated at other times.

~ ~ ~

My phone pings with a new text, bringing me back to the now. I'm hoping it's from Julia but am not surprised that it's not. It's from Lucas. *Just come back home.* I want to send back that I don't know where that is exactly. I decide to ignore it instead. There is no need in worrying him with my demons. And those suckers are dancing full force today.

Don't get me wrong. I love Rhode Island and its charming living. Nothing is cookie-cutter there. Homes and businesses are unique and sturdy in their ample age. The place feels rich with history. There are always festivals and activities on the horizon. This northern home has provided many an adventure since I had arrived. There has been an abundance of savory lobster rolls and rich clam chowder consumed, just let me tell you. My stomach arouses awareness with a snippy growl as I have these thoughts. *Growl all you want.* I can barely swallow my acrid emotions today, much less food. Ignoring my hunger, I picture the house Lucas and I have worked hard at making a home. Our home.

I'm crazy about our home. It is firmly planted on the shore as though its roots have been maturing over centuries, so it can weather any storm wanting to stir up ruckus. Adirondack chairs sitting patiently in the small yard, and cedar shake siding lends a beach cottage impression to our condo. It's a homey place that seems to always be welcoming guests to come grow a sit, and the waters paint an ever-evolving coastal portrait for them to admire. I love it, but I feel as though I am only a visitor, and I'm just wandering around this life until I can figure out where I belong.

I expand my lungs to full capacity with the savory air one last time before releasing it with a heavy sigh. I stand and dust the sand off as best as I can but know some it is sneaking away with me on my trip. I don't mind its company. Standing straighter in hopes of bringing forth some bravery, I head back to my car to continue this journey. It's a trip I can make in one long day if I set my mind to it. But today my mind just isn't up to being set.

Easing back onto the highway, I open the sunroof and turn on the radio. Of course, the first station selection is an all eighties and nineties station. Figures. The music of my youth—*stolen youth*. My anxiety starts to get the better of me, so I crank up the music, which is none other than Madonna belting out "Holiday," She persuades me to sing along, and the next thing I know, I'm screaming to the top of my lungs.

Out of the corner of my eye, I notice a truck full of teenage boys driving alongside me, witnessing my little episode. Feeling embarrassed, I turn the blaring radio off and stare forward, hoping they will just go ahead and finish passing me in the fast lane. Instead, they hang right beside me. They are probably thinking they have stumbled upon a mad woman—maybe I am.

The guy in the passenger side sort of hangs out the open window and hollers at me. "You all right?"

I holler back sarcastically. "Why no!" Without waiting for a response, I roll up my window, return my gaze forward and continue my screaming fit as I drive on.

Chapter Four

"Come sit with me and watch a little TV before your mother returns from all of her *chores,*" Evan said sarcastically, rolling his eyes for effect. Julia and I just giggled happily at being a part of his inside joke. He knew how we felt about Jean and her spoiled ways.

He beckoned us to join him on the cramped couch. It was one of those stupid antique couches that seemed to be made for petite people. It's funny that a family full of above-average height members would have such a piece of furniture. It never made sense to me.

Evan sat sprawled out in loose jogging shorts and a snug tank top. He patted his lap as I stood there, trying to figure out where I wanted to sit. "Just sit in my lap, little miss." He grinned mischievously at me.

I hesitated long enough for Julia to jump at the opportunity. We both had schoolgirl crushes on Evan. With me being only ten, I had a hard time trying to understand those feelings. Julia was fourteen and more comfortable with them, I guess.

We sat there watching music videos for a while. I kept glancing out the corner of my eye to Evan and Julia with uneasiness. He had started out rubbing her shoulders, but had moved to her lower back. I guess there was no harm in that, but what I found a bit weird was his hands were under the back of her shirt. This continued until Evan couldn't sit still any longer and decided it was time to dance.

Grabbing me by the waist, he murmured, "You're dancing with me first, little miss." We walked like an Egyptian before a slow song took over. He pulled me close and whispered in my ear with his humid breath uncomfortably hot. "I saw you watching earlier. Don't be jealous." With that, he placed a soft kiss on my neck, causing my gut to twist in discomfort. Evan plastered my unwilling body tight against him. His invasion was wrong. In that moment, my innocent crush on him crashed to the floor and shatter to millions of sinful shards. At only ten years old, I didn't like his groping hands trespassing where no grown man should on a child, or his probing lips. It felt gross, as though each touch tainted me. I wanted no part in it.

I tried to wiggle free that horrible day, but Evan seemed to only get more worked up—heavy breaths and continuously pressing body. I hated the feel of him, and my skin crawled with disgust. My chest felt like it was being pinched in a vice grip, and I could hardly breathe. It all felt dirty. I was scared and confused. As I stood in my family's den, life began to descend a dark, slippery slope, and I began to lose myself.

~ ~ ~

Tap, tap, tap…

Tap, tap, tap…

The tapping on my driver's side window startles me out of the nightmare and brings me back to the now. I try to focus on what's causing the tapping, but it takes me a while to regain my composure. The tap picks back up, and I finally notice a police officer peeking through the window at me. Looking around, I notice I've parked on the side of the interstate without really realizing it. Thank goodness, I got off the road…

"Ma'am, are you okay?" He taps again when I don't respond. "Ma'am?"

I finally find enough sense to power the window

down, but say nothing. The humid air rushes in and caresses my cheeks.

"Do you need some assistance?" the concerned officer asks.

I clear my throat. "No sir." My throat feels constricted, and I try to clear it again. He stands cautiously with his head slightly bent towards the open window, waiting for more. "I'm heading to South Carolina for a family emergency. I think it just all got the best of me. I… I just need a minute to pull myself together," I stutter. I try to reassure him with a smile, but can't. My lips fail me and continue to grimace. I see my dazed weariness reflecting off his aviator shades.

"Please be careful." He tips his hat in a courteous manner. After a lengthy moment of hesitation, he finally leaves me alone.

I press my head to the steering wheel and force deep breaths in and out. I don't have the gumption to get back on the road just yet, so I sit a while longer and work on conjuring up a good memory—something that will encourage me to keep moving forward. If I don't, I know I will be heading back to Rhode Island and the comfort of Lucas. Deep down, I know that's not an option. It doesn't take long before a beautiful, older black lady comes to mind, Miss May Wilson—my saving grace. My lips finally decide to tilt slightly up as her comforting image settles my mind. Miss May is just under five foot in height and 'bout as round as she is tall. A hug from this woman is the only one I have ever welcomed without apprehension—it's a protective shielding hug. Some of my best memories were made at my dad's restaurant, and those were mostly due to this special lady. I coveted the opportunity to be her shadow at any chance I got. She is pure goodness.

Jean may be a culinary genius, but she lacks one important ingredient that Miss May possesses—heart. The woman cooks love right into everything she serves.

Now I'm not bragging here, but simply stating the facts when I tell you The Thorton Seafood House is the best meal on the Grand Strand. There are more awards than wall space. These awards are kept in my father's office because there are too many to be put on display. My dad also thought they took away from the beach house ambiance of the restaurant. Really though, no award was needed to entice customers through the door. The only advertisement my dad ever needed was by word of mouth. I have never seen a time when the porch wasn't lined with people patiently waiting their turn to eat.

My dad believed in serving only the freshest seafood. If he couldn't get it fresh within the day, then he simply wouldn't serve nor sell it. The local docks supplied him abundantly. Now, lots of southern seafood restaurants serve a country buffet along with seafood, such as fried chicken and BBQ. My dad didn't believe in that. He said seafood houses should serve seafood and seafood only.

That's all fine and dandy as long as you have a gifted cook to back it up. My dad definitely had that with Miss May. We kids would like to always be right up underneath her. It was hard not to gravitate towards this lady. Miss May is like a warm, welcoming place who just draws you into her comforts and somehow sooths all the wrongs. We all adored her.

~ ~ ~

"Miss May, how come your name is the same as one of the months of the year? Ain't that weird?" A young John Paul asked her this one afternoon in her kitchen at the restaurant. Yep. That's right—her kitchen. We each had pulled a stool up to her work counter and were *supervising*. Every now and then, she would need something out the pantry or fridge, and we would just about fight over who would get it for her. She was such a pleasing woman, and we all wanted to please her right back.

Miss May chuckled at John Paul's question as she continued to pick through a container of crabmeat. "'Cause my folks had so many young'uns, that's the only way to keep they's birthdays straight. My older brothers are June and August. My younger sisters are December, January, April, and September."

"Ain't you lucky you were born in a month that's not too weird," John Paul commented with a wrinkled nose and a reassuring nod of his head, causing Miss May to laugh wholeheartedly. That woman's laugh was contagious and we all joined in. She laughed with her whole body and her face would light up like none other. She could barely laugh without crying. Man, that woman could really laugh…

She began assembling some of her award-winning hush puppy batter. Hush puppies are a legend around these southern coastal parts. It is said that fishermen would come in from the sea and set up to frying their fresh catches right on the docks. The problem was they would be hounded to no end by the local dock dogs for their dinner. To get the dogs to leave them alone, the fishermen would fry up balls of the fish batter and feed it to the pesky animals to shut them up, hence the name hush puppies. Miss May called hers hush babies. Her award-winning crab cakes are legendary, too. Just as the fishermen had to pacify the dogs to keep them out of their fish, so did Miss May to keep us out of her crab cakes. No matter how busy she would be, she would always take the time to whip us up a fresh batch of her mouthwatering treats. Those sweet balls of cornmeal batter would melt in your mouth.

That afternoon, with the name history lesson complete, that little lady set out to hush us up. We all stood around watching and patiently waiting as she drained the fried dough on a paper towel, transferring it all into a carryout tray along with a cup of honey butter. "Here now. Take 'em and let this here ole woman with a funny name get back to work," she said with a wink to John Paul.

She handed him the container then proceeded to give each of us kids a kiss on the top of our heads as we filed by her to the back door of the kitchen. The restaurant and seafood market are backed up by the inlet, and we enjoyed spending the afternoons exploring at low tide. To visitors, the smell is a bit unpleasant. Some people would describe it as a putrid smell, but we locals are born with an immunity to the low tide stench.

Once Jean roped Evan into helping her out, our days at the restaurant became limited. And as I grew closer to my eleventh birthday that dark year, the more lost I seemed to get. Miss May became my only ally in those days.

My first disappearing act, albeit unsuccessful, was one afternoon that early spring. Evan was becoming progressively weirder to be around, always wanting me and Julia to sit in his lap or wanting us to lie on the couch with him. Always with wandering hands and stolen kisses.

I tried to deter him by not washing and wearing some of the boys' outgrown clothes. This won me no friends at school, but that was the least of my problems in those days. In my almost eleven-year-old mind, I thought I could gross him out enough that he would only want to pay Julia attention. She seemed to not be bothered by his wandering hands that much, so I thought it was okay. And once Evan grew strange, a peculiar filth seemed to embed in me anyways. I felt I could never wash it off.

After school that day the disappearing act began, I did a mad dash inside to grab my fishing pole. The boys had reluctantly agreed to let me join them. I was in the washing room where I kept my pole, and that's when Evan cornered me.

He slid his hands around my waist and eased me against the corner, out of sight. "Just where are you running off to now, little miss?" His pale eyes held mine captive and bile rose in my throat. My body always reacted with sickening dread when he touched me.

"I umm…fishing…" Before I could continue, he ducked his head and brushed his lips against mine.

"You don't have to be jealous over Julia Rose. You know I'm crazy about you too." He then tried to nudge my lips apart with his own, but mine became like stone. I tried to squirm out of his grasp, with him looking offended by that.

"Please let me go." I squirmed some more, but he still wouldn't release me.

"Did that make you uncomfortable, little miss? I'm sorry." He pulled back slightly with a look of repentance painted carefully across his handsome features. "That's how my family expresses love. That's all I was doing. Julia Rose likes it. Says she wishes your family was more loving."

I knew our family was different. Love? I didn't even know what that word meant. But I surely didn't think it was supposed to make you feel sick to your stomach and scared.

The front door banged open abruptly and Evan quickly freed me, so I took advantage of the moment and burst out the back door. I started off in a run and didn't stop until I made it to the kitchen of the restaurant. I scooted in the door and stopped to catch my breath with my entire body trembling. Miss May stood by her worktable preparing something I can't remember. I was bent over with my hands on my knees, feeling as though I was about to pass out. She began, "What..." but paused, taking in my demeanor. I looked up and shook my head, not being able to speak.

Miss May wiped her hands on her apron as she started over towards me, but stopped when she noticed I took a cautious step back. "What in the world got ahold of you, young'un?"

I darted to the back corner and hunkered down without saying a word. I didn't think I could if I wanted to. I was totally freaked out, and that fear had somehow stolen my voice. I thought if I was just near her I would be okay. She checked on me once as I hid behind a large stack of bread pallets but didn't say anything else. An hour or so passed before my dad stormed through, looking for me.

"Miss May, have you seen Savannah? I just got a phone call that she's missing." I could hear the panic in my dad's voice from where I hid.

"Yessir. She been 'round here for a bit. I'll send her to yo' office in a minute."

My dad must have agreed because I heard him step back out of the kitchen.

A mad rage came over me and I stormed over to Miss May to square off with her. Before I uttered a word, she grabbed me by the shoulders and looked me dead in the eyes.

"I done told yo' daddy that I caught sight of you. I had to tell 'em. He my boss and I ain't gonna be lyin'." She nodded her head sternly to emphasize her point.

I stood there nearly choking on the hurt and tried to look away from her intense stare, but she gave me a slight shake to get back my attention.

"You more than welcome 'round here as long as these here two eyes don't catch sight of you."

I stared into her chocolate eyes, confused.

"Do you understand me, child? I ain't gonna lie, but if I don't actually see you then I won't be lyin', *right*?" She eased so close until our noses almost touched. She widened her eyes to convey her message.

And that's when I finally caught on to her drift. And that was the beginning of my disappearing acts.

The afternoons that Evan was at the house, I would escape to the back porch of the restaurant or to the storage room in the kitchen. Snacks of hush puppies or french fries and sweet tea would always find me. Miss May knew I was there, but when my dad came storming in, proclaiming I had disappeared again, she would always reply the same. "These two eyes ain't laid sight on her today, sir." I knew my dad didn't believe her because he would always look around and let out a loud huff before stomping out of the kitchen.

I overheard her mumbling under her breath after he departed one afternoon, "That fool need to quit worryin' where that girl sneaks off to and start worryin' why."

I did show my appreciation to my saving grace by helping her out in any way I could find. Sometimes I would snatch a basket of fresh corn and shuck it all for her so she could put it into a Frogmore stew. Or I would pick through endless amounts of crabmeat until my fingers were pruned from the damp meat and slide it back to her when she turned her back to me. I didn't care how tedious the task was, as long as I got to stay away from Evan. I would have been willing to scrub the men's bathroom.

She saved me from months of unknown mistreatment, and how did I reward her? I ran away from her, without a second glance, the moment I got my chance. The realization that I wronged so many in my quest to escape the ones that wronged me was becoming a sharp regret that seemed to be piercing me deep within…

Chapter Five

The sun seems just as tired as I am and is beginning to droop in the sky quickly as I make my way farther south. I know I should just drive on through, but I decide to put off the inevitable for just a bit longer. I hit the GPS screen on my dashboard and do a quick search for the closest beach resort. After finding an appealing stop, I follow my car's direction to my destination.

The beachfront resort and spa has ended up being my easiest decision of the day. I take a deep cleansing breath as I enter the vast lobby, which feels heavenly after being in the cramped confines of my car all day. The space is draped in tranquility from whispering water fountains and sumptuous tropical plants. I scoot up to the check-in counter and get lucky. The place is booked solid, being that it is tourist season, but had a last-minute cancellation. I hurry through check-in and find more peace in my oceanfront luxury suite.

The first thing I do is open the glass doors to the balcony so I can listen to the soothing melody of the peaceful seashore. Some of the tension eases away as I stand by the window and watch the waves roll in under the moonlit sky. I've always found the vacant night beaches to be such a seductive mystery. I feel as though we are sharing an intimate secret that no one else is a privy to know about. I gaze over this natural wonder for a while longer and allow it to emit its calming effect over me.

After getting settled, I call my best friend, and he answers on the first ring. "Hey," I say. "Just letting you know I've stopped for the night. Traffic's been bad and I don't feel like driving in the dark."

"Savannah? What's wrong with your voice?" I hear the concern in Lucas's voice.

My little screaming session earlier plays through my head. It's left my throat feeling like sandpaper got ahold of it in a severe way. "It's nothing. I just think I'm allergic to the South," I say dryly.

"You know you can just forget about the whole thing… Or I can catch up with you so we can face this together. Please let me be there for you, love."

"That's awfully tempting, but I think this is something I need to take care of on my own." I really don't want him to have to be in the midst of the chaos I was about to step into. For one thing, the way my family deems fit to treat each other is embarrassing. Lucas deserves to be spared from as much of my issues as possible. "I'll call you tomorrow. Love you."

"Love you too. If you change your mind, you know where I'll be."

I hang up the phone without replying. Sitting here on the edge of the bed, I rub my shaky hands over my knees as the demons begin to dance. I roll my shoulders over and over, but I am unable to shrug them off. As I glance around the room, my gaze land on a cocktail menu sitting on the nightstand. Drinking was something I left back in college, but tonight I just want to hush those blame demons. Before I can come to my senses, I call in an order. Maybe the booze will help with my *allergies*. The hotel operator sounds confused and a bit amused as I order a buffet of various drinks like a pure idiot.

After the cocktails arrive, I fill the large soaking tub and select an orange fruity-looking concoction to medicate myself while I soak. I toss in some complementary bath salts and ease into the steaming water that tingles along my skin. After I get settled, I turn on the jets, hoping to work out the knots in my shoulders. I reach over to the side of the tub to retrieve my fancy glass and take a test sip. The first stings of the alcohol on my tongue remind me of a home remedy Jean used to give us kids when we were sick. It was a combination of vodka, lemon, and honey. I don't know if it cured anything besides keeping us out of our mother's hair while we were sick. That potent potion would knock you flat on your butt. Needless to say, we slept a lot when we were sick. I guess that was a good thing for us all.

I rest my head on the back of the enormous tub and sink a little farther down. As I watch the water whirl around in all directions, the demons pick up on their dancing. *I'm lost…I'm bored…I'm worthless…I'm so confused. Just slip under the water. Just let it overtake you and the pain will be gone…*

I chug the rest of the sharp syrupy liquid and set the glass back down, nearly dropping it in my haste. I sink farther into the steaming, vigorous water and feel as though I'm losing control. All of a sudden, the room starts feeling too hot and overwhelming. The water seems to hold me captive, and I can't lift my arms with my body feeling like lead. My fingertips start to tingle and I know I have to get out of the tub before the attack overtakes me. It's like this ugly monster has crept up on me from nowhere, with its claws drawn. I finally muster the strength to climb out and end up staggering into the sink vanity. The immediate pain in my side distracts me enough from the attack so that I can grab a towel and stumble to the bed. It's too late to take my medicine and now that I dabbled into the poison of alcohol, I don't have a choice. I select another toxic drink and gulp it down in one long swallow as I try to fend off the panic from overtaking me, but I know it's too late. My hands are trembling, and my heart is racing at a skipping, hiccupping rate. I stretch across the bed and watch the room blur away.

~ ~ ~

"She's dying, Momma." The words bellow from my trembling lips as I stare down at the breathing corpse that once was my sister. "Please do something," I beg.

"Julia Rose is just being a drama queen," Jean snaps as she stares down at Julia too. Jean's arms are crossed over her chest, and she is spitting mad. Her perfectly curled blonde hair is dancing in a hushed quiver with her rage.

I ease my sight from my mother and back towards my sick sister. I know I'm not looking at a drama queen, but of a broken girl. It takes one to know one—even though our forms are broken differently, I've learned broken is still broken, regardless. Julia lies on her side, facing away from us. It pains me to see her hipbone jutting out under her gown in an unnatural way and her bony arm lies limply over her wasted away waist. I slowly walk to the other side of the bed and continue to stare down at her. Studying her features, I take in the hollowness and severely sharp angles. Her eye sockets are sunk in her ashen skin, and it makes me so scared. I try to capture her attention, but she only gazes to the corner of the room. It's like she's here in this puny body, but gone completely in spirit.

I point over at the sodden sheets Julia is laying on. "But—"

"She's just a lovesick teenager and I won't play these immature games with her!" Jean growls at me and then turns her attention back to Julia. "Enough is enough. I know you miss Evan, but seriously, Julia. You are just a child. He's too old for you anyways. Just get your butt up and eat already. I don't have time for this!" She storms out of the room, leaving me alone with my sick sister and my overwhelming fear.

I find a clean spot on the bed and have a seat. I cautiously sit here looking down at her, scared that she is going to die and leave me alone with the memories. Alone to survive the demons by myself. I'll never survive them alone. I need her to carry the burden with me. I know it's selfish of me, because it's obvious the burden is killing her right before me. My hand reaches out to touch her, but think better of it. I can't tolerate touch anymore, and I want to comfort her in this moment, but cannot get over my own fears to do so. *We are both so broken*.

I sit a while longer, but cannot figure out a solution. And I really cannot stomach being in this room for another minute. The pungent smell of ammonia and body odor attacks my nose, and I am unable to inhale without the assault. I try to stand and escape, but the filthy bed sheets begin to wrap around me, pulling me farther onto the bed. The more I fight against it, the more I am consumed. The sheet snakes its way around my neck aggressively, leaving me gasping for the vile air. My vision darkens frightfully. And by the next window of clarity, I find my sister and me being swallowed up by the sinfully tarnished bed. She ends up rolled on top of me, staring a ghostly stare with her pale, vacant eyes. I try to scream, but the overpowering ammonia steals my breath. I'm choking. Gagging. Gasping…

~ ~ ~

My trembling body nearly clears of the bed in a jolt as the awful dream finally releases me. It's one of my many repeat nightmares. Asleep or awake, I can get no peace. The only action I can muster is to lay here for a while, trying to get my breathing and heart rate under control. I breathe deeply, trying to chase the lingering ammonia and stench from my airway with the salty ocean air filtering through the room. That pungent smell is one I will never be able to forget. The whooshing sounds of the waves softly rolling onto the shore outside filter in also from the open balcony door, so I place my focus there. I try to conjure up the images of the night ocean as I concentrate on my breathing exercises. I can see the ghostly white caps peeking from the water ever so often and the twinkling night sky watching from overhead. *Breathe in… Breathe out…*

Once I calm down, I check the clock on my phone and disappointingly discover that I have only slept for a few hours. I feel like I have already battled an entire night's sleep. I lick my dry lips and try to swallow a pasty swallow uncomfortably. I'm parched, so I wearily grab a watered down drink and sling it back, only to have my stomach protest. I dart to the bathroom just in time for my body to exorcise the alcohol.

After the retching finally passes, I wash my mouth out with some complimentary mouthwash by the sink, for which I'm thankful. My mouth tasted like a sewer. Fatigue pushes my body onto the cool marble bathroom floor. It feels heavenly on my fevered skin. Now I remember bitterly why I don't drink. Stupid lesson learned—*again*.

As I lay on this bathroom floor, I can't help but think about my sister and the reason behind this nightmare I have just endured. She performed her own disappearing act after the darkness of Evan Grey. Julia withered away at such a fast rate that the rumor around town was she was sick with some type of cancer. My mother did nothing to dispel the rumors either. She stayed so mad during this time in our lives. It was the first time my sister had caused any disturbance to our family, and it rubbed my mother wrong something fierce. Jean dared my father to do anything about it, saying she was just being rebellious and would eat when she got good and hungry. But I knew better. My sister had no intentions of eating ever again. She had made her mind up while lying up in that room, and I knew nothing was going to change it. I took matters into my own hands.

There was only one option, and that was to call Jean's estranged parents. They had spoiled her up until the grandbabies were born, when they realized their error of their ways. That spoiled brat couldn't see past herself to care for her own. They encouraged my mother to be a better parent, and this earned them the boot out of our lives. I had not seen them in well over six years by the time I made that fateful phone call. Jean scheduled a spa appointment for an entire day's pampering that early spring day, saying all of the stress of Julia's mess had earned her the treat. Scared out of my mind, I arranged for my grandparents to sneak Julia away. At that point, she was nothing more than bones and dried, gray flesh. Her hair had thinned considerably too, and I had to fight the overwhelming urge to be scared of the thing that my sister had become.

I remember them entering Julia's room and my grandmother going to her knees at the first sight of my sister. It was a memory filled with pity and absolute shame. She finally picked herself up off the floor to make her way onto the bed. She lay there holding my sister, crying, while I helped my grandfather pack a suitcase. He spoke very few words, and I knew he was in shock at the sight of Julia also. My grandfather finally encouraged my grandmother to release Julia so he could gather her skeleton in his arms and carry her to their van. They both gave me a sympathetic look as they drove away, leaving me on the curb with the weight of what I had just done crashing down on me.

By the time Jean entered the house that late

afternoon, I had Julia's bed stripped down and the room aired out of the stench left behind. The bedding ended up in the outside garbage. The soiled material was past the point of no return.

I was lying on the rope rug in my room, listening to the stereo, when Jean stormed in, yanking me up off that floor quicker than I had time to comprehend. Fury was radiating off her, and it scared me.

"Where's your sister? I know she didn't walk out that door on her own," she shouted as she shook me.

I was beyond upset, and the fact that Jean openly knew that my sister was too sick to walk out on her own devastated me. Yet she did nothing about it. She was more worried about keeping up her image in front of the town than to take care of her sick daughter. I hated her in a way I wish wasn't possible in that moment. It felt purely evil, and I had thoughts about my mother that I'm too ashamed to admit.

She shook me in a violent snatch one more time. "Tell me!" She let me go with a slight shove so that she could light a cigarette. I hated the smell of it, and she knew this as she puffed the smoke right into my face. The acrid smoke attacked me before I could close my airway off, causing me to choke out a cough.

"Your parents took her to get some help," I muttered while staring at the floor.

She took another long drag, and my room began

to fog with the vulgar smoke, setting my eyes on fire. "Just how do you suppose they knew to do that?" She looked nervous in that moment, like she might have been caught doing wrong. This one sign of weakness from her gave me just enough courage.

I looked at her with as much hate as I could muster. "I *suppose* I called and told them she was—"

Jean didn't allow me to finish. This smart-mouthed comment earned me a handprint across my cheek. With my cheek on fire, she pushed me back to the floor. I was too busy clutching my cheek to catch my fall, so my head banged into the corner of footboard of my bed. The skin on my scalp felt a little wet, but I was too stunned to check it. My attention was on my mother, who was pointing that cigarette at me as though she wished it were a gun. In that very moment, I had my first suicidal thought. I had desperately wished it was a loaded gun and that she would use it on me. The standoff between us teetered for mere minutes, but boy did it feel like a lifetime to me. I do believe we both had a death wish for me during this.

She shook her head and stormed to the door. "I don't want to see sight of you for the rest of the day," she said before slamming my door shut.

Later that night, I crept to the bottom of the stairs

and spied on Jean while she was on the phone with her mom. She was demanding that they tell her where Julia was and to bring her back. Jean backed down when words such as child neglect and social services entered their conversation.

"Fine. Keep her. I was at my wits' end with her anyway." The nervousness trembled in my mother's voice. Something that was not present often. "I… I tried to get her to eat. Just ask her." The conversation ended with little more commentary than that. She turned around and caught me listening, and I knew I was about to get the beating of my life. Instead she seemed to not think I was worth her effort. Jean retrieved a bottle of wine and a glass and disappeared into her room for the rest of the night. So I went back to my room and pretty much hid there for the next ten months. That was how long it took before the facility for eating disorders would release Julia to come back home. Those ten months alone with Jean were a living hell. Life was lonely, and I felt even more lost.

~ ~ ~

Shivering and aching all over, I wake up on the bathroom floor and feel right disappointed in myself. Here I am, in a luxurious hotel suite, and I end up spending the night on the blame bathroom floor. *What an idiot.* The crick in my neck and my sore back rebels against movement, but it eventually allows me to rise off the floor and go straight to the shower. I release the towel that is haphazardly wrapped around me and step into the hot spray, trying to wash off the restless night. I don't ever sleep well. Most nights, I end up roaming around the condo with a nagging restlessness keeping me company. Last night was a bit rougher than my norm. Too many memories chasing me around, and let's not forget about the stupid alcohol idea.

After the shower, I down two aspirins with an entire bottle of water. By the time I'm dressed, the resolution to not go to Bay Creek is firmly in place. I am on the verge of a complete meltdown and it's just not worth it. I pack my bag with determination and head back to Lucas and to my safe life—the only place I should be.

Okay. So not even a half hour down the taunting road, I find myself making a U-turn and start heading back south. Ugh. I have to do this. This unpleasant task has to be followed to the very end. It's time to face all the demons and just have it out—no-holds-barred.

Two more long frustrating hours pass before my

stomach reminds me I haven't eaten in well over twenty-four hours. I pull off the interstate and find a quaint country diner. As I walk through the door, the aroma of savory eggs and sausage frying sends my stomach into a mean growl. The smells remind me of a local diner set right on the beach in Bay Creek. It is rightfully named the Beach Shack because it resembles a dilapidated beach shack with well-worn clapboard siding and a rusty tin roof. It serves the best biscuits and gravy I have ever eaten. It's tradition for locals and tourists alike to indulge on the greasy, delicious fare before hitting the beach for the day.

This diner is pretty neat as well. It resembles an old farmhouse with blue gingham curtains and tablecloths and roosters perched around the perimeter as though they are keeping an eye on the place. The old wooden floors creak when I enter as though to welcome me. The hostess, who is wearing a gingham apron and an old-fashioned farm dress, greets me and escorts me to a table near the front. I end up ordering biscuits and gravy to compare to my childhood memories. They are okay, but not as rich and creamy as the one back home. *Home*? Yep, I just slipped, didn't I?

I sit for a while and overanalyze my slip-up. Boy oh boy. I can't believe I called Bay Creek home. Honest mistake, I suppose. Speaking of which, it's time I stop lollygagging and get on with it. Well... Soon. I'll head out *soon*.

While I try talking myself into heading out, I end up ordering a fudge brownie, hoping it will give me the boost I need to get back on the road. The decadent treat reminds me of an amusing memory and I sit at that table and laugh loudly with myself over it. That laugh has been the only thing to feel right in these last few days.

I did get a bit of revenge on ole Jean over the ordeal with Julia. Jean's only other indulgence besides fine wine is fine gourmet treats. Well, let's be more honest—her whole life is an indulgence. But gourmet treats are close to the top of the list. Of course, local gourmet isn't good enough for the brat. She has to have her decadent treats delivered all the way from New York. She had discovered the most scrumptious cookies on one of her many vacations without us and had set up a monthly delivery of the treats. Great, right? For Jean maybe, because no one else was allowed to eat any. These little fudgy jewels are double chocolate chip cookies with tiny chips of toffee and almonds nestled throughout in rich chocolate goodness. They are made from the finest ingredients, and this is evident in the price tag. I thought about ordering my own box over the years, but the allure of them isn't so great when not being told it's forbidden.

Ain't it funny how that works? We always want what we can't have, simply for being forbidden.

Jean forbade us to touch them. Of course, each one of us had made the mistake of snatching one of the melt-in-your-mouth cookies at some point or another, and we ALWAYS got caught. My mother would make us pay for our wrongdoing. My father didn't even dare touch her precious cookies. She acted as though she was the only one deserving of the fine treats. Yep. Spoiled rotten brat.

Well, one day I was home alone and missing Julia something awful. Jean wouldn't tell me anything about how my sister was doing. She said it was my punishment for what I did. And so I was sitting in the living room, folding a basket of laundry when the deliveryman dropped off her monthly cookie order. I dutifully brought the package to its designated cabinet. I hesitated for just one split second and that's all it took for the evil idea to take root.

I placed the box on the counter and stared down at it as I resolved to what to do. My first idea was to eat every single one of them, throw the box out, and deny their delivery. Then I thought some more and a smile crept over my face when the brilliant decision resolved. For me to be deemed a chronic procrastinator, it took me no time to act on this decision. Retrieving the cayenne pepper from the fancy spice rack, pure giddiness washed over me. I worked a knife under the seal without damage so that I could glue it back once my task was complete.

Then I walked the cayenne pepper and cookies outside to a picnic table to the far edge of the backyard. And just let me tell you, I pulled each cookie out, giving it a good wet lick before sprinkling it heavily with the cayenne pepper. The dark fudgy texture of the cookie seemed to absorb the cayenne instantly. No red speckles were visible. After licking and dousing each one, I took the package back in and super-glued the seal shut and placed the box in its rightful cabinet. I then dashed upstairs to scrub any evidence from my mouth, laughing the entire time. I was finally going to get one up on that witch, and it felt so good. Now, call that evil or callous or whatever you want. I choose to call it creatively one-upping my enemy. She deserved it and you ain't changing my mind about it. You know you're giggling right along with me.

That night after supper, Jean dismissed us all as she prepared to enjoy her freshly delivered treats. I watched from the hallway as my mother placed two generously sized jewels on a dessert plate and made herself a cup of tea. As she sat down, John Paul tapped me on my shoulder and just about made me yelp in surprise.

"What are you doing?" he whispered with a smirk. I guess his instincts warned him I was up to mischief, being that he is an expert on the matter.

I said nothing, shook my head, and tried to shoo him to go back upstairs, but he wouldn't budge. So I reluctantly let him stand over my shoulder to watch the anticipated show he had no idea he was about to witness.

Jean sat and took a small sip of her tea before seeming to decide it was still too hot. She then selected a cookie off the plate. She sniffed it, and I thought I was busted right on the spot, but then she took a substantial bite. She chewed for a few seconds as though she was trying to decipher it. Confusion, then panic, ran across her face in a cartoonish manner. It was all I could do to hold it together. She spit the cookie out all over the table and started rubbing her napkin across her tongue. When that didn't help, she grabbed up her tea and took a good scorching gulp before spitting it out in a spray all over the table. She jumped up, causing her chair to tumble over as she ran to the sink. She drank and drank and drank straight from the faucet, heaving like something possessed.

I pushed past John Paul and shot upstairs to my room for a good laugh. Later on that night, he eased into my room with an amused expression on his face.

I was lying on my makeshift bed on the floor. This was where I had slept for the past eight months. If this seemed strange, John Paul kept it to himself. He just sat beside me and snickered as he playfully nudged me with his foot.

"What did you put on those cookies, Savannah?"

"I don't know what you're talking about." I ended up laughing right along with him. Now that, my friends, is a good memory. I just wish I had more of them kicking around.

Chapter Six

I grab a to-go cup of coffee and hit the road once more. A few uneventful hours pass before my phone starts singing. I try to sound upbeat as I answer. "Hello. This is Savannah."

"Where are you?" John Paul asks. Before I can answer, he continues his rant. "Why are you dragging your a—" (My brother has a mouth on him. Sorry.)

I interrupt him before he can spit the curse word out completely. "Oh! It's so nice to hear your pleasant voice this lovely morning. No need for ugly language. I should be there in about another hour or so."

"You should have been here *yesterday*. This ain't a casual visit, but here you are just shooting the breeze like our dad didn't just die."

This is the slap of reality I didn't want, but

needed. Yesterday's call felt like a dream, and in this moment, I realize that it is a permanent situation. I have lost my opportunity to have a relationship with my dad. When I ran from my demons, I ran from him too.

"I'll be there soon," I say through a tight throat before ending the call. I power the phone off and drive silently the rest of the way on autopilot.

I love my brother, but his own personal demons have scarred him—some immediate and some surfacing over time. The last time I saw him was about five years ago. He was in his mid-twenties then, but already seemed to have lived a rough long life. I guess in some ways he had.

He spent his days on the beach in a lounge chair sleeping off hangovers or on a surfboard. His nights were spent at the restaurant where he *helped* my dad run things. John Paul's idea of helping was wooing all of the attractive female tourists. With his long, sun-bleached hair that touched well past his shoulders and rugged good looks, this was no problem for him. He is as good-looking of a man as Julia is as a beautiful woman. They are both very striking, and people tend to stare. I look nothing like them. I've already told you that, though.

John Paul always has an endless supply of tall-tales to share. One of his favorites was the time he tossed a baby green garden snake at my feet, and I cried like a baby and passed out, which landed me in a big pile of cow manure. He said I walked around smelling like crap for weeks. The true version of that story was he raided my parent's liquor cabinet and got smashed. His drunk-self found me hanging out with some friends in an old barn near our house. That sucker tossed a copperhead snake at me. The poisonous creature bounced off my shoulder and struck a garden rake beside me. Unfortunately, the only part of the story he had correct was I did cry like a baby. That was the last time I hung out with that crowd due to my embarrassment over his drunken taunting and my crying fit. This is the short simpler version of that tale. Please don't ask for the longer and more complicated one. I just ain't up for sharing it.

His friends couldn't get enough of his farfetched stories and were always begging J.P. to tell another one. And boy, can he spin a tale right out of thin air. Everyone calls him J.P., but me. Evan was the one to call him that first, so I never had the desire to call him anything but John Paul.

Yeah, so one night a buddy made a crucial error when he asked my brother to share the story of what happened to our cousin Bradley. Needless to say, that certain buddy ended up in the emergency room and

John Paul ended up in jail. That was the last time anyone ever mentioned Bradley's name in front of John Paul. I'd say that was a hard lessoned learned.

Just thinking Bradley's name causes pain to course up and bite me harshly, so I tamp that down as far as I can and focus back on the road.

The closer I get to Bay Creek, the sicker I feel. I dread beyond dread having to come face to face with my mother again. She had such a big part in me running away in the first place, and now I blame her and myself for robbing me of any time I could have had with my dad. He was a hardworking man, and I know he loved us, even if he didn't have enough hours in the day to express any of it.

Jean is a different story. I've learned in my short life a valuable lesson—some battles are unwinnable, and the best thing to do is knock the dust off your shoes and move on. Jean is a battle I will never win. All my memories of her are the same. No matter what, at the first sight of her I have always felt a jolt of apprehension as to what was going to be wrong. She is unpleasable. I know. I tried unsuccessfully for years to do nothing more than to please my mother, and I failed miserably.

After calling my grandparents about Julia, it seemed that Jean just wrote me off completely. I spent my teenage years trying to make up for it too—

getting perfect grades, keeping up all of the house chores done without complaint, and working part-time between the restaurant and the seafood market. It was all fruitless. She always found me to be imperfect and my attempts beyond flawed.

~ ~ ~

"Just what are you doing to that chicken?" Jean almost shouted as she came up behind me at the stove. I could feel the hate in her voice slap my on the back.

I was cooking supper and had dazed off into my own little world. I couldn't help it because I was so darn tired that evening. I had just completed a shift at the market after school. And after supper, I would have to do the dishes, a load of towels, and finish a midterm paper. My brain was fuzzy with all the tasks completed and frazzled with the ones that still awaited me. The repeated nightmares had already begun to keep me company most nights. So a good night's sleep had become something of my past.

My mother's shouting only rubbed my exhausted-self wrong. So, without thinking better, I blurted out sharply, "I'm making blackened chicken. What does it look like?" I turned to meet her glare with my own to only earn a handprint across my face.

She snatched the tongs out of my hand and made herself useful in saving supper, which was fine by me.

I watched as she quickly scooped the chicken out of the pan and demanded I hand her a clean one. I was none too happy about that because it meant more dishes for me later, but I figured for the safety of my face, it was best to keep that complaint to myself. I gave her the pan and stood holding my throbbing cheek until she began barking out other orders to me.

"Get me the garlic and rosemary," she commanded. I watched intently as she gently peeled the skin of the chicken back. She made a paste with the garlic, rosemary, and some butter, which she spread over the chicken before smoothing the skin back over it. She placed the chicken in the clean heated pan, and without looking away from the sautéed chicken, she barked for me to slice some shallots. Once I was done, I nudged the cutting board in her vicinity while maintaining my distance. She tossed them in the pan.

"Now hand me my glass of wine."

I did as I was told. I figured it was time for a drink after having to put up with me. To my surprise, Jean doused the chicken with the white wine instead. She did amaze me with her culinary techniques. Even though I earned another slap in my face, the meal had been worth it. I often use that exact same chicken recipe in my own kitchen, minus the animosity.

~ ~ ~

It is late morning as I hit the city limits of Bay Creek. Relief washes over me that I've made it as uneasiness seeps through me over the exact same point. A beautiful driftwood sign with lots of brightly colored flowers planted along the base welcomes visitors to this picturesque town. It's a lovely place too. The country and seashore landscape mingle together and allures people right on in.

I slowly drive past my childhood home and take a quick glance at it. Besides a fresh coat of white paint and freshly landscaped lawn, the two-story colonial looks exactly the same. Cars line the driveway as well as along a lengthy stretch of the street. The wraparound porch has mourners scattered about it. All the guests have either a plate of food or a cup of drink, as they huddle in groups, deep in conversation. I'm sure the house is packed full of guests tending to Jean's every need. I can't bring myself to hit the brakes and before I know it, I am a turning off our street. I set a course for the six-minute drive to my dad's prides and joys. Crossing over the familiar waterway, the clinking and clanking sound of the ancient drawbridge welcomes me back.

Within mere minutes, I am sitting in my idling car in the parking lot. I eventually turn the car off and climb out to inspect the places. They look exactly as they should with two exceptions. One is the fresh coat of paint. And the other is the fact that it is smack-dab in the heart of tourist season and these two prominent establishments sit here abandoned. It's an eerie feeling to be here alone on this balmy summer day. The quietness allows for the ocean's tune to lull through the empty parking lot in a way I have never heard. The air is not filled with the usual aroma of succulent seafood being cooked up inside. Only the briny salt air is present, and this scene leaves me feeling hollow.

After choking back the hurt, I walk up the porch of the restaurant that is lined with lonely rocking chairs swaying mournfully from the breeze. On the door is a wreath with an explanation as to why the tourists will miss the best beach meal they could have found.

We are sad to announce the untimely passing of proprietor, Mr. John Paul Thorton II. We will keep you posted as to when the businesses will reopen.

People have left cards and notes tucked throughout the wreath, offering their condolences. In this moment, the impact of it all finally hits me. I've lost my dad… Lost him and there's no changing this bitter fact that I can hardly comprehend.

Not being able to take it, I run down the block to the beach and stumble to a stop in the sand. He's gone. *Really gone*. And I have run out of time to make amends. My chance is lost to know my dad and to let him know me. The hurt is crushing and strikes me with such a blow that I am brought abruptly to my knees. If the beachgoers find my meltdown strange, they don't act on it. I'm left alone to dance with a few of my demons for a spell.

I rock back and forth in the sand for a while as I fight off one of my attacks. *Breathe, Savannah. Breathe. In… Out… Breathe.*

The sea breeze has whipped my hair across my face, so I don't see it coming when strong hands slide under my arms and pluck me from the sand in one swift snatch. Before I know it, I am pulled around and encircled in a vice grip embrace. His shaking vibrates through me, and it's obvious he is close to tears. We say nothing to one another in an understandable silence. Needing some space from the beachgoers, he eventually leads me back to my car. He holds my hand the entire way, and I rein in my anxiety over the physical contact. *He's not gonna hurt you*. I'm guessing his worry is that I'll run off again is why he won't let go of me. He's no dumb blond, because that is exactly what I'm thinking about doing. Once we reach the parking lot, he turns to face me, and I get a good long look at him.

"You've cut your hair?" I ask my brother. His long surfer locks are gone. I had not seen my brother with short hair since grade school. John Paul is sporting a short, yet perfectly messy, style. It looks good, but it's not him. He is too rough and tough for such a preppy look.

He weakly smiles as he rubs his hands through it, as though he can't believe it himself. I stare at his red-rimmed eyes with concern and wait for him to find his voice. I guess he is unable to speak, because he swoops me up in another hug. He's still trembling, and I begin to hurt for the pain he is going through. I suddenly feel selfish for taking so long in getting here to him. Not once in the past two days have I considered how he feels for losing his dad. A dad that he knew well compared to my own relationship. And he has been here going through it all alone.

"I'm sorry," I whisper against his shoulder. He nods his head in agreement, but still says nothing. "John Paul?"

"*Your* mother made me cut it," he finally chokes out, making us both laugh at his way of forming the sentence. Neither one of us much claimed her through the years.

"Great day. I've really missed you," I confess honestly. "How'd you know where I was?"

"I watched your butt sneak by the house earlier. Only two possibilities as to where I'd find you. Here or at Miss May's."

We walk over to the market's porch and have a seat. We rock for a bit before I ask, "How is she?"

"Madder than a wet setting hen at you."

"What? Why?"

"You disappeared on us over five years ago, Savannah. Ain't that enough?" There's a pucker of hurt between his blond eyebrows and I feel guilty for being the cause.

"I suppose," I admit.

We sit staring over the empty parking lot for a little longer, catching up. I know I'm just putting off the inevitable, so I finally agree to follow John Paul back to the house.

I catch myself holding my breath as we walk through the front door. It took nearly an hour to make it through the mourners on just the porch. Using my bag as a protective shield to keep the condoling guests at arm length, I've been able to control my anxiety of their nearness. It's all so overwhelming. I step over the threshold and the first thing I notice is that the interior has been updated with paint and the wood floors have a freshly polished gleam. My eyes take all this in before I spot my mother in the den. She is surrounded by a group of ladies doting over her. As soon as her eyes make contact with my own, a steady stream of tears rush down her face. She is heartbroken, and all at once, I'm heartbroken for her. I want to run over and throw my arms around her and make our relationship right and be the daughter she needs me to be.

The moment is lost with the first slash of her sharp tongue. Who was I kidding? Some things never, and I mean NEVER change.

"What took you so long? I've needed you here!" Jean snaps out so bitterly that I can almost taste bile. A room full of disappointing eyes find me embarrassed.

"I... I um, got here as fast as I could. Sorry," I mumble while I study my shoes.

"Humph."

My defenses kick in, forcing my head back up, and I smart off in true Savannah fashion. "Well, where's your famous Julia Rose? Why isn't she here to hold your hand?"

Jean turns a violent shade of red. Good. I want her embarrassed too. Might as well not have to be alone in this, right? I feel the warmth of embarrassment not only in my cheeks but all over.

"You know as well as I do, her busy career is not

easy to get away from. Maybe you don't understand since you do nothing for a living." She crosses her arms as we square off. I stand there clutching my overnight bag as though it's my security blanket. "She's trying her best to get here. You have no excuse."

I don't waste anyone's time with a reply. I turn and walk through the crowd and head upstairs to my abandoned room. As I open the door and glance around at a room that looks exactly as I had left it, I am overwhelmed and then pushed to my knees with times past.

Still clinging onto my bag for dear life, I feel the tingling begin in my fingertips and then sneak up my arms in piercing stings. Before I can focus on an escape, I am paralyzed. This one has hit me hard. My eyes lose focus, blurring the room, and my heart rate is skipping around. Breathing is labored as though my lungs have rebelled against me. I have lost this battle, and the demons push me way under. As I tilt forward, the wood floor rushes towards me before all goes black.

Chapter Seven

The summer is brutally hot, and I feel sweat trickling down my back. It's the kind of humid heat that pushes against you, thick and uncomfortably. Wiping my damp forehead, I watch my dad pack suitcases in the car. Jean was on her way to another vacation—a week in Hawaii, and this time she so graciously invited our dad. This was a first, and surprisingly, my dad agreed to go.

"Can I please stay with my friend Chrissy? Please Daddy. Her mom said it was okay." My whiny pitch begs out to him to agree.

"Sweetheart, you know your mother already said no. She wants you here with Julia Rose," Dad said as he closed the trunk with a good thud. He patted me on the shoulder as to say sorry, but that made me even madder. I turn my attention to Jean as she sauntered down the steps in a new sundress that looked all fresh and tropical.

"You always get a break and I'm sick of never getting one!" I kicked at a nearby bush for good measure and shot daggers in her direction with my scornful glare.

"You are just a child," Jean hissed. "You haven't earned a break yet!" And with that, my dad loaded her up in the car and set out to the airport.

A week stuck with Evan made me nauseous. Something bad was going to happen. I just knew it. My eleventh birthday was a few months back and Julia had turned fifteen just before school let out for summer break. My dad finally agreed to let us start staying alone in the afternoons. We hadn't seen Evan for nearly two months and it was wonderful. But Dad drew the line about us staying overnight alone, so Jean talked him into letting Evan stay with us.

The week passed with John Paul and Bradley coming and going as they pleased, with us girls having to stay put and do chores. I began viewing Evan as a chore too. The wandering hands and kisses were tiring to dodge. I set out to not wash the entire week, but Evan always called me out on it in front of the boys and would embarrass me into washing. I refused deodorant, though. My hope was to repel him, but he seemed to take it as an inviting challenge instead.

I got fed up pretty quickly and headed out to work at the market or restaurant each day without permission. I knew Dad would find out when he returned, but I would gladly take the consequences. I wasn't sitting around that house, like some open target for whatever that sick man decided he wanted to do to me next. I remember sitting in the kitchen with Miss May while she worked that first afternoon. I had already washed up some dishes for her and was waiting for another task to be ordered.

"Child, why you rather work here all day instead of enjoying yo' summer break like the rest of them young'uns?" She looked up at me and waited for an answer.

I fidgeted while deciding how to answer her. She tapped the table in front of me with her knobby knuckles to summon an answer I really wasn't too keen on giving. I let out a huff. "I hate him, and I don't want to be around him."

"Who?" she asked.

I met her gaze. "Evan! I hate him!"

"That's a strong word, girl. I don't take too kindly to lettin' it be said so easily."

"Well, it's the truth," I said, screeching out each word.

"Why you hate him?" she nearly whispered, trying to get me to calm down.

"I ain't telling you, so don't ask!" I snapped at her.

She stood there eyeing me quietly for a spell, and I could see her resolving some things. I just weren't so sure on what she was resolving. She eventually nodded her head once as though her decision on the matter was made.

"Get me a box of pudding from the pantry and a small bunch of bananas," Miss May ordered. I did as she asked but wasn't too thrilled with it. She knew that each one of us young'uns hated a banana. It was the one thing I think we all agreed to never eat. I personally couldn't get over the mushy texture and always ended up gagging.

I handed her the pudding and watched as she combined it together with a white powder and milk. "What are you doing, Miss May?" I asked confused. I had never seen her make this particular dessert.

"I'm making Evan a treat," she answered as she began slicing the gross bananas into the pudding mixture.

"Why?" I gagged at the gross, sickly sweet scent of the fruit. I took a few steps away from the table and covered my nose.

"Cause you done 'n acted rude and I ain't

standin' for it." She cut me a look. It was as though she was trying to get me riled up with her for some reason. And she knew it didn't take much to rile me up. "You gonna give it to him with no lip."

I crossed my arms and huffed out, "Well, I ain't giving that devil a treat. You can forget it!"

"If you don't give it to him and apologize for your mean self, then I'm gonna take to beatin' you like yo' daddy never has." She crushed some vanilla wafers on top and placed a lid on the plastic container. As she handed it over to me, Miss May instructed, "Now get yo' white butt out my kitchen and don't come back 'til you deliver this."

I snatched it out of her hand and stomped out the door. I eventually made it home with the vile dessert. I may have stopped along the way to spit in it… I stormed into the house, slung it on a shelf in the fridge, and slammed the door shut with a satisfying bang. Evan and the boys were at the kitchen table, looking at some surf magazine. My beating and a banging drew their attention. I whipped around to leave and found them all eyeing me curiously.

"What's that in the container, Savannah?" John Paul asked.

"Nasty banana pudding," I grumbled. The boys grumbled their own disapproval for the gross treat as well.

"Why the crap you bring junk like that home?" John Paul complained.

"I can't believe you would even bring that mess in this house," Bradley commented with a wrinkled up nose. We Thortons are something serious over our distaste for bananas.

"Miss May *made* me," I muttered.

Evan hopped up from the table in excitement. "I love banana pudding." He beamed in delight. With that declaration, he grabbed a large spoon from the drawer and retrieved the dessert from the fridge. He sat back down and tore into the pudding like he hadn't eaten in days. The boys and I started gagging from the awful odor and made quick exits—them slamming the back door with their hastily getaway and me running upstairs. I was still mad at Miss May, so I decided to hide out in the attic for the rest of the afternoon instead of going back to her. It was stifling hot up there, but it was a sure guarantee no one would look for me there—one person in particular. A sweat-drenched afternoon sounded heavenly compared to the alternative.

Later that night, I heard a very sick Evan in the bathroom across the hall from my room moaning in pain. He whined about it being the worst stomach pains he had ever had. His *stomach virus* lasted only until the next day, but he was too weak to bother me or Julia for another day after that. I was thankful it allowed me a brief reprieve from him—thanks to Miss May and her mystery ingredients. Needless to say, the leftover banana pudding made its way into the trashcan without Evan indulging in it anymore. I think he knew what she did. There was no love lost between the two of them.

When Thursday rolled around, the boys boomed with excitement. They had been invited on a three-day camping trip with the Cox family down the street. The Coxes acted like they enjoyed spending time together and doing the whole vacation thing as a family. The boys always got invited. I never did. I think it's because they only had boys, but I still would have liked to have gone.

Panicked with being left alone, I begged the boys fruitlessly not to go up until the very minute they left me.

"Please don't go."

"No way! This is going to be a blast!" John Paul replied when I begged.

I crossed my arms over my bowed out chest and glared at him as he gathered camping supplies from the garage. "Then I'm going to tell Daddy and Jean on you. They said no leaving the house overnight!"

"Don't be a brat about it, Savannah," he said as he threw a flashlight into his duffle bag. Bradley was cramming one in his too, but he gave no commentary.

"It's fine. I gave them permission." Evan's voice came from behind me and made me jump. I spun around and gave him the stink eye, but it only made him chuckle. He wandered back into the house as the boys kept packing all kinds of junk. I watched him until the door closed. I would have brought him another Miss May dessert, but I don't think I could have gotten him to eat it.

I eventually stormed over to the sidewalk's edge and slung myself down on the curb. Every so often, I would huff as loudly as I could to let them know I was still there and still not happy. Bradley would give pause to eye me, but John Paul just ignored me completely. They passed me as they began their trek to the neighbor's house with their camping gear in tow. They were too excited to wait to be picked up and decided to head over and help with loading up. They looked like twins almost, in cutoff camouflage pants with all sorts of pockets, black T-shirts, and tattered Chuck Taylors. Both boys had a head full of long, wavy hair, just in different hues. They did everything together. You never saw one without the other. It made me even more jealous that they were so close. I wanted that with Julia, but our relationship had shifted away from each other over the last year. I felt lonely all the time.

Bradley hesitated beside me. "You okay?" he asked with concern in his green eyes.

"Please don't go." I begged. "Please don't leave us alone with him."

"Stop being a brat," John Paul said again over his shoulder.

"I'm not being a brat, you jerk!" I hollered back.

Bradley slightly nudged me with his shoe. "Sorry, Savannah. It's just… Well, we really want to go camping so bad is all."

"Stop messin' it up for us," John Paul said as he continued walking.

"It's just three days. I promise to take you fishing when we get back, okay?"

Bradley waited for my reply, but I didn't give him one. I just sat there, staring down at my scuffed-up Converse sneakers. They used to be John Paul's shoes until he outgrew them, and I took them as my own. Boys' clothes seemed so much more practical and comfortable than girls' clothing, so I mostly wore his outgrown clothes. Jean hated this.

"Savannah?" Bradley tried again, but I continued to ignore him. So with a shrug of his shoulders, he followed behind John Paul.

I sat out there willing the boys to return with all my might. By the time the sky darkened completely, I gave up the hope. I had stayed firmly planted to that sidewalk for hours and needed to pee something fierce, so I reluctantly went inside.

I sensed that it was bad before witnessing anything as I crept into the dark house. Tiffany was singing about her thinking we're alone now from the living room's stereo, and Evan was laughing in the kitchen. I rounded the corner and spotted Julia sitting at the table in just her panties and bra, causing the hairs to rise on my neck. *Bad…This is bad…*

I oddly remember her bra was the same baby pink bra I had just gotten for my birthday. I was wearing mine, coincidentally. I remember it being itchy and damp from sweat. Bra wearing was new to me, and I already hated it with a vengeance.

"Now the party can begin," Evan said as he walked around the counter towards me, startling me again. He was only wearing a pair of shorts. His bronze chest was striking, and my focus was glued on its own accord. "You enjoying the view, little miss?" He laughed with too much self-assuredness. Punching the cocky son of a gun in the gut is what I really wanted to do in that moment. I was trembling in anger. I felt caught in his snare, and I knew he had won. And boy, did that tick me off something fierce. Yet, I stood there froze in fear.

I looked over to give Julia a questioning look, but she wouldn't meet my gaze. Something was wrong, besides the fact she was nearly naked. I looked back to Evan as he eased closer to me like an animal stalking his prey. He had a half-emptied liquor bottle in one hand and was rubbing his chest with the other hand.

"It's time for a toast, my beauties." His words came out in a slur. "Pick up your glass, my sweet Rose." He nodded his head towards the glass that I had not noticed sitting on the table before her. It was filled with the amber liquid. She hesitantly picked it up, but paused. He made a tilting motion towards his mouth with his empty hand, and she mimicked him with taking a sip. Her eyes seemed to tear up and she shuttered a bit as she swallowed.

"That's my girl," he crooned. He eased uncomfortably close to me and draped his arm around my waist. "Oh ladies. We are going to have such fun tonight," he whispered against my neck. He then moved to stand in front of me, and held my cheek as his glassy eyes studied me. "Now it's Miss Firecracker's turn." The words came out like an order as he held the bottle to my mouth.

I jerked away and shook my head in protest.

"No? That's not the way a party works," he said lazily with a crooked grin. He offered the bottle again. I still didn't take it.

"Just drink it, Savannah," Julia gently urged. I

looked over at her, but she still wouldn't look at me.

Before I could refuse again, Evan grasped ahold of my jaw tightly in his hand. While holding my mouth open, he tilted the bottle up and began pouring the harsh liquor too quickly. I started gagging and ended up spraying the vile stuff all over his bare chest. He slid his grip to my neck to hold me in place as he drained the remnants in the bottle before setting it down.

"Now, now, little miss. You've made quite a mess on me." He ran his free hand over his wet chest. "Now you are going to just have to wipe it off."

I stood in shock at his words. Was he serious? How could this be happening? I felt like I was stuck in some bizarre dream I couldn't escape. He dragged me closer, urging a paper towel in my hand and guided it to clean the alcohol away. Then he poured another shot and demanded I drink it. I had no other choice but to do as he said. I gagged but managed to keep this one down. As it hit my stomach, my insides felt like they were on fire.

After an inappropriate kiss, Evan released me and headed over to Julia. He held his hand out and gestured for her to join him. "Come on, my sweet Rose. Come dance with me."

She stood stiffly, and that was when I noticed the bruises blooming along her thighs and back.

Confusion cinched my gut as I tried to comprehend why she was riddled with bruises. *Had he beaten her? Why?* Evan and Rose circled the room in a slow dance. My heart raced as I watched my sister quietly cry while dancing with that devil. Their dance eventually led them upstairs, and I was left in the middle of the kitchen alone, in shock and standing in a large puddle of urine.

I gradually unglued my feet and shuffled upstairs to my room. I could hear noises that I didn't want to identify coming from my sister's room. I gathered a clean outfit and dashed to the bathroom across the hall. I locked the door and then propped a step stool under the knob in hopes of barricading myself in.

After peeling my soiled clothes off, I showered numbly. I drew a bath after the shower to prolong the bathroom visit as long as I could. As I sat in the tub trembling, I watched the doorknob come to life. Evan knocked once he realized I would not be willingly opening the door for him.

"You've been in there a long time. Are you okay?" he asked through the door as the knob jiggled again. "Why's the door locked?"

"I'll be out soon," I stammered. I didn't move until I heard him walk away. I quickly dressed and hesitantly peeped in the hall. It was clear, so I darted over to Julia's door and knocked.

"Julia. It's me. Are you okay? Can I come in?" I asked urgently as I continued to eye the hallway for any sign of Evan's return.

"Just go to bed. Lock your door," she said in a tired voice. I wanted to be locked in her room with her, but did as she told me.

I locked the door before crawling in my bed and hiding under the quilt. I willed the nightmare to be over, but, oh no, it would not be that easy. Not even an hour had passed before it began. I lay in the dark room and listened to the doorknob jiggle around in protest to the lock, followed by a quiet knocking that I ignored. Then came the rustling sound of a tool being jammed forcefully into the lock. I jumped as though those knowing sounds had jolted me with electricity. All I could do was just lie there and wait. The nightmare was worsening, and there was absolutely nothing or no one to save me from the inevitable. Nothing.

As the demons of fear danced around frantically, the door swung open with Evan filling the space. His bare chest heaved up and down with his excitement. The hall light filtered around him, and his face glinted in the unnerving nightglow, adding to the wickedness.

"It's our turn to dance, little miss," he said in a slurred voice as he turned to close and lock the door behind him. He moved through the dark room and joined me in my bed.

It was the first of many sick dances that night. He was like a ravenous beast on the prowl, in and out of our rooms. His perverted acts continued until the early hours of the sun began to rise. When his sick pleasures were finally satisfied, he gathered up our bloody sheets and hid the evidence of the innocence he savagely stripped away from my sister and me. Innocence that was forever stolen and normalcy completely lost.

With the scent of pungent sin tinging the air, I staggered to the bathroom to begin an unrelenting, unsuccessful quest to scrub the feel of that monster off my torn body. *It has never come clean.*

Julia and I stayed in bed the following week with the *flu*. Jean gave us ample supplies of her home remedy elixir after she returned tanned and rested from her vacation. Never did she mention finding the signs of what happened, but I have my suspicion she knew. Evan was never asked to come over again. Thankfully, by the end of the summer, he moved back to Chicago.

Julia gradually left me too, and sadly, I never got her back.

Chapter Eight

Finally floating back to reality, I find myself sprawled face down on the floor of my bedroom. The aroma of lemon furniture polish surrounds me. The panic attacks very rarely escalate to the point of blacking out, but this one hit me hard. I lie here for a little longer and try to get my bearings. My bag is sitting beside me, so I dig out a halved Xanax and gulp it down without water, hoping it will chase the remaining remnants of the attack away.

As I lay here waiting for the detached feeling to free me, I notice I have landed on my rope rug. I run my fingers along the woven material, soften in age. It was my bed for nearly a year after Evan raped me. I had refused to even touch the bed and would sleep on the floor every night. I requested an entire new bed and mattress set for my twelfth birthday and was relieved when it was delivered. Having that reminder gone helped some.

I finally gather myself into a sitting position and am contemplating an escape, when I hear a knock on the door. After another impatient knock sounds, I slowly stand to answer it. I pull the door open and stare down at one of Jean's short, pudgy friends. She is in her late sixties, maybe early seventies, and looks her age with gray hair and crow's feet—unlike Jean. My mother is still blonde and wrinkle free. I didn't inspect her closely to be sure, but I suspect a nip and tuck has occurred by now.

This lady must finally decide I'm not going to speak because she stammers out weakly, "Sweetheart, I hate to bother you, but don't you think you need to be making your way over to the funeral home?"

"Why?" I look at her confused.

"To make the funeral arrangements, of course." She steps away from the door to encourage me to be on my way, but I just stand here, leaning on the doorframe for support. "Your poor mother can't bring herself to do it. *We* all think it's best for you to take care of it."

I stare at her, wondering just who in the heck are *we*?

"And be sure to go to the florist too." She bobs

her head reassuringly.

I roll my eyes at her. *Who does she think she is? Really?*

Without saying a word, I grab up my bag and make a beeline to the front door. I make no eye contact, and the guests pretty much leave me alone. I do a quick glance around in the hopes of finding John Paul and roping him to going with me. Of course, he's nowhere to be found.

Alone. I have always done everything alone in this family. I guess this is no different. I point the car in the direction of the funeral home and set out to begin the task of burying my father—alone.

The funeral home director knew dad better than I did, so he made the unbearable task as simple as he could. I was out the door in less than an hour, after picking a nice wood carved casket, writing an obituary, and setting the time and date for the funeral service. His assistant helped to put the memorial cards together. She had already received a photo from the family. When I saw it, I had to sit down for a spell. It was a picture of my dad sitting at the end of the Bay Creek Pier. It was early morning so the sun was rising behind him and sparkling vibrantly off the ocean waves. His salt-and-pepper hair was dancing in the breeze, and his grey eyes were squinted from laughing at something. My heart throbbed as I held it in a shaky hand and wished beyond wishing to have been there in that moment, laughing along with him. Oh how I wish I could hear that laugh just one more time. But time is up…

I arrange to drop a suit off before crossing the street to the conveniently located florist. I know my dad wasn't big into flowers, so I keep the choices simple. I order several beautifully potted beach grass plants and sea oats. I figure after it's all said and done, these can be replanted at my dad's pride and joys—the restaurant and seafood market. I know Jean won't be pleased with this choice because it's not grand enough, but I know Dad would have approved. And that's who I want to please with this choice.

I choose another route home. I'm in desperate need of some peace. If I can just see her, I know I can feel better. I know I will be able to get through this. My body is relaxed from my medication, but my soul is stirring and churning in a way that I can hardly stand it.

Miss May is making her way out of her house, wearing her Sunday's best with her silver hair freshly curled, carrying a covered casserole dish as I pull up. The sight of this round, petite woman is instant comfort. I have no idea how I have been able to bear being away from her for over five years.

"Well… Just who is this standing before me after all these years?" She wraps her free hand around my waist.

I stoop and return her hug as I whisper, "Nobody hoping to see somebody."

"Nonsense." She pulls away to get a good look at me. "This ain't one of yo' disappearin' acts is it? I'm allowed to see you?"

"No ma'am. Just a visit." I stand here squinting from the sun.

"I'm sorry 'bout yo' daddy, child."

"Me too." I point at the dish in her hand. "I catch you at a bad time?"

"Nope. Perfect timin'. You can accompany me to my church social." With this, she hands me the warm dish and heads over to her car. She starts digging around her in gigantic purse.

"Miss May? Don't tell me you still drive?" I ask skeptically.

"Child, I may be old as dirt, but ain't nuttin' wrong with my eyes." She turns her attention to my car. "Fine. You drive us in yo' fancy Mercedes Coupe." She walks over and starts climbing in the passenger seat.

"Since when do you speak car?" I place the dish in the backseat and then climb in the driver's seat. I've already made my mind up that I'm only going to drop her off.

"Since all my great-grandson wants to talk to me about is cars. As long as that boy wants to talk to me 'bout anything, I'm gonna listen." She buckles her seatbelt. "Well now, let's go."

"I'm not dressed for church." I look down at my jeans and plain peasant blouse, which are wrinkled from traveling and the impromptu *nap* on the floor of my bedroom earlier.

"Long as you ain't naked, you dressed right for God." She knows I'm reluctant about the whole church-going thing. "I ort to have whooped yo' folks for not havin' you young'un's butts in church." She shakes her head and presses her lips together firmly.

"I... I go to church some."

"Just what kind of church might that be?"

"Methodist." I think… Or is it Presbyterian? Lucas goes most every Sunday, but I only agree to join him every now and then.

"I suppose that'll do," she says with a sassy smile.

I unenthusiastically put the car in drive and follow her directions to church. When we pull up, I notice her church brand of choice is Baptist, which is indicated on the sign by the road. We stow her dish in the fellowship hall and make our way to the church sanctuary.

"I thought we were here to eat?" I whisper as we

take our seat in a pew near the back—to my relief.

"We are. First we get our spiritual meal, then our physical," she whispers back.

I lean close to her ear. "I'm just really in the mood for the physical. I think I'm going to pass on the first portion." I make to stand up, but that little lady grabs hold of my blame arm and won't let go. "Miss May, I ain't got this much free time. Jean will surely bless me out for this long disappearing act." We are playing tug-of-war with my arm, and I wish I could simply disappear right now.

"You takin' me home. Now stop with all them excuses." She keeps her vice grip hold on my arm, so I give up.

The service opens with us singing who knows how many songs that are followed by a long, melodious prayer that actually lulls me to doze off until an elbow finds my side abruptly. I look over and Miss May sits there like she didn't do what I know she just did. Rubbing the tender spot on my side, I focus my attention to the tall, portly man behind the pulpit, but cut my gaze one last time at Miss May. She still doesn't acknowledge me, so I try to get comfortable for the long haul. A quick glance around confirms my suspicions. I'm the only white girl present with jeans on. *Only* in both aspects. Great.

I hunch down as best as I can, but Miss May gives

me a less powerful nudge in my side and says, "Sit up straight."

Trying not to sulk, I reluctantly sit up and focus on the preacher as he slides his glasses on and opens his Bible. Everyone else follows suit with the opening of the Bible thing when he announces he will be reading Jeremiah 1:5. Miss May tries to share hers with me, but I just brush her off with a slight nod and listen. She places her well-worn Bible on her short lap and follows along.

"Before I formed thee in the belly, I knew thee; and before thou camest forth out of the womb I sanctified thee…" He stops here and takes pause as he scans the congregation. His gaze hits on me, and I know I stick out like a sore, bright white thumb.

Sorry, preacher man. Don't mean to distract you.

He moves to the side of the podium and props his elbow there. "My brothers and sisters, don't you realize, God created each one of us. And before we entered this world and took even our first breaths, He approved of us… *People*! There are no mistakes with *God*!" He shouts with long drawn-out pronunciations of his words and is rewarded with loud shouts of *amen*.

The preacher moves back to his spot behind the podium, where he dabs the corners of his mouth with a folded handkerchief. He goes back to reading more scripture, but I don't follow along. I'm stuck on the statement he just declared. I have always viewed myself as a mistake by God. You know, like he just had an off day when He thought it was a good idea to stick me in the Thorton family. But this man just stood before me and declared me *wrong*.

I stew on this but the preacher eventually gains my attention after a while. "We as humans are the ones to make the mistakes. God ain't made no junk. Oh no, sisters and brothers!! He ain't in the junk making *b-u-s-i-n-e-s-s*. He in the miracle making *b-u-s-i-n-e-s-s*." He punctuates each word by pounding the podium with his fist, exaggerating each syllable. More amens and shouts. "We the ones who make the mistakes. We make mistakes, and we let others' mistakes make a mess of our lives." Amens roar from the crowd some more. "Oh, but our heavenly Father gives us the choice. That's right. He lets us choose if we gonna let them mistakes haunt us or we can let it go and live this life He has blessed to us!" The continuous pounding of the podium echoes his statements all around in the supercharged sanctuary, and everyone is nearly shouting now.

My arms are covered in goose bumps, and I feel the urge to bolt. Miss May must sense this because she places my hand in hers in another one of her death grips. I glance down at our interlocked hands and then at her, but she just keeps staring forward. I try to pry my hand free when I catch a slight shake of her head. *Humph!*

"Jesus said that He came so that we can all have life and have it more abundantly. That means He desires us to be with great plenty. Of what, you may ask?" People shout out back, urging him to tell us. They have been having a conversation with the preacher, and I guess God too, the entire service. "It means He wants us to have a great plenty of… Peace! Happiness! Love!" More amens. "You live and love like you should. You lay them burdens down to Him and ask Him in." He covers his heart before he proceeds. "You put down them demons haunting you from yo' past. And all the good 'n plenty can be yours!" He is shouting and walking back and forth across the small stage and is sweating profusely. I'm sweating too. I watch him enviously as he dabs at his forehead with the handkerchief, wishing I had one of them dang things too.

Sitting in this unfamiliar pew, listening to these unfamiliar words, I'm right miserable. *I'm so lost…I'm so confused…I'm worthless…*

"Don't lose yo' self in this world. Don't let the confusion of doubt and past pains make you feel worthless," he continues, and I'm beginning to think this sweaty dude has a direct line to my thoughts. It makes me nervous. He points directly towards me, and I near 'bout faint. "God made you and He approved of you and don't you dare let anyone, especially that devil, tell you no different!"

~ ~ ~

I end up asking Miss May to find a ride home after the service. I've lost my appetite with everything pressing down on me. I just needed to be alone, and she seemed to understand. She's always seemed to know when to push and when to back off with me. I've been taught many a lesson in my youth by Miss May. Whether it was a recipe lesson or a life lesson, I have always kept them stowed away.

One of her last gifts to me before I left for college was a life lesson. It was the day I was to leave and was feeling pretty weighed down. I had earned a full academic scholarship to USC and purchased my first car earlier that year—a Volkswagen Beetle, powder blue with a black convertible top. It was old and well broken in, but I could call it all mine. Tips from waitressing and summer bonuses that I diligently saved for several years had allowed me it pay it off in full.

I knew I should have been excited. And I was, but I felt all alone in that excitement. Bradley and Julia were long gone, and John Paul's presence was pretty scarce.

I had just finished loading my stuff into my little car at the house when my mother walked past me to her own car.

"I'm off to the salon," she announced. She acted as though she was completely blind to the fact that I was leaving. I know it shouldn't have hurt. Really. But it did anyway. Ever since that nightmare of a summer and then me defying her, Jean had totally acted as though I did not exist in her world.

"You have fun with that," I said perky enough for her to cut me a look as she closed her car door. I stood grinning at her until she pulled away. I might have muttered a few choice words, but let's not repeat that.

I swung by the restaurant to say my goodbyes to my real family. The staff had been better to me than any blood relative ever had been. The family businesses were also the only fond memories I had of my dad. From having quick meals to helping him do invoices—it was our moments. Moments that I have to cling to now, because I am realizing how much I have cheated myself out of by running away.

I remember walking into the quiet restaurant a little before opening time and was shocked when people jumped out from every nook and cranny to shout surprise! Both the staff from the seafood market and the restaurant crew, along with my dad, presented me with a cake and ice cream. We ate and laughed as they celebrated my departure.

Nearing opening time, they began saying their goodbyes and presented me with various presents. First was from my dad. It was an envelope thick with hundred dollar bills. He hugged me and requested that we kept that between just the two of us. He disappeared into his office after that. Then I was completely overloaded with gifts. Most of the staff knew not to attempt a hug, so they presented me encouragements along with gifts. My arms became overfilled grocery bags of mac and cheese and peanut butter and other easy food choices, a USC sweatshirt, a USC T-shirt, a messenger bag, several phone cards, some more cash, and some other stuff I can't remember. But it was a lot of stuff! My hands were completely full by the time Miss May walked up to me with a huge wicker basket full of baked and canned goods in one hand and a gallon of sweet tea in the other. She knew me well, that's for sure.

"There's no way I can carry that, Miss May." I laughed. It was just us two in the kitchen now due to everyone else having to get to work.

"Your load is pretty heavy, ain't it child?" she asked. I began to laugh again, but then realized I was about to receive a lesson. She was subdued looking and had tears in her eyes. "Come on, child. I'll help you carry this load for a spell." She then headed to the back door of the kitchen. I was parked just off to the side of the restaurant. We walked silently. I remember sighing in relief when I freed my hands of everything into the backseat. I turned around to grab her gifts and noticed that the tears had spilled onto her dark cheeks.

"God's blessings are so much easier if yo' lay all your baggage down first, ain't it?" She handed me her gifts to make the point. She didn't release the handle of the basket once I claimed it in mine. "God is even willin' to take our baggage. All's we gotta do is be willin' to hand it over to Him." She released the handle with a knowing nod. We just stood there staring at each other somberly. She knew I had demons I carried around, although she just didn't know specifically what they were caused from.

"Have a good life, my child. Don't let no baggage rob yo' of the happiness God gots in store for you."

I hugged her one last time after receiving my Miss May lesson. I drove away that day, to find my new start, with a peculiar sense worrying in the back of my mind that I was just missing a crucial point from her. I know now how crucial it had been.

Don't we always wish we knew then what we know now?

Chapter Nine

It's well past dark as I pull into the driveway. I can see in the glow of the house lights that mourners are still lingering around. I had really hoped they would have paid enough respects by now, but I keep forgetting that I'm back in the South.

After I shuffle through the crowd on the porch to push open the front door, I am greeted by two elegant flower arrangements in the foyer. They are exquisite with pale pink peonies gathered with creamy, smaller peonies, cascading sweet peas, and dainty foliage. The fragrance is a heavenly floral perfume. I greedily steal several deep breaths of their aroma before I fish the cards out and find that one is addressed to me and the other is to the Thorton family. Both have been gifted by the Monroe family. Lucas's mom, Kathleen, has impeccable taste and is one of my dearest friends. She knows my flower of choice is a peony. I detest a bouquet with any rose in it. I've always regarded that flower as to only belonging to my sister, Julia. She is a Rose, not me.

I grab up my bouquet and stow it on my dresser in my room so that I can enjoy it during my undetermined sentence. I drop my purse on the floor and send Kathleen a quick "thank you" text before following my nose to the kitchen. It's been a long time since the biscuits and gravy, and my stomach is letting me know all about it. I stop in my tracks as I take in the transformation of the kitchen space. Gone are the off-white Formica countertops and old tan appliances. They have been replaced with sleek granite countertops and stainless steel appliances. The old oak cabinets have also been replaced with crisp white ones that are adorned with brushed nickel nobs and pulls. The only thing original is the wood floors, which have been recently resurfaced. This is not the outdated country kitchen I grew up in. This is a chef's kitchen. The walls are a fresh sky-blue, and are dressed with beautiful black-and-white photographs that beg me to walk over to study them. One picture has captured the two businesses. These structures look like antique beach houses in the photo, with deep covered porches and rocking chairs. The other photo is a landscape shot of the beach I like to visit. I run my fingers along the frame edge and come to a stop when I notice the photographer's signature scrawled along the bottom of the canvas.

"Your brother is a gifted photographer, don't you think?"

I turn around and find a familiar yet aging man looking past me to the photos. "He is," I answer a bit confused. I had no idea John Paul had any other talent besides telling tall-tales and wooing women. I have missed more than I had expected.

"Sweetheart, I'm sorry about your daddy. He was a great man to work for," Mr. Chester says. He is my dad's seafood market manager. Or he may still be. Who knows. "Are you hanging in there?"

"I think so," I mumble as I scan the crowd. "Do you know where my mother is?"

"She was given something earlier to help her rest. She's already gone to bed. That poor woman has just about grieved herself to death…" He catches what he has just said but we both know it's too late to take it back, so we ignore it.

I quickly change the subject. "Wow. Wonder when my parents did all this?" I ask as I motion around the renovated kitchen.

"Your dad kept himself quite busy since he

retired earlier this year."

"Retired? My dad? Are you sure?" I can't fathom him ever doing that willingly. I rub my temples in the hopes of making all of this clearer, but it's not working.

"Yes. He announced at the Christmas Party that it was time to spend more time with his lovely bride." Mr. Chester moves a little closer and says quietly, "Between you and me, your dad was waiting for you to decide to come home so he could hand it over to you. He wanted you to sow your oats and didn't want to rush you, so he temporarily handed things over to John Paul."

Well, that explains why he is at the funeral home. Jean had managed to worry him slap to death in only six short months. I push my own guilt from Mr. Chester's words down as far as I can. I'm at a loss as to why Dad ever thought I would come back home to run his businesses. Nothing against the restaurant and market, but *no*.

I don't want to hear any more, so I set out to look for my brother. I find him at the door, practically shoving people out.

"Thank you for all of your help, condolences, and food." John Paul echoes this repeatedly as he shows people to the door. I realize it is now after ten, and I still have not eaten by the time he has closed the door for good for the night. He senses this, or is hungry himself, because he guides me back to the kitchen. "Let's eat."

I set my sights on the bounty of food that practically covers every surface of the kitchen. This is a southern tradition, unlike what I have encountered up north at wakes, which resemble more of a somber cocktail party. Here in the South, it's like a family reunion with endless supplies of food that is always more than can be consumed. Southern folks love to love on you with food. Feeding you gives them a purpose in these sad situations. Right now, I'm super glad of this because I'm starving. I scan the counters and spot more mac and cheese casseroles than needed, several pots of chicken bog, a spiral-cut glazed ham, potato salad, butter beans, fried squash, fried chicken, fried shrimp, homemade biscuits, and any type of dessert you could imagine. It looks like a bakery shop has been unloaded in here.

I pop a deviled egg in my mouth before grabbing a paper plate. I dig a fried chicken leg out of an aluminum pan and set my sights on the desserts. I find my favorite right away and cut a considerable chunk off. It's an old-fashioned chocolate cake made of twenty thin layers, and the smell of the fudgy icing sets my mouth to watering. I'm unable to resist, so I run my finger along the edge of the cake plate and scoop a large glob of gooey goodness into my mouth. Oh boy, this stuff is so good. So good, in fact I cannot resist another glob. As I suck the stickiness off my finger, I catch John Paul staring at me with a smirk on his face.

"What?" I ask around a mouthful of fudgy icing.

He shakes his head. "Wish I had my camera. You've smeared that crap all over your chin. Looks like you been eating sh—"

I playfully pop him in his mouth with my sticky hand before he can spit the rest of the ugly word out. I've never been a fan of that kind of language, and he knows it.

He jumps away from me, laughing. "Gross, Savannah. Don't put that nasty hand on me." He bats my hand away.

After grabbing a glass of sweet tea, I leave him in the kitchen and head to the porch swing. I glide slowly in the night's soothing silence as I enjoy my greasy chicken leg and scrumptious cake. John Paul joins me by the time I've made a substantial dent in my chunk of cake.

"Here," he says as he sits beside me, trying to hand me a glass of wine. "This will go better with your dessert than tea."

I shake my head, refusing it. "I'm not much of a drinker. All it does is give me nightmares and bad headaches."

He shrugs his shoulders and downs all of the wine in one long gulp. He places the empty glass on the wood-planked floor and then sets out to nurse the beer.

"Where's your food?" I ask.

"Not hungry," he says. I try not to worry, but he looks a bit gaunt tonight.

We rock in silence as I finish the cake. It was almost too much, and I think I overdid it, but it will be worth the bellyache. As I toss my empty plate Frisbee-style over to the garbage bin on the porch, the front door opens. Two ladies shuffle out, surprising John Paul and me.

The short, pudgy one from earlier says, "We put the food away. We'll be back in the morning. Good night, children." They both wave goodbye.

Once they drive off, we burst out laughing.

"Where in the world were them two hiding?" I ask.

"I don't know. I thought I kicked everybody out earlier." John Paul chuckles.

"They must have been upstairs tending to *your* mother." We laugh some more before settling into the quietness of the night.

I finally break the silence after a while. "When was the last time you saw Dad?" I glance over at my brother and really give him a looking over. The dark circles under his red, swollen eyes are evidence to his loss, and it causes a deep ache of anguish for him to resonate in the pit of my stomach.

"Only three nights ago," he says. "He popped in the restaurant at closing and helped me finish up the night duties. We ended up hanging out in one of the booths for a couple of hours afterwards, just running off at the mouth. He told me how proud he was of me and encouraged me to keep up my photography business." He pauses before muttering in disappointment, "I've been debating on giving it up."

"I didn't know you were into that. I think it's great. Those pictures in the kitchen are impressive." I compliment him, but he seems far away. I place my hand on his arm. He looks over at me with tear-filled eyes. A thought clicks into place. "You took that picture of Dad on the pier, didn't you?" John Paul nods somberly. "I would love a copy of it, please." He nods again.

We swing another stretch before John Paul speaks again. "I knew that night something bad was going to go down. I just didn't know it was going to be this." He hangs his head and quietly weeps. After he regains his composure, he whispers, "He really listened to me that night when I was telling him about a photo shoot I just wrapped. Not the normal way with him grunting every now and then through the conversation and not really listening, you know. The way he normally would. It was a great final gift the other night."

I'm grateful for my brother and jealous at the same time. I have no final gift of time with my dad. I have blown it and understand there's no second chance in this situation. I can't manage another word, so I leave John Paul on the porch to mourn alone and head upstairs to do some of my own.

After changing, I settle on the bed and call Lucas from the neon-pink phone on my nightstand. This was a phone Julia insisted I have in our youth, but I never really used it, being the loner my young days.

"Hello?" The calmness echoes in his quiet voice as it always does and is an instant salve to my tender heart.

"It's me. I needed to hear your voice…I miss you too much." I feel the tears prick my eyes but know they won't escape. I'm not a crier. I wish I were. Maybe then I could wash away some of this overwhelming grief.

"I can get on the road right now. I can be there by midmor—"

"It's okay." I bet he is already on his feet, heading to his closet to pack. "You've got that business meeting tomorrow." I hear a door close, and am pretty sure it was probably the closet door.

"You know I would cancel it for you." Lucas lets out a long sigh of resignation.

"I know, but don't, okay?"

He gives up and moves on quickly. He has learned over the years that I'm a bit stubborn. "Your voice sounds better. I guess you cooled it on the screaming exercise?"

I roll my eyes. I can't get anything past him.

"I told you it's my allergies against the south." I try to laugh it off. Lucas remains quiet as expected at my lie. "Look. It's been an exhausting day and I was only in Jean's presence for not even five minutes. Tomorrow is gonna be worse. I best be getting to bed. I love you."

"Love you too. Good night, love."

I hang up the phone and turn over. I pull the cover up over my head and try to pretend I'm back at our condo and he is just working late. I miss him and want him here, but I'm not that selfish. He doesn't need to be stuck in this mess. I finally drift off to sleep after tossing and turning for about an hour. At my last glance of the clock, it's one in the morning.

~ ~ ~

"Come on man! Momma said we could. Don't

chicken out on me now," John Paul says. He is trying so hard to convince Bradley, who's being quite hesitant about this stunt. "You know everyone is looking forward to this latest feat. This is our coolest idea by far, dude." They stand there—one blond and one auburn, and both of equal height and weight—near the edge of the overgrown field, contemplating. They are more like brothers than cousins.

The two teenage boys are known for performing daredevil stunts for all the kids in the neighborhood—whether it includes a surfboard, skateboard, or anything with a motor. Consequently, neither one ever walks away unscathed. They end up with broken bones and stitches quite often.

I move a bit closer so I can hear their conversation better. "I don't know, J.P." Bradley hesitates. "We don't know what's in that grassy field." Bradley's uncertainty on attempting their latest stunt is loud and clear. He has already chewed every bit of his fingernails off up to the quick and is now chewing on the skin around what's left of his thumbnail.

"Okay, okay," John Paul replies, raising his hands up. "Let's check it over real good first." I can tell he has his mind made up on performing today, no matter what. "You know everyone will be pissed at us if they come out here in this blame heat and we chicken out, dude." John Paul runs his hands through his long hair.

The grassy field is located down a dirt road and isn't being planted this year, so it's pretty secluded and deserted. It is overgrown with waist-high weeds in some spots. I keep checking around my feet for snakes as I follow behind them. They quickly scope it out for any hidden obstacles while the cicadas keep whining out a warning. I hope those blame bugs hit their crescendo soon, because the volume is echoing around the field in an annoying buzz.

After the boys decide the field is safe enough, John Paul can barely contain his excitement. He's practically skipping around, high-fiving some of his buddies as he passes by. The crowd of kids begins to gather at the edge of the field.

"What are they going to do this time?" someone in the group behind me asks once I settle in my spot at the edge of the field. I have no idea, so I let someone else answer.

"J.P. is going to drive that old, beat-up car around the field while Bradley walks on top of it from the front to the back," another kid answers.

I slipped out of the house earlier to come out here and watch the stunt. Now that I find out exactly what the stunt is, I want the boys to heed to the cicadas warnings. I know it's no use to try to talk them out of it, though. I reluctantly stand on the sidelines with everyone else and watch nervously. The heat is searing my face and thick beads of sweat blanket the back of my neck in the late summer afternoon. It's nearing suppertime, so I'm hoping this won't take long. My heart is pounding so intensely that I can see my shirt bouncing off my chest. My gut just knows this isn't going to end well.

After John Paul slides behind the wheel, a strenuous roar yells out from the massive car with the engine coming to life, and "Smells Like Teen Spirit" by Nirvana booms from the speakers in a static-filled thump. The old radio system is just butchering a perfectly good song, but no one seems to mind.

Bradley jumps on top of the hood and sits on it with his long legs crossed casually as the beast of a car slowly begins to creep across the grassy field. The ancient thing creaks and vibrates over the uneven ground. It is a mammoth of a vehicle. Maybe it will make it easier for the lanky teenage boy to keep his balance. I keep my fingers crossed. He has a stern, very determined look on his face. Good. That means he is concentrating. I can only hope John Paul is taking this as seriously. I slide my attention to him sitting behind the wheel, one arm hanging out the open window. He is tapping the side of the door in the rhythm of the music. The humidity flicks his hair in every direction in the breeze, but he seems to not mind.

Once Bradley seems to work up enough nerve, he stands on the dented hood. The thick metal pops and groans in protest as he plants his feet. Slowly he straightens his posture and extends his arms away from his sides to help with balancing. He looks as if he is surfing a massive wave. I begin to relax at this thought, for both boys are excellent surfers. Carefully, he steps over the windshield onto the roof and then makes his way towards the back of the long rusty car. Once he reaches the trunk, the crowd lets out an earsplitting roar. He gives us a thumbs-up before turning around cautiously.

The car passes in front of us. "Are you ready to go a little faster?" John Paul yells out of the window, trying to antagonize his cousin. "That was way too easy, bro!"

Bradley shakes his head aversely but agrees, and so John Paul increases the old car's speed gradually and heads away from us once more. The pile of junk sounds like it wants to choke off in defeat, but instead the speed creeps up slowly. Bradley begins to make his way towards the front of the car in the same manner. His demeanor is more confident with the second pass, and he is maneuvering through the stunt a little faster. The spectators are cheering and whistling with excitement, but the cicadas are stilling shouting their disapproval. With a quick glance at me and a slight grin working from the corners of his mouth, Bradley proceeds. His shaggy hair flairs out all around him, and his face is tinged pink from the heat and excitement.

As he is reaching the rooftop once again, the car wobbles in response to an uneven groove in the field and Bradley loses his balance and nearly sails off the side completely. John Paul instinctively decelerates without hitting the brakes to slow the speed. The crowd gasps as Bradley safely recovers his balance. Thankfully, his foot landed on top of the passenger side rearview mirror, and so he is able to use it to help climb back on top. A spasm of panic shoots through my stomach and I have to remind myself to breathe. Within seconds, Bradley is standing straight up on the roof and waving his arms in the air with victory. Everyone joins in with their own victorious roar. John Paul, wrapped up in all the excitement of the moment, isn't paying attention to where he is going and drives through another uneven area of the field.

With the car shaking from the bumpiness, Bradley loses his balance once again. Only this time he is unable to catch himself and he soars over the hood of the old car as it plows into a deep rut on the far edge of the field. Everything flashes in slow motion at a hastened speed in a confused instant.

Bradley lands right in the path of the car and before he can roll out the way, it pins him up against the earth. John Paul immediately puts the car into reverse, but the rut is just too steep to get it out. The car only whines and sputters with smoke bellowing out of from all directions before it abruptly chokes off. I watch hopelessly as the wheels sink in the soft soil even more. The earth begins to whirl around us before we can will ourselves to move forward. As the crowd erupts in horror, John Paul jumps from the driver's seat screaming. My cool, laidback brother is gone and a madman wailing at the top of his lungs has taken his place.

"I'm sorry! I couldn't get it to stop! I'm so sorry!" John Paul screams. He just repeats this over and over again as he tries to lift and pull the solid piece of death trap that's on Bradley. Several guys from the crowd try to help but it still won't budge. John Paul tries to dig Bradley out, but the soft dry dirt quickly fills back in every time. He digs until he is black from dust and his fingertips trickle blood. Everyone is running around crazed. Everything is chaotic. We are frightened and in shock over seeing the awful accident happening right before us. I can taste the bitterness, and the field begins to spin out of control. I try swallowing it back down, but my throat refuses until I relent and vomit. I vomit until dry heaves seize me and render me destitute. I just stand here by the two boys in disbelief as John Paul keeps pulling on Bradley—one wild in pain and one still in death.

"Please, bro. Please move. Please, please, *please*!" John Paul cries. "Please God. *Please*!" He has Bradley under his arms and is yanking with all his might, still screaming.

I vaguely notice the put-put puttering sound of the tractor echoing through the field. The farm machine is hooked to the bumper of the car in an instant, and it only takes minutes for the tractor to wrench the heavy car off Bradley. But it is already too late. We gather around his broken body in shock. His shirt has been torn and exposes deep bruises and cuts on his abdomen. His left arm hangs in an unnatural angle. My cousin's long legs, which have always seemed so nimble, are now oddly still—broken and bleeding. Bradley's green lifeless eyes stare past us as we stand trembling in confusion and shock. Sweat, tears, and overwhelming grief cast their own effects in our features.

Time feels as though it stands still for hours, and I don't think the horrifying scene will ever end. No one leaves us. They all stay until adults arrive and demand them to go home. Dad shows up. He collapses beside John Paul and tries unsuccessfully to grip his shoulders. My brother's body is shaking uncontrollably, and he is still screaming. His movements are jerky and chaotic.

Suddenly—but not really—the sun seems to abandon us. The world turns an eerie dark. The field is only lit up with sporadic flashes of blue and red lights as police and rescue vehicles file in and out. In the midst of all the commotion, John Paul sits beside Bradley, rocking back and forth. His painful screams linger over and over but with no voice. He can only squeak at this point, grief and pain having stolen his voice. Even the cicadas finally fall silent. I find the night's quietness peculiar, and this is the point where I find my voice and begin to scream for us all—John Paul, Bradley, Daddy, and me.

My screaming angers the night, and the ground begins to move and dissolve around my feet. I still don't relent. I scream repeatedly in yelping cries. I want it known that this is not right. This is not fair. The night warns again as I feel my body sinking and slipping dangerously close to the edge of the guilty car. As the soil moves, it tugs me closer to Bradley's torn body and John Paul. We are being swallowed up by the earth. I blink the abrasive dirt out of my eyes, only to discover we are imprisoned in a grave and the bloody soil is seeping slowly in on us. I continue to scream until my mouth fills with dirt, which finally mutes me.

~ ~ ~

I nearly jump out of the bed as the dreadful dream finally releases me. My hands bat at my mouth, searching for invasive dirt, but find none. A shiver skirts me, bringing awareness of the cold sweat dampening me. Gasping and moaning, I let my anger out on the bed and begin punching the mattress over and over again. This nightmare has plagued me for years, along with my others. I punch some more, wanting those images to leave me the heck alone. I'm so sick of this night routine.

I can't take it anymore, so I climb out of bed and pace the expanse of my room for a while. I want the anxiety to taper down without having to take a pill. I'm sick of those dang things too. My shaky hands fumble with the window latch for a few aggressive moments before I can open the window up, causing the glass panes to rattle in protest. I lean way out to take several deep breaths of the humid air and demand my body to calm down.

The panic finally subsides, so I slip out of my room and ease to John Paul's door. It's open, so I glance in and am disappointed at finding it empty. I look back down the hall and find it empty as well. I don't want to go back to my haunting room, so I walk in his and am amazed at what I find. The bedroom walls are covered in hundreds of photographs. I know instantly that my brother has taken each one of these spectacular images. There are many vivid ocean shoreline scenes and a few of surfers on the waves. The intense action captured in the images is awe-inspiring. The waves whirl around the surfer or the sun's rays are filtering through the scene in such an artistic way. These are not amateur photos, for sure.

I find one to be exquisite amongst the grouping. It's of the beach during an intense storm. The sky is painted just as I had seen it only the other day. The waves are crashing the shore harshly, and rain is pelting the sea with big splashes. The camera catches the water being raised from the splash, midair, and I'm astounded by the clarity. It's breathtaking, and I'm wondering if I can sneak it home with me. The scene looks as though John Paul hit a pause button to capture the perfection of Mother Nature raging against the sea. Oh yes, this baby will be mine.

I glance over at the opposite wall with the intention of heading back to my room, when my eyes get a good look at the photos. My stomach seizes as I take in the repeated image of the grassy field where Bradley lost his life. My brother has made a memorial in his room to our cousin, and it sends a deep ache through me. Reining in the emotions as best I can, I shuffle in the direction of the wall to learn a bit more about my older brother.

I ease closer and study the unnerving collage of photos. Some are black and white while others in are striking color or aged antiqued. Some are in the daylight and some at night. No matter, they are eerie and laced with grief. My skin pricks with goose bumps rising all over my body. My eyes focus in one spot, and I start to decipher the images before me in a slow, meticulous fashion. I don't want to miss anything. A long time passes as I take in scene after scene of the floor to ceiling collage. One night shot has a huge, glowing moon hovering over the field. Another one captures a rare ice storm with the secrets of the haunted field hidden under a thick sheet of ice. I take in the photo beside this one. It was taken during a severe-looking thunderstorm. The field is drenched and mournful in the gloomy illumination as lightening cuts through the sky ruthlessly. You can feel the animosity in the storm's fury. I scan another that has been tinted in a russet red. It reminds me of dried blood, and I know that was John Paul's intention. This gallery here in my brother's bedroom is unnerving and mesmerizing all at once. There are hundreds. And I can see my brother's pain in each one.

I stand in astonishment for a long spell, studying

each photo in reverence and sorrow at the same time. My brother is an artist. An absolute genius with a camera. And I've missed seeing him develop this. I'm just beginning to realize how costly my disappearing act has been.

After taking a few shaky breaths, I head back to my room and think back over my regrets. Miss May had warned me of needing to abandon my disappearing acts. Did I listen? Of course not.

I ran away shortly after Bradley's funeral. Life had become unbearable with losing Julia and then him unexpectedly. John Paul took to hiding in his room with liquor bottles he snatched either from the house's liquor cabinet or from the restaurant. He became a dark individual. My dad seemed to grow quieter after the accident, and his eyes always held a weariness that wasn't there before. Jean showed her behind as only she could and had to be admitted to the hospital for a nervous breakdown. Whatever. It amazes me that someone who never had a kind word to spare for Bradley could be affected so greatly by his death. Whoever wails the loudest, right? Not. Our family's relationship grew more and more distant after this tragedy.

The nightmares of those images from the accident haunted me both day and night. The panic attacks started gradually during this time. I just couldn't take it anymore one afternoon, so I ran away, straight to Miss May's house. I remember her opening the front door with a discerning expression on her face, and I immediately began to shout at her.

"Stop looking at me!!! You don't see me!!" I screamed. With understanding, she quickly closed her eyes. I took off and hid behind her couch and cried myself to sleep. I awoke later that day to find a blanket draped over me and a pillow placed under my head. I had not slept that hard in forever, it felt. My nightmares had already begun to get the best of me. Insomnia had become a way of life for me early on. A sandwich and glass of tea were on the floor at the end of the couch. As I lay there debating whether I felt up to eating, there was a knock at the door. Of course, it was my dad.

"Miss May, I'm here for Savannah," he said in a tired voice.

"I ain't seen her, sir," she said in her own tired tone.

"Ma'am, I have put up with you and my daughter's disappearing games for years. Do you think I'm really that stupid?" His frustration was undoubtedly strong.

My dread began to fade away and be replaced with acute anger at precisely the same moment as Miss May's. "You mean to tell me that you knew

Savannah was back there in that kitchen with me all those times? You sir, had enough blame sense to know where yo' daughter was hiding, but yo' fool-self never manned up enough to figure out the *why*?" Miss May shouted. I had never seen her so upset in all my life. That woman never lost her cool. "Shame on you, you blind fool. You didn't see the most important part… No, I guess I should say that you chose to *not* see the most important part, since you *is* so smart." She was spitting the words out full of vinegar.

It had gotten so quiet that I finally peeped around the edge of the couch to see if I was left alone. Still at the front door, my dad stood with his shoulders hunched over in defeat and eyes focused on the floor. Miss May just stood in front of him, intently staring up at him.

After a while, she finally spoke, "When Miss Savannah is ready to reappear, I promise to send her straight home. Not until then. Do yo' understand, Mr. John?"

He must have realized this would probably be the only choice he would receive and nodded his head in agreement. Without another word, he was gone. Relief sunk in for just a brief moment before Miss May slammed the door and faced the couch.

"Get yo' white butt out from behind my couch

right this minute!" she said. "This here game of yours is over. It's time you quit actin' like yo' momma."

Then it was my turn to snap. I came charging out from behind the couch and began screaming at her with all my might. "Don't say I'm like that witch! I hate her!" I screamed.

"Then stop actin' like her! What's that ole witch do every time things get tough? Huh? Answer me right now!"

"She runs away," I reluctantly admitted.

"And just what does yo' stubborn self do when things get tough?"

"I run away..."

I couldn't believe this mess. How did I end up being anything like Jean? I was so disgusted with myself that the realization caused me to sink to the floor in shock and shame. Miss May left me to my thoughts on that revelation for the rest of the night. The next day, I decided to go home. That moment in Miss May's home was the last time I have been able to shed a tear. It's as if I released all I could for Bradley before slamming up walls to guard my fragile heart.

Chapter Ten

As the first hints of sunlight begin peeking through my peach colored curtains, I decide sleep has eluded me, and it is pointless to try to get any now. I roll to my side and close my eyes to the new day for just a bit longer.

Hurt…all I feel is hurt. I lay here and beg my memory to give me a reminder of a better day with my dad. I conjure up as clear of an image of him that I can. He is tall and lean in this memory. His clear grey eyes match mine, as well as his dark, wavy hair. His is dusted with some silver, though. The crow's feet around his eyes and laugh lines only accentuate his handsome features.

He is barking with laughter in this flash of memory, and I grab hold of it for dear life. This is a good one, and it feels like a treasure that I have just discovered again after a long forgotten season. Snuggling back into my quilt, I let the memory perform its soothing act…

It's a warm Sunday afternoon and both the restaurant and market are closed as we are preparing for the end of the season celebration. Dad always treats the employees with a bountiful feast and fat bonuses. I'm finally old enough to receive one, and I'm beside myself.

The place is lively with beach music singing lazily in the background while we prepare for the festivities. A small group has paused in their tasks to dance the Carolina Shag. The couples hold one of their partner's hands as they do the smooth steps. They are laughing as they spin around and go back to the dance steps. I can't help but watch with a smile for a few moments before heading back outside.

My job for the day is to set out crab traps and haul them in often for the crab boil. I've already hauled in one batch and am back to check the traps for a second round. Prepping the traps is gross. I have to stuff the bait basket with raw slimy chicken parts before casting the pods out into the inlet. And let's not forget the trickiness of emptying those ornery suckers once caught. Blue crabs like to hold on for dear life, and you have to carefully pry them off. The odds of being pinched are ever in that favor. Yes. I was pinched earlier in the day. I look down at the red whelp on the top of my hand and scoff at it.

I take my responsibilities from my dad seriously, so forging ahead with this unpleasant task is a must. I find the trap to one of the pods has come open, so I pull it onto the dock and replenish the bait. I lob the clunky trap over the water and lose my balance, casting myself in the inlet right along with the trap.

I emerge from the murky water and try to stand, but my feet quickly sink into the sticky mud. I end up falling backwards. Roaring laughter echoes over the inlet as I reemerge for the second time. I find my dad standing on the dock in hysterics, holding his stomach as he laughs at the hilarity.

"Daaadyyy!!" *I whine while trying to dislodge myself from the snares of the inlet mud. Trust me. This stuff is like gloppy glue and it has no incentive to let you go.*

"I told you to gather us some blue crabs and your behind goes swimming instead." He's still laughing.

"It ain't funny!" I begin to gripe but end up snickering over the situation too.

"You might as well make yourself even more useful and gather us some fresh baby clams," he says as he scoops up a wire clam basket.

I'm 'bout to whine even more that he should just help me dislodge myself when he starts sliding off his Sperry Top-Siders. Then he hops right into that murky mess with me, still laughing. I'm floored that he just did this and I know Jean will surely scold him over the fact that he has just infused the pungent inlet water into his new-collared shirt and shorts. But he seems to have no care in the world in this moment except to share a chuckle with me.

We glide along the low tide surface to dig the little clam jewels out of the mud and place them in our basket. During this impromptu clam harvest, Dad tells me how proud he is of me for the hard work I put in during this summer. He also says that he will go with me to pick up the car soon. He talks car for a bit and I have no idea what any of it means, but I don't mind. I focus on just simply enjoying the timbre of his voice. I memorize the late sun dancing along his grey eyes and watch as the water drips from his nearly black mane. He is my dad, and I have his undivided attention in the middle of this Atlantic creek. I feel important and loved.

We glop along until the tide comes in enough to unstick us from the mud. If you can imagine trying to slosh through an enormous vat of foul-smelling chocolate pudding with a heaping amount of glue added, then you can just about get the idea of how one is in a mess if stuck in a creek bed.

Later this evening, my dad and I laugh and chat through our share of garlic butter–soaked steamed clams on the back porch of the restaurant, where Jean exiled us. She said we were stinking up the place with the pungent odor of the inlet clinging to our skin and now dried clothes. I don't mind one bit. It's a very rare occasion for me to have my dad all to myself.

I resurface from this comforting memory with a rare smile. It feels good, but I know it won't last. There's a lot to face, and I am just stalling now. I shuffle through the stack of photos I helped myself to from John Paul's room once more, and then head downstairs for a much-needed caffeine fix. My hopes are to beat Jean waking up so I can enjoy my coffee and maybe another piece of cake alone. Disappointedly, I find her sitting at the table with her own cup of coffee. She is in her dressing gown, but her shoulder-length blonde hair is curled and her make-up painted on tastefully. Typical Jean.

Without a word, I go straight over to the coffeepot and pour myself a large cup. I can feel her eyes boring into my back—judging me and belittling me with her every thought. I toy with the idea of going out to the porch to have my coffee in peace, but decide to be civil and sit at the table with her.

"Did you take care of everything yesterday?" She drawls the words out as she gazes out the set of French doors that I just notice have replaced the picture window.

"Yes. I just have to drop Dad's suit off at the funeral home in a little while," I say, and then ramble off the details. "The service will be the day after tomorrow. It's gonna be held at the Oceanfront Chapel. I thought he would like it there since it was the church he attended as a child, and that's where Bradley is buried." I stop there because I can sense it coming as I watch dissatisfaction cross her face. I inwardly brace myself.

"Maybe you should have asked me what your father would have wanted before you stormed out of here yesterday." Her voice is laced with bitterness, and I wonder if she ever gets tired of the taste of it. "Why'd you think you have the *right* to assume all that? You are nothing more than a *stranger* to this family."

"I was *ordered* to take care of everything without bothering you. That's what your busy-bee friend instructed." I'm so furious I'm beginning to tremble. "I can do nothing right!"

"Explain to me why we are dragging this out for two more days?"

This throws me for a loop. I actually thought she would be glad to have the extra days for the attention. I smart off a response. "It gives your hotshot daughter ample time to decide to find *her* way home."

She snorts at this. "No need in being so snide. Julia Rose has a busy career. I don't expect you to understand that." She looks me over with her nosed wrinkled like I might stink.

"Just what do you mean by that?"

"Exactly what it sounds like. Your sister is earning a living while you lay up in your condo with nothing but time on your lazy hands." She crosses her arms on the table and glares at me. *She's a fine one to talk.*

"You're right, Jean. I'm absolutely worthless." I grab my cup of coffee and start my escape back upstairs. The day has just started, and I have already had to spend too much time with the witch. "Just write down what you want changed and I'll take care of it," I say over my shoulder.

"Just leave it," she says. "It's too late to be changing things around now."

I raise my hand up in surrender and leave her be. Slamming the door for good measure, I go over to the bedroom window and stare out to the backyard. The voluptuous oaks shadow most of the grassy space while they seem to be guarding the lone gardenia bush. Breathing in a deep gulp of the country air, I can smell the heavy perfume of the white flowers from up here.

I chug back my cooling coffee before heading over to my closet. After scrounging around, I'm able to find a pair of jeans and old Hard Rock T-shirt. I change into them and pull my long brown hair into a messy bun. I head to the bathroom to brush my teeth and wash my face. I skip make-up all together in hopes it peeves my mother. Taking a few deep breaths, I go back to the kitchen.

Of course, Jean is at the table with a fresh cup of coffee, but now she is dressed in a black dress suit. A few of her friends are already back manning the kitchen. One is just finishing up a few dishes while the other one is placing muffins and pastries onto a platter.

Without looking up, Jean says dryly, "I know you are not thinking about leaving this house looking like that."

I scoot over, grab a foam cup since I forgot my cup upstairs, and begin preparing a to-go cup of coffee. "Sure am," I mutter.

"You look like crap. You need to get properly dressed," she says too calmly.

I grab a napkin, place several donuts in it, and shove the bundle in my bag for later. I snatch an apple fritter and take a very unladylike bite, cramming my mouth as full as I can. I turn to face Jean and the spectators to our little conversation. My mouth smacks on the doughy goodness for a bit, and then I answer her through my full mouth, "Well…I'm a grown woman, and I can look like crap if I darn well please." As soon as I do this, I wish I could take it back. What's the point in being snide with her?

I try to smooth things over before exiting the kitchen. "By the way, Dad did a great job remodeling the kitchen." I should have known better. I know I should…

"Don't you go thinking all of this will be yours one day," she snaps.

A bitter laugh rips from my snarling lips. "You have no worries on me *ever* wanting to reside in the house where Evan Grey ripped my innocence away!" My words lash out full of venom. My eyes sweep across the kitchen, and the realization of spectators enters my view. Their jaws drop open and my mother dribbles coffee down the front of her top. I really didn't mean to spit out that tidbit at the end. It just slipped, but it was worth seeing my mother's reaction. I have not enjoyed such a response from her since the cookie incident.

I have had enough so I whirl around, grab the business keys off the hook, and slam the door—leaving them silently stunned.

~ ~ ~

I drop my dad's suit off with the receptionist at the funeral home and make a hasty exit. Funeral homes creep me out. Plus, I'm still reeling from my encounter with Jean. I have no idea why my dad was over the moon about her. I guess love really is blind.

I decide to go meet with the other two loves of his life. At least they are welcoming, and more importantly—quiet. I park in front of these two structures that are such a major part of me. They are identical buildings that have loyally kept each other company year after year. The structures resemble two vintage beach houses that have been removed from their lanky stilts. White clapboards dress the outside, and the grey, weathered cedar shingles shield the structures from the coastal sun. Swaying palmetto palm trees are tucked around the perimeter, with one standing between the twins. Small discreet signs painted in sea-blue sway from the porch rafters. I know the exact name of the color because I helped my dad pick it out before I disappeared. The one to the left identifies The Thorton Seafood Market in white script, and the one hanging on the right building's porch identifies it as The Thorton Seafood House. But these two beach jewels need no sign to be found. People just know. Yes. It's that good—award winning good. I've already mentioned that didn't I?

I stare a bit longer before trekking across the crushed seashell parking lot. My mother harassed my dad constantly throughout the years about getting the lot properly paved, but he actually stood his ground on keeping it original.

After unlocking the market door and stepping inside, my nose discovers a smell that I have never smelled emitting from this place. It reeks of old seafood and overripe produce. This is a gourmet specialty store. Seafood has always been of the highest and freshest quality. If my dad couldn't get it from the local docks or in his shop within a few hours of being plucked from the ocean, then he simply wouldn't sell it. Frozen was a big NO. Another unique quality of the market is that whatever seafood dish you can dream up cooking, you can find the needed ingredients waiting patiently on the shelves and bins. So to be assaulted by such wrong smells hits me deep in the pit of my stomach, and I worry a special Thorton era may be coming to an end.

I walk down the aisles, skimming my hands along the way. My eyes sting with wanting to cry, but my body won't give in. I focus on the lovely packages as I walk by and push the hurt away. There are so many batter mixes, everything from hot and spicy to sweet and fruity. The sauce varieties are just as endless in choices.

I grab a large garbage can by the register and head to the produce area to weed out the spoiled items. It's not a very large section so this takes no time. On autopilot, I then head to the seafood display.

I know what my dad would do, so I do it also. I dump each bin of fish and shellfish into the trash. It's not fresh and needs to be tossed. I work in silent anguish as I scrub the bins after tossing the trash in the back dumpster. My last task is to mop my way out before heading next door.

I'm at the front door of the restaurant and have to force myself to unlock the door and step in. It's almost unbearable. The quietness echoes as I walk over the worn wood-planked floor. I glance around the lonely dining area before heading to my favorite spot—the kitchen. It's impeccably clean as it has always been. I do a quick scan of the refrigerators and toss a few items. There's not much to take care of in here, so I make my way to my dad's office.

I brace myself before pushing through his door. The familiar scent of my dad's spicy cologne assails my senses as I walk in. I expect to find him sitting behind his desk, but it's empty. My eyes sting and my throat constricts, but still no tears. My chest tightens as I ease into his chair. I push the pain away as much as I can and focus on the task at hand.

I check the numerous messages, which are mostly customers wanting to pay their condolences. I record a brief message on the phone service. "This is Savannah, and on behalf of the Thorton family, I would like to thank you for your concerns and well wishes. An announcement will be posted by next week with information as to when the businesses will reopen." I pause before continuing to clear my throat and add, "My father loved these two places, and he held his customers in high regard. Thank you for being such a special part of his life." I end there because emotions take over, and I just can't say anything else.

I lay my head down on his desk and mourn… I sit here tearless, but mourn just the same. I mourn for what we had—the camaraderie here in this very place. I mourn for what we lost. I mourn not getting to know my dad better. I mourn him not knowing me. It's too late. He's gone and there's nothing, absolutely nothing I can do about it now. No second chance. No redo.

After a while I stand to leave, but a framed document hanging proudly on the back wall grabs my attention. I walk over and discover it to be my college acceptance letter. This surprises me. I didn't realize my dad even had it. I always thought it was hidden in my junk somewhere. I pluck it off the wall and take it with me. After locking up the front, I head out back to visit the inlet. I notice the tide is nearing its end of lazily heading out for a while and will soon decide to come back. I pull an old rocking chair from the back porch, deposit it near the bank, and have a sit for a spell to wait on the tide's return.

I let the creek sounds lull me into a lethargic state while I rock to the tempo of the soothing breeze. I study the lively creek bed as it mysteriously comes into view. Hermit crabs are scampering about, looking for hidden treasure and nosy seagulls roam around to see what they can find for a snack.

The bank is littered with the inlet's natural waste. Empty shells of all sorts are scattered about—oyster, clam, crab, and shrimp shells. Fish bones are left discarded about as well. Eventually, the inlet's rich mud will reclaim this natural waste. It's amazing how this ecosystem works perfectly without any assistance from man. And if we leave it alone and not abuse it, this inlet rewards abundantly. I have never seen a time it didn't give generously in the form of fresh seafood. Crab traps have always been overly occupied, and treasure hunts for clams have always been plentiful. This major part of the ocean owns my heart just as much as the sandy beaches and rolling waves. Maybe the love for the inlet is a local thing or just my thing. I hold it dear and respect it greatly for always giving to my family so generously.

A squawking sound draws my attention to a muddy part of the bank towards my left. I find a seagull waving his wings in the air, bickering with a crab that he is the rightful owner of a wayward minnow flopping in a murky puddle. The grouchy crab raises his snapping claw in challenge as he dances in front of the minnow. A snort of amusement slips out of me as the cowardly seagull admits defeat, flying away and leaving the crab to his meal.

I watch for a while until the framed acceptance letter beckons my attention where it is resting in my lap. Dormant memories of those years echo sweetly through me, causing a wistful smile to pull at my lips. They were typical college years to an outsider, but they were of much significance to me. College is where I found my other saving grace. It's where I met my Lucas.

Lucas Ray Monroe is the best thing about life, even though I know I don't deserve him one bit. I did absolutely nothing to earn him, yet he offered me his love like it was a divine ruling for him to do so.

I met him in my freshman English class and felt drawn to him immediately. I was intrigued by this quiet guy who always seemed to be near me. He has always exuded a silent peace that just draws people in. Lucas is the kind of guy that when he speaks, people hush up and take notice. He is one who doesn't waste words. And man oh man, is he pretty to look at. He has an all-American look about him with playfully curly brown hair and an always clean-shaven boyish face. Those curls summon any sane female to want to test the luscious texture of them. We are clear on the fact I do not put myself in the category of sane, so my hands easily kept to themselves back then. The only wicked thing about him is his hazel eyes. Some days they gleam like pure gold, other days they can be a brilliant green, and creamy brown eyes sometimes make an appearance as well. His body is lean and just under six feet in height. Lucas has a confident glide to his walk that is never rushed but always gets him where he's going with plenty of time to spare. I haven't figured out how to have his calming peace, but I really want to possess it too.

We hung out at the beginning of freshman year and have never parted since. He sort of held a big brother position with me. I made some dumb freshman mistakes and he was always there to rescue me. I would call inebriated and he would quickly and quietly show up to drive me back to the dorms. Or I would totally blow off class and he would show up afterwards with a copy of his notes and hand them over without a word. He was a constant stabilizer, and I was so drawn to it.

I know college is supposed to be a place to develop an education on a particular career, but I was completely clueless on what I wanted to be. I barely knew who I was, much less knowing what I wanted to be when I grew up. College for me was an escape from my life so far. I went in without declaring a major. I honestly had no ambition to succeed in anything but staying away from home.

Freshman year was definitely a learning curve for me. My dorm roommate Phoebe and I spent too much time partying and goofing off, and the evidence showed up swiftly with my poor grades. The slap in the face from reality didn't reach me until that summer break. I was back home working at the restaurant. My dad showed up in late June with a note from the university. He handed the thick envelope over right before my lunch shift. Thinking it was my fall schedule information packet, I crammed it in my bag to check out later. I didn't even open it until after a week had passed. And when I did finally open it, I nearly exploded in panic. The note declared I was on academic probation and had only the fall semester to show drastic improvement or they would be revoking my scholarship. And that was all it took to straighten my behind out. There was no way I would be going back to Bay Creek on a permanent basis, so I did what I had to do when I returned.

I may have been motivated but my returning roommate, Phoebe, was not. She continued with the partying, and it near about made it impossible to study. Most nights our dorm was filled with a rowdy crowd, which normally led to sleepovers. So after spending too many nights on the smelly couch in the common room, I knew I had to find an alternative living arrangement.

I asked Lucas to help me find an apartment, and this led us to a discussion about the spare room in his apartment.

"That's sweet, but I just don't think it's a good idea." I brushed his offer off as gently as I could.

"Why?" he asked that fall afternoon as we walked to the library. There was a bit of a nip in the air that day. I remember it being quite a refreshing change from the thick humidity that these southern parts are plagued by.

"You're a guy. I'm a girl," I stated matter-of-fact. He eyed me with those curious eyes for a moment before shrugging his shoulders and continuing down the sidewalk.

I knew he wouldn't say anything else, but expected me to explain just the same. "I don't trust you." I remember blurting that out like an idiot. What I really meant to say was that I was scared to be that near him. I didn't want him to mess up what we had with crossing that invisible line. Lucas nodded his head like that made perfect sense and dropped the subject.

The following week, the campus was abuzz with

fall break coming up. Not me. I was too busy panicking over not having my grades high enough. I had midterms to worry over, so Lucas agreed to let me study most afternoons at his quiet apartment while he went to the gym with his buddies. He was lucky. His parents provided him an off-campus two-bedroom apartment. Yes, I was totally jealous.

When I arrived that afternoon, I found a note on the dining table. I opened it and a set of keys fell out. *The room is yours. Take it. I installed a lock on the door. These are the only two keys to it. No one will bother you here. You can trust me. Take these keys as my promise. – Lucas.*

I picked the keys up and stared at them for a moment as I measured the weight of the decision in my hand. It was nearly an irresistible offer, but I just wasn't sure. Trust issues wouldn't let me. So I studied and left before he returned. I sat my own note on the table with the keys thanking him for the offer, but declining.

I ended up failing the statistics exam the next week, and I was right disgusted with myself. I studied as much as possible, but the sporadic sleeping schedule, mired with my usual nightmares, was becoming my undoing.

After receiving my exam grade that morning, I walked in a deep gloom to Lucas's apartment to bid him goodbye. He was heading home for the small break, but I had decided to hide out in my dorm instead of facing Jean for Thanksgiving. I had a feeling I was going to have to see way too much of her soon enough after flunking out of college.

I let myself in his unlocked apartment as I normally did, and tripped right over Lucas's suitcase. I laid there stunned for a moment before he strolled out of his room. He stood over me with a curl hanging in one of his amused eyes. The teal-blue shirt he wore was causing his eyes to shine with a unique green hue that day.

"Walk much?" he asked in an even tone, which made me want to crack up.

"You booby-trapped your door, hotshot," I said as he helped me stand.

"How about a peace offering then?" he asked as he released me to shove the suitcase out of the way. He pushed the curl back into place as he waited for me to comment.

"Yeah? What's the offering?" I asked as I headed to take a seat at the table, where the bedroom keys continued to patiently wait on me. Lucas stood by the table without taking a seat and I wasn't too pleased. He was ready to go home, but I wasn't ready to let him.

"Stay here while I'm gone." This is all he said as

he slid the keys in front of me. Without another word, Lucas grabbed his suitcase and walked out the door. I stood to follow him, but he raised his hand up with a wave and shut the door behind him.

I sat a little longer, taking in my surroundings while I reevaluated his offer. My gaze eased over the apartment. The open concept was masculine with crisp, grey walls and dark, chunky furniture. The small living room was dominated by a dark grey micro suede sofa that you could just sink into because it was so plush. A black leather recliner and massive TV joined in the mix. The only wall décor was a giant framed Gamecocks emblem. The table I sat at matched the black chunky coffee table, so I guess they came as a set. The kitchen was a generic apartment setup with grey Formica counters and a black fridge and stove set. Nothing fancy, but incredibly tidy for a young man.

Curiosity finally won out. I walked to the vacant bedroom to take a peek, and was surprised at what I found. The last time I had glanced into the room it was bare, with white walls and a mattress set without a bedframe. The space had been transformed into a beach-themed room with light blue walls and gauzy, cream-colored curtains. The bed had been outfitted with a comforter set in a thick, striped pattern in delicate shades of blue and cream, and framed by a wicker headboard. A large seascape picture of the ocean and beach shore that glowed warmly under a tender sun dressed the wall behind the bed. In awe, I skimmed my fingers along a cream-colored, distressed dresser that sat quietly in the corner carefully holding a vase full of seashells. After circling the room in admiration, I took a seat on the edge of the bed, sinking slightly in the softness. A conk shell rested on top of the nightstand, giving me permission to pick it up. I raised the iridescent shell to my ear and let it whisper the secrets of the ocean to me for a while. I let out a sigh of receipt. It baffled me as to why Lucas would do this for me, and I was more astonished by how well he really knew me.

I stayed that long weekend and never left. Every night, I locked myself in my room but he never tried to enter that space. Believe it or not, but for the remaining two and half years of college, Lucas never stepped one foot into my bedroom. When he made a point, he didn't do it halfheartedly. But I promise you I never forgot to lock that door behind me and even placed my desk chair under the knob every single night I slept there. Most importantly, my grades improved and I was able to stay in college.

Lucas's apartment was deemed the hangout spot because his buddies were either exiled to dorm life or a frat house. Most weekends you could easily find a small gathering. The typical activity was a big screen viewing of some ballgame and consuming large quantities of pizza and hot wings. Beer keg parties were found at the frat houses and sexual menageries were hidden in dorm rooms. But Lucas's place seemed to be the safe haven where people could leave the peer pressures and social expectations at the door. I know that was exactly the way I felt about it.

Lucas's friends were a loyal, tight group, and I was surprised at how easily they welcomed me in. Don't ask me how someone as damaged by the male species issues as myself would actually feel comfortable being surrounded by such a bunch. I'm a tomboy through and through, so I know that made it easier. Sports and pizza were right up my alley. I also trusted Lucas, and I knew he wouldn't let anything happen to me. Oddly, he was the first and, up until this day, the only male I completely trusted.

It didn't hurt that the guys got a lesson early on in our friendship about my no contact rule. This became crystal clear one afternoon while watching our Gamecocks team crush the opposing team at an away game. Miles made the mistake of grabbing me up in a fierce bear hug in celebration. The result of this landed Miles with a broken nose. After what I endured with Evan, I had vowed to myself to never be touched by a man against my will ever again.

My fist landed one brisk blow before I knew what came over me. "No one touches me!" I screamed at the stunned group of guys before retreating to my room for the remainder of the evening. I know someone took Miles over to the on-campus clinic to get his nose checked out, but I suppose the rest stayed and helped Lucas clean up. I was too embarrassed to find out either way.

The next morning, while sitting in silence at the dining table with a cup of coffee, I caught Lucas studying my bruised knuckles as though he was waiting for my hand to explain my bizarre outburst. My hand gave no explanation, and Lucas seemed to think better about outright asking.

Honestly, I had no regrets about punching Miles. He is a great guy, one of my dearest friends to this day, actually. He was just excited over the game, but I showed Lucas and myself that I had limits and would not stand to be pushed over them.

Lucas respected my boundaries and never attempted to cross them. Not until midway through our junior year at least. If it weren't for the overwhelming attack that crushed me, he would have received a broken nose that night just as Miles did.

I reluctantly remember that miserable day, with Jean on a constant phone war with me. She had been calling almost every day, trying to persuade me into not finishing the spring semester so I could move back to Bay Creek to help complete some renovations planned for the family businesses before the tourist season got underway. I think she was secretly trying to make me live up to my reputation of not being able to complete anything I started. Heaven forbid I prove her wrong. But she forgot to take in the fact that I'm just as stubborn as I am a procrastinator—so I showed her.

"You need to come home to help your father out. John Paul hasn't got an ounce of gumption when it comes to the market or restaurant," Jean said. "You're being selfish and just wasting time at that school. You don't even have a major."

I had heard this conversation repeatedly since I arrived my freshman year and was sick of it. I had finally declared business as a major. I did this just so I could be in more classes with Lucas, but that was beside the point.

After hanging up on her and shutting my cell phone off, I walked into the kitchen where Lucas was loading the fridge with drinks. He was getting ready for a movie night with the guys, and had rented the latest Die Hard movie for us to watch. I leaned against the counter and shuffled through the pizza menus he had set out. I skimmed my eyes over him as he continued to load the fridge. It amazed me how

Lucas could make a tattered black hoodie, faded jeans, and bare feet look so appealing. He was too dang adorable with his curly hair still damp from his recent shower. He glanced over at me and caught me checking him out. I am who I am, so I answered his questioning look with a so-what shrug.

Never one to tease me, he gave me a slight smirk in acknowledgement before asking, "What type of pizza do you want to order?"

I shrugged my shoulders in answer. He seemed to catch something off with my silent gestures, so Lucas closed the fridge door and leaned against it to study me. "What's up?" The worry glinted in his golden eyes. He didn't miss much and was able to read people remarkably well. I suppose this comes in quite handy in his business profession as well as having such a closed-off wife.

"Nothing."

He pushed away from the fridge, grabbed the kitchen phone, and placed a call. "Hey man. Something's come up. We're going to have to cancel tonight."

I didn't wait for the rest of the conversation. There was no need in trying to make Lucas change his decision. Once he made up his mind on something that was that. I was embarrassed for being the reason for the cancelled plans, so I retreated to my room to sulk. Nearly an hour later, I decided to take a drive.

When I opened the door I was surprised to find Lucas sitting on the floor in front of me.

"What on earth are you doing sitting in the hall?" I asked, confused.

"Making sure you didn't try for a fast getaway." He chuckled quietly as he stood. "Will you tell me what's wrong?"

"I don't want to talk about it," I said and then tried to close myself back into my room.

Lucas stepped closer to the door threshold but was careful not to cross it. "Come on, Savannah, we'll just hang out if that's what you want. I promise not to ask one question all night."

I could tell it really bothered him that I kept things to myself, but he was good at his word and didn't ask another question all night. We ended up making it into a joke. He tortured us with CNN, something neither one of us ever watched, for nearly a half hour before I caught on to what he was doing.

"Sorry. I promised not to *ask* you anything, so I can't *ask* you what you want to watch," he said remorsefully.

"You're not funny," I said in a deadpan voice. We both knew he was incredibly funny. I grabbed the remote and manned our television programming for the remainder of the evening.

He later brought me a glass of root beer from the fridge, knowing of course that I couldn't stand the syrupy sweet taste of his favorite soda. Thinking it was plain soda, I took a big gulp and gagged. He'd dramatically shrugged his shoulders with a sheepish look and said that he couldn't *ask* me what I wanted. That earned him a punch in the arm. He eventually drew me out of my funk, and we spent the rest of the night watching a comedy channel. Laughter really is good medicine.

Or it seemed to be until I dozed off on the couch and right into a nightmare. It was the one where I was dancing with the devil in a dark field that was engulfed in flames and he had tried to smother me by holding me forcefully against his chest. I snapped out of the nightmare in a panic and totally lost it when I found myself locked in a sleeping Lucas's arms. He somehow ended up lying behind me on the couch with his arm wrapped tightly around my waist.

Instincts kicked in and I began to try to push him off. I struggled until he woke up with a start to find me freaking out. The tingling sensation had overpowered my entire body and the hyperventilation was past the point of no return. I wiggled my way to the floor and started crawling languidly across the room to get away from him.

"Savannah?" Lucas asked frantically.

I could barely hear him over the ringing in my ears. I had no voice, so I couldn't answer him. All I could do was shake my head no and hold my hands out to keep him at bay. I backed myself into the hallway and couldn't unscramble my thoughts enough to figure out how to get through the darn thing.

Lucas was nearly freaking out himself by witnessing me in such a meltdown. He would take a step closer and then back off in an anxious dance once he realized it made me panic even worse. I watched as he dragged his hands through his hair and then raised them in desperation before running out of the room.

He had just been witness to one of my hidden demons and there was no escaping it. The trembling overtook my body and my vision blurred before going completely dark.

I woke up in the emergency room, not knowing how I managed to get there, with Lucas by my side. Embarrassed and defeated, I said nothing as I watched him watch over me from his chair.

"You had a severe panic attack." He answered my unspoken question in his hushed voice. He sat up straighter in his chair but made no move to near me, and I was thankful. "They gave you a sedative and said I can take you home after you wake up." His eyes were a vigorous green on this night and held many questions that I had no desire to answer.

I was beginning to worry I had let this man get too close to me. I felt the need to confess. He had a right to know that there was no healthy future with me. Without meeting his gaze, I admitted, "I don't want to let you down Lucas, but I'm too damaged and it's too dark inside." I placed my hand sluggishly over my broken heart.

He shook his head slightly before walking out of the small hospital room. With no other choice, I focused my disappointment on the IV pricking the top of my hand. My nose and eyes stung as though they were summoning tears, but I knew they would not arrive. I knew I needed to let Lucas go. It wasn't right to include him in the nightmare I lived privately.

I was wrestling with going home to Bay Creek permanently as I lay there. It was the only place I sort of fit in, and I knew I could dig my grave there and no one would be affected or stand in my way. As I contemplated this, Lucas returned with a doctor in tow.

"Good morning, Savannah. I'm Dr. Jacobs." While the grey-haired doctor looked over my chart, I glanced at the clock and discovered it was well past three in the morning. He signed a prescription pad before tearing it off and handing it over to Lucas. "I'm prescribing you a small amount of Xanax to hold you over until you can make an appointment to see a doctor about your panic attacks. Take one pill at the first sign of an attack and never mix it with alcohol. If you don't have any questions, I'm going to send a nurse in to remove the IV and let you go home. Is that okay with you?" He waited for an answer, so I nodded my head. I guess at three in the morning that was answer enough because he shuffled back out the door.

Later that same day, after sleeping the remainder of the sedative off, I awoke parched like a dry desert. I shuffled out of bedroom to find some relief and came to a halt by the door. I found Lucas sitting in the hall across from my room as though he were keeping guard. With his knees drawn towards his chest and head resting on the wall, those hazel eyes looked up and beg for answers. I had never seen him in such a state of dishevelment—emitting weariness both physically and emotionally.

"All I wanted to do was hold you last night," he said. "What did I do wrong, Savannah?"

He was blaming himself for my issues and I had to let him off the hook. I joined him in the hall and slid down to the floor, careful to keep distance between us in the cramped space. His somber eyes never left mine, and I knew I needed to help him understand none of it was his fault.

"You did nothing wrong. I told you, Lucas. I'm damaged." He began to shake his head no, but I stopped him. "I'm serious." I placed my hand back over my heart for emphasis. "I'm *broken,* and there's no fixing it..." My voice strained in defeated pain.

"We can get you some help."

"I don't think I'm fixable," I said, but he kept shaking his head in silent protest.

"You won't know until you try, and I think it's time. I've watched you for three years now carrying this burden around and letting it cripple you."

I sniffed the stinging sensation away in my nose as I sat there trying to talk myself into disappearing. This lifesaver sitting before me was making it nearly impossible. Lucas was like warm sunshine, and all I wanted to do was to figure out how I could bask freely in it for the rest of my life.

He seemed to sense me wrestling with my demons so he ever so slowly eased his hand across the floor, welcoming me to take it.

Shaking my head, I whispered, "I... I don't like to be touched."

He studied me carefully before commenting, "Then you've never been touched right."

I scrutinized his hand but refused to take it. "I

can't, Lucas." Refusing him caused me to ache in a peculiar way, and I was confused by it. I wanted to make him happy, but I knew I couldn't in that moment. That made me mad with myself. I felt worthless.

We sat in a mournful trance until the sky darkened that evening—silently calling a stalemate.

A few weeks passed before I reluctantly agreed to meet with a counselor through some outreach organization the college provided students, but antidepressants and Xanax became my crutch. I'm sure the counseling might have worked if I had participated honestly. The generic questions of *tell me how you feel – is there anything you would like to talk about* and *how does that make you feel* – just didn't cut it with me. I mean really, why on earth would I tell a stranger about my deepest, darkest secrets? I knew it was a waste of both mine and the counselor's time. After dancing around the truth for a few months, I did both of us a favor and quit.

Lucas was better than any counseling session. That man is like a salve that immediately eases the constant sting just by being near. He never stopped offering me his hand over the spring semester. He was always placing it palm-side up between us on the couch, on the console between us in his Jeep, or in the movie theaters. He never pushed the issue but also never gave up in his offering.

More weeks passed before I began testing the waters—gradually evaluated the feel of his palm with only my fingertips at first, but would retreat hastily. Lucas never seemed bothered by this apprehensive dance, but patiently kept at his offering. Eventually I would let my hand linger on top of his and he was wise as to not try to grasp it. He seemed content with just letting me do the touching. And I found much comfort in the warm smooth skin of his hand. For his hand never stole anything from me. He only wanted to give, and that struck me in a way I can't even describe now.

This continued to the point where I was desperate to admit to him why I wasn't worth his efforts, so he could move on. He had made it his mission to cure me of my physical contact phobia but there was no way he could grasp the magnitude behind the cause. Call me drama all you want. But after the innocence of touch has been torn from you, then we can talk. Touch made me feel dirty and sick. I didn't understand a touch that could be anything but that. It was all I knew. Lucas was so foreign, and I just couldn't accept it.

One afternoon after finals were complete and I knew I would be heading home in a few days, I reached a point where I had had enough. I hid out in my room that afternoon until I worked up enough nerve to face him. I found him lounging on the couch, one long leg stretched over the back of the couch in a boyish manner, scanning a Sports Illustrated magazine. His USC T-shirt had ridden up, showing off a span of his perfect abdomen, and I nearly ran away right then and there. He was and is a beautiful man, but beauty didn't come with an assurance of good for me. Another problem. Yes, I have many. We've already discussed that though.

Lucas caught sight of me before I could slide back into my room, halting my retreat. He tossed the magazine on the coffee table. As he sat up, he patted the couch beside him. "I think you should just stay here with me this summer," he said as I eased beside him. "You can help me with my homework," he said with a wink. He was taking extra summer courses, but I was not.

I sat there staring at his welcoming hand between us, but ignoring its meaning so I wouldn't lose my nerve. "I'm not worth this effort, Lucas." Of course, he began to disagree until I shut him up with a confession I knew he was not prepared to receive. But he needed to know my phobias weren't some naïve schoolgirl issues.

I began rambling about being raped in rapid fire so I wouldn't back out of the confession. I explained that it was impossible for me to ever come clean from it. I watched disgust furrow his features as I told him of the sick nightmare of Evan. It was the first and last time I have ever uttered the nauseating details of that dark time. It all flowed out vehemently. I was determined to let him have it all so he would finally get the silly notion out of his determined head that he could fix me. He needed to move on and find someone who wasn't so tainted and broken. It was as though a dam of hurt burst, and I found myself pouring out the details of Bradley's accident, Julia's battle with anorexia, and Jean's abusive words and her relentless palm that seemed to always be ready to slap me back in my place. I told him about how poor John Paul was drowning in a bottle of liquor. We are definitely a messed-up bunch if there ever was one.

I will never forget him quietly pacing the floor as I admitted it all, his mouth set sternly and his eyes dark with rage.

We shared a room filled thick with silent tension for a long spell until he turned a harsh gaze towards me that I had never seen him wear. "We live together, Savannah. I thought you were my closest friend. How could you just keep all of this from me?" His quiet voice was filled with disappointment.

I tried swallowing the panic long enough to get out the door. I was desperate for a disappearing act and had resolved to make my leave and head back to Miss May. As I turned the knob, Lucas came up behind me, grabbed my arm and spun me around. Instinct took control, I flinched and braced for him to strike me. I waited with my eyes clamped shut, but they shot back open when I felt his arms wrap around me. His embrace begged me to allow him to give me comfort. I allowed it for just a short time, until my breathing started to become erratic. I pulled away and eyed him in confusion. I couldn't understand why he would want to touch me after what I had just shared with him. Did he not get that I was soiled beyond ever coming clean?

Lucas placed his palm lightly on my cheek as he spoke, and I hated myself for not being able to restrain the flinch. He didn't let him deter him though and kept his hand gently in place. "I will never let something so horrible ever happen to you again, Savannah." Desperate determination resonated in his tone as his sympathetic eyes assessed me. "And I will never push you into anything until you are ready. You just have to be straight with me about things. Okay?"

Lucas never mentioned that night and the sick things I shared with him ever again. He wasn't someone who dwelled on matters for too long. He dealt with them and moved on. I wish it was that easy for me. I know if I ever needed to talk about it, Lucas would welcome the conversation—just as he knows I never will.

I know I've not told you all the details of those sick episodes with Evan Grey, and I feel that some things are best to not be shared. They were dark and revolting, and I'd rather not speak of it. I doubt seriously that you would want to know, anyway.

Only a few short days later, I had my bags packed for Bay Creek to begin another summer. I remember the apartment coming to life with the low murmurings of music while I packed a few last items stacked on my bed. The slow, melodious song eventually beckoned me to the living room where Lucas stood waiting, his hands in his pockets and rocking on his heels slowly as his eyes took in every inch of me, making me shiver. Curious, I stood a few feet away. I knew he was up to something, but I was not sure exactly what. He had kept a cautious distance from me ever since I had made my confession, and I was beginning to think it was finally sinking in that it was best to leave me alone.

Lucas pulled his right hand out of his pocket and invited me over. "Come dance with me," he said softly, without moving forward. We stood before each other as the song played around us.

I stayed in my spot with apprehension cautioning

me. "What?"

"I said dance with me," he repeated, but made no effort to initiate the dance. I knew he was waiting me out. Lucas's eyes conveyed an entire message as he confidently waited—*it's time...let me show you*.

I'm not a romantic and had no clue really as to what romance meant up until that very day, but for some reason I recognized the romanticism in that moment between two college students standing in the middle of their apartment, adorned in ratty T-shirts and jeans. It wasn't the scene but the feelings radiating around the space as it mingled with the sultry ballad.

"Okay," I said finally, feeling I owed him at least this moment. I walked over and stood before Lucas as I eased my hand gingerly into his awaiting one. He held it ever so softly as he slowly wrapped his other hand around my hip. He led us in a leisure dance. Was I confused? Yes, but I waited. Lucas never did anything without purpose.

After silently dancing for a while, he gently threaded his hand through my hair. Panic ebbed at me, and I immediately tried to disengage myself, but he held me firmly yet tenderly in place.

"Try, Savannah. Please. Just trust it," he said breathlessly as his mysterious eyes whirled in gold hues, conveying to me a promise of safety. He released my hand, glided his fingertips along my cheek and curved them feather-soft over the line of my jaw. His touch was but an intimate whisper across my skin, causing me to ache in such a way I had never experienced. The gentleness ignited peculiar sensations, causing me to want to weep. I held my breath, hoping that those feelings would never end. They felt strange yet alluring at the same time.

Lucas slowly leaned forward, holding my gaze while caressing my cheek with his warm breath. It was such a ghost of a kiss that I wasn't even sure his lips connected to my skin. We danced another long stretch until he guided my shaky hand to his mouth, placing graceful kisses of assurance on each fingertip before pressing my hand over his pounding heart. The strong quick rhythm revealed his desire, yet he took things no further than dancing and innocently touching me. That heart was begging me to trust him, and oh how I wanted to be able to do just that.

With his hand holding mine in place over his heart, he whispered, "This is me expressing my love for you, Savannah." My attention was drawn to the slight tremble skirting along Lucas's mouth, giving away hidden emotions he had masked with his cool demeanor. He licked his full bottom lip as he traced my own with the tip of his index finger so lightly that it nearly tickled. "Can you feel that?"

"Feel what?" I asked breathlessly against his fingertip. I couldn't look away from him. It was like we were in some trance, and I never wanted to escape it. It was a whole new world in that moment.

"This is me loving you," he answered as he continued to rock us to the rhythm of the song. I vaguely recollect the same song playing on repeat and we had already danced it through at least a half dozen times at that point. Lucas was in no rush to make his point. He took things slow and was conveying so much with each action. I paid close attention too because I wanted to miss none of it.

He combed his hand through my hair once again and asked, "Does this feel wrong?"

I answered with a shake of my head. I surprised myself when I felt my body lean into his touch.

Dropping his hand, Lucas circled around me. Feeling his protective presence behind me, I demanded my body not to stiffen when I felt his hand brush my hair over my shoulder. His warm caress landed softly on the exposed skin of my neck before beginning a slow, soothing journey across my shoulders and down my arms. He nuzzled into my hair as he worshiped me simply with his delicate touches. Never urgent. Never aggressive. He was relaying his message to me in an achingly sweet gesture.

Eventually Lucas circled back around and pulled me tenderly into his embrace—holding me but barely. He delicately rubbed away the tension in my back with his capable hands as he whispered into my ear, "Does this make you feel good?"

I inhaled the clean masculine scent of him and shocked myself again when I cuddled into the crook of his neck. "Yes," I whispered. And it did. I had never experienced something that felt so nice and so right. It didn't make my stomach hurt nor did it cause panic to build. It felt good and pure. And I just knew if I could somehow completely bathe in this pure love, surely I could be cleansed. I wanted the past wiped clean. My body trembled from that very want.

"This is what love is supposed to feel like. This is how God intended it." He paused to press a kiss to my temple. "Please stop letting the past rob you of this gift God created for us to share. Allow us to have this gift. I want you, Savannah. I want you to let me love you. And I want to be loved by you."

Love was something I had very little understanding about, but the overwhelming desire in that moment demanded I love him completely. I just didn't know if I knew how.

The dancing and caressing continued until finally Lucas pulled my face delicately up to his and tenderly warmed my lips with his own. His whispered words were breathed over my lips. "I love you, Savannah." His emotions were thickly laced in his words so much so he had to pause to clear it away. "This is what love feels like." He offered another delicate kiss only to the corner of my mouth. "It's giving… and it's accepting." Conveying no more words, Lucas released me. A few seconds of silence danced between our still bodies before he left me and the apartment.

His declarations of love and promises of protection glued me in my spot. I stood in the abandoned room and quietly released a few demons that day.

Chapter Eleven

A ruckus draws me out of my thoughts, as a scraggly group of children come scurrying up. Ignoring them, I turn my attention back to the inlet and watch the water slowly begin its way back home. It's peaceful all of two seconds before it's interrupted by all kinds of twangy chatter. I glance over at this little motley crew, barefooted and dripping wet. This bunch reminds me of days long ago spent exploring the mysteries of the inlet with John Paul and Bradley.

A blonde-haired girl, who I'm guessing is around the age of eight, speaks first. "Where's that lady with them hush puppies?"

"Where's Miss May?" an older boy in his teens asks. He seems like the leader of the group. He's a lanky kid who needs several good meals for sure.

I continue to rock in my chair. "Sorry. She's not here today."

The group erupts in groans of protest.

A young girl with chocolate skin and eyes pouts. "Her promised us hush puppies for today."

"Yeah! She promised," another little blonde-haired girl pipes in. I'm pretty sure they are twins.

My head darts between all of them as I try to take in all of their whining. "Sorry," I say again. "No hush puppies today."

One of them nosy young'uns pulls the framed acceptance letter off my lap, and I grab it back quickly. This little guy, with his hair falling in his eyes, is in serious need of a haircut. He asks, "What's that you holding?"

"My college acceptance…"

Before I can continue, one of them scoffs, "You too old for college." Them boogers laugh at that.

I'm only twenty-eight for Pete's sake! "Am not!" I snap back. "Besides, I've already gone *and* graduated."

They all once again ramble at the same time. Questions are circling all around me and I don't know, nor do I think I care, enough to answer any of them.

"What are you then?"

"Um…" My brows pinch together in aggravation.

"What's your name?"

"What you doing out here anyways?"

"I was really wanting me some of them hush puppies," Hair-too-Long whines.

"She promised, and my Pappy said you ain't 'pose to break a promise," the youngest one pipes in.

"Yeah! Mine says that too," agree the twins in unison.

They continue to worry me to no end until I decide I am going to have to hush them up. I stand and head to the kitchen door. "Y'all stay here and try not to fall into the inlet and I'll go see what I can do." I say, and they cheer.

I check the fryer first and set the temperature before heading to the pantry to gather the ingredients. I grab up the container of self-rising flour and the one containing cornmeal. Balancing the sugar container on top, I carry the load to the worktable. I ease over to the refrigerator and pull out milk, eggs, and butter. Once everything is spread before me, I pause to set a pot of tea to brew. With that underway, I dump nearly equal parts of flour and cornmeal into a mixing bowl. I combine them and add a good heap of sugar and a dash of salt. I have watched Miss May perform this same recipe so many times, I need no measuring. Even with the five-year absence, this task feels like second nature.

After all of my dry ingredients are combined, a dollop of honey, two eggs, and just enough milk to bind it all together in a thick batter joins in. I move my mixing bowl along with two tablespoons over to the fryer. I scoop up the batter with one spoon and use the other to swipe it into the hot oil. It sizzles and bubbles and the frying aromas engulf my senses into a contentment state. Instinct says the oil is right, so I continue to plop batter into the boiling liquid.

While the dough browns, I pour the brewed tea into a gallon pitcher and dump in a hardy helping of sugar. After filling the remaining pitcher with ice, I set it by a tray with a stack of glasses. I rotate the fried dough to a basket covered with brown paper towels so the excess grease can drain off. I then set another batch to frying while I whip up some honey butter. By the time I have transferred the succulent treats to a fresh basket, my stomach lets out a growl in excitement. I gather the tray and pitcher of tea and set out to have an impromptu picnic with a bunch of local young'uns.

They all gather around me and sit on the bank patiently. I place the goodies down before them and sit crossed leg as they are doing. "Okay. Let's eat," I declare as I pop one in my mouth. This is when I notice they have all bowed their heads, and the oldest one eyes me disapprovingly. I reluctantly spit the hush puppy in my hand and bow my own head. The boy blesses the food, and then they tear into those hush puppies like a ravenous bunch of animals. Before I can down three hush puppies, the basket is empty and their tea glasses drained.

"Good grief. Did you even taste the dang things?" I ask as I sip my tea grudgingly. I really wanted more than just *three* hush puppies. I fried at least three dozen!

They ignore me, so I declare our visit over and begin gathering their glasses.

"Wait," says one of the blondies. "Tell Miss May we ready for our lesson."

"What?" I ask confused. "I already told you she *ain't* here."

One of the twins skeptically props her lime-green polished hands on her little hips. "Then who done an' cooked this up?"

"I did, I have you know," I sassed back.

She continues to study me as though she doesn't believe me. "Then I guess you get to give us a lesson too."

"Look, I already gave you little punks enough." I head to the kitchen, but they all moan and groan like I have just ruined their lives.

"You gotta teach us something," the younger blonde whines.

"I got nothing," I say, giving a quick nod of my head, and more grumbling breaks out.

"You old enough, you gotta know something," pipes in Hair-too-Long.

Okay, so there they go with that old crap again. They want old fart advice then I'm gonna divvy some out. "Listen up, you brats." I call them this because they call me old and that makes it right, so don't judge me. They laugh at this, thinking I'm being funny. I ain't. *Brats.*

I flick my hand, summoning them closer as I lean towards them like I'm about to share the mysteries of the world with them. I look around as though I'm making sure no one else can hear and this automatically causes them to lean closer.

"Never take a laxative and a sleeping pill on the same night," I stage whisper in all seriousness. They stare at me dumbfounded for a few moments before the understanding eases across their nasty little faces. Now they are literally rolling around on the ground at my feet in laughter except for the oldest one. He just stands there with a smirk on his face as though he gets me. I think I may like that kid.

One of them looks up at me and says, "That ain't no lesson!"

"It sounds like pretty sound advice to me. I mean, who wants to mess themselves while sleeping?" I wrinkle my nose for emphasis. "I read that somewhere and let me tell you, I ain't ever forgot it." I conclude my *lesson* with a wave and head once again for the door.

"What's your name?" one of them yells.

"Pudding Tang," I say. Ain't no way I'm telling these kids my name so they can go tell their parents that Savannah told them such mess.

I laugh at this unexpected afternoon while I clean the kitchen. Once I'm done I send Lucas a text. I wish I had the wits to share my encounter with him but decide to save it for another time.

Me: *I love you.*

Lucas: *I love you more.*

Me: *I miss you.*

He fires right back: *I miss you more.*

I perch on a stool at the kitchen counter with my tea while memories of that last significant year of college keep me company. Lucas showed me what real love was that year. I know what you're thinking so let me just go ahead and clear that up for you. Lucas showing me love did not include sex. Some heated kissing sessions maybe, but that was as far as I'd let him go.

He joked around one night after I pushed him

away. "What? Am I going to have to marry you just so I can get lucky?" I knew he was just trying to ease the tension caused by my apprehension. Panic attacks were always begging to emerge, and it took a lot to keep them in check—especially when I allowed him in my personal space.

In the midst of that turbulent time, Lucas took it upon himself to become my ally against panic attacks. Sometimes he could chase the attack away with joking, while other times it demanded attention and we would have to declare defeat.

One night I awoke from one of my reoccurring nightmares and could not shake the panic from me no matter how hard I tried. I just didn't want to take a pill. My stubborn self wanted to prove to the attack that I was boss, but I was losing the battle rapidly. I paced the length of the apartment for a spell with no relief before deciding to plop on the couch. As the attack latched on, my skin pricked and I broke out in a cold sweat in defense. Lucas begged me to give in and take the dang pill as he tried unsuccessfully to comfort me, but all I would do is shake my head. So that man of mine had at one point reached his limit with both me and the attack. Before I could comprehend his actions, Lucas had picked me up off the couch and carried me right outside in the midst of a rain shower. The cold rain sent a shock over me that demanded I focus on it. We were soaked through within seconds. The combination of the cold rain and the whooshing sound worked like magic.

Lucas set me down on my feet abruptly and began dancing me around the small court yard silently, surprising me further. Under the watery glow of the courtyard lights, he was stunning with his shirt plastered to his well-defined chest—my strong protector. And I knew I was in love, no matter the fact that I didn't really understand it. Now I realize love is something that occurs on its own accord with or without your permission. I certainly did not give permission. But it happened.

The feeling of ease had washed over me right along with the rain that night as Lucas lightly pushed my soaked hair away from my face. The look of awe and affection soften his features as he skimmed his knuckles along my cheek and whispered into the rain, "Beautiful." And that's exactly what he has always made me feel like, even though I carry such a vulgar, ugly past. Even in my worst moments, he has never made me feel that I meant any less to him than in our best moments.

We danced with our shoes splashing through water puddles until I was able to brush the remnants of the attack off. As he twirled me around, I couldn't help but giggle with relief. My saving grace had not given up on me and somehow figured out how to guide me through many stormy issues with steady patience and unconditional love.

There are days now that the attacks start winning. It's like the tension of my demons build up until my body demands I release it. The tingling and rapid heart rate will start taking effect, so I will go seek out my protector. All I have to do is walk up to him and say I feel like dancing in the rain. He will drop whatever he is doing, take me by the hand, and escort me outside. Rain or shine, day or night, Lucas will help me dance away my attacks. Sometimes it is a slow silent dance and other times it's a silly dance that is always performed in front of whoever may pass by. I think this helps too—being aware that others see me. It helps me snap out of it. Well…most of the time.

I'm not going to even go near the honeymoon night episode with you. Let's just say, the marriage bed did not go smoothly for quite a long time. Unfortunately, a few panic attacks escalated to the point of emergency room visits. Some demons were harder to battle.

I'm getting ahead of myself a bit. Anyway, that year of my life flew by too quickly. I was one of those students who actually didn't want school to end. One of my biggest problems about finishing school was that I still had no earthly idea what I wanted to do with the rest of my life. I was content with how things were, but I did have enough sense to realize it couldn't last forever. My worst fear after graduation was I would have to crawl back home to Jean. The closer graduation came, the more it sunk in that I was going to have to do just that. I dreaded the reality of actually having to go back home. I had no other choice, and I knew Jean would relish in my failure.

Lucas's future was totally opposite of my own. He already had things lined up perfectly. He was moving back up north. The graduate program that he had been accepted to was near his home. He was looking forward to being back near his parents, which was beyond my understanding. Our families were total opposites.

Lucas was born into a successful, loving, upper-class family who's very close knit. His dad, Robert Monroe, was the CEO of a multi-million dollar investment firm that he founded, until Lucas took over after graduate school. Although my father-in-law is a very wealthy businessman, family always comes first. He absolutely adores his down-to-earth wife, Kathleen and he is the doting father to three sons who each look like he could have spit them right out of his mouth. All three boys have the trademark Monroe look of curly, brown hair and hazel eyes.

Robert Jr., also known as Robbie, is the oldest, with Jackson following behind him by only sixteen months. The baby, Lucas, followed Jackson by only eighteen months. Stepping stones, just as their parents had wanted. Poor Kathleen threw in the towel once the third boy arrived and gave up on the chance of ever producing a daughter. Never one for negativity, Kathleen loved to brag about being the only girl in the house and that her men treated her as the Betty Crocker Queen. They absolutely adore her. Lucas grew up in a house that he described as always smelling like fresh baked cookies and always overflowing with laughter.

Robbie is the athletic son. Football and wrestling were his main priorities during high school. After earning his master's degree in business, he gladly joined in the family business.

Jackson has always been called the brainy middle child. He loves graphic arts, and can play a piano so sweetly it can make you cry. Well, you maybe. Not me. I wish. The high school valedictorian went to an Ivy League college and now heads up the advertising branch of the company.

Lucas is a mixture of his two older brothers. He played soccer in high school and graduated with honors. He chose to go to a less prestigious college so that he could explore life down south for a while. He promised his parents he would go to a graduate school close to home so that he could intern with his father. And he did. Lucas and his brothers are such well-rounded young men. Definitely a bunch of momma's boys. They are a reflection of a stable home life and sound child rearing from their parents.

Even though his dad is a very dedicated businessman, he never works past five o'clock and never on weekends. This is how he runs his company, and he is just as successful as the CEOs who worked themselves to death. He shared one quality with my dad, and that was how well they took care of their employees. That had always stuck out to me about my dad, and it was nice to see Lucas's dad was the same way.

I was desperately sad at the idea of having to be apart from Lucas, and the ache grew severe the closer we got to graduation. It also broke my heart that it didn't seem to bother him at all. He was so excited about getting on with his future—grinning nonstop and even a bit more talkative than his norm. I finally had to come to the realization that I was only a part of college life for him and now he was ready to move on. I didn't blame him per se, but it still stung.

Two weeks before graduation, Lucas came home with lots of empty boxes. I was depressed at the sight of them. I knew it was the end of the contented life I had with him, and it was time to pack those comfortable memories up. I stood there frowning at the boxes, while he looked at me with a silly grin.

"You didn't think this mess was going to pack itself, did you?" And with that we began packing up the apartment. First we sorted through what was mine and what was his, which was mostly his. We boxed it all up separately. I let it be known that this was not something exciting to me. I stomped around and would snap at him when he was too cheerful. I definitely showed my grouchy side. I figured it didn't matter if he liked how I was acting or not. "Us" seemed to be coming to a close right along with college. We were still packing the day of graduation.

"Would you mind sorting through a few boxes in the back room while I finish up in the bathroom?" He said this so chipper that it push an instant frown on my face. He was so excited because his parents were driving down to watch him graduate. He was also graduating at the top in his class. I was proud of him as well and envious at the same time. Lucas had his act together, and he had a well thought-out path awaiting him. Not me. I was completely clueless and the only path I saw had a dead-end.

I had sent my parents an invitation, but my dad called to inform me that they would not be able to break away due to the busy tourist season erupting.

All I could think about was how that was a bunch of bull. I also sent Julia one but I never received a reply from her. Only an envelope with two one-hundred dollar bills came with her address on it. I guess she was too busy to pick up a card or to scribble a few lines on a piece of paper. I sent her a blank thank you note in return. Julia always got my wicked sarcasm, and I knew she would totally get it with the blank card. I should have been more appreciative that she took enough time to throw some money in an envelope for me. After all, it was more than what I could say for my own mother.

After the phone call with my dad, I threw myself a little pity party. After about an hour of that whiny crap, I got good and mad. I came to the conclusion that I had made it through the past four years of college all on my own, and I definitely didn't want them to show up and take any credit for my hard work. That's what I tried to convince myself of anyway. The closer the time came for the ceremony, the more I wished the jerks were going to be there anyway.

"Come on grumpy butt, get the lead out. We've got to get your stuff out before my parents show up and start asking too many questions," Lucas said as he walked by and placed a kiss on my cheek. "There are two boxes in my room that I think some of your stuff got mixed in."

I hesitantly made my way to the back to his room as Mr. Happy-go-Lucky had asked of me. I began slinging the boxes open, mumbling under my breath the entire time about how it was mostly his crap and he should be the one to go through it. I completed one box. Shoving it out the way, and quickly moved to the next. I was so ready to be done with it. When I tore open the last box, I found a small satin jewelry box sitting on top. I had never seen it before, and so my nosy-self decided to find out what was inside. As I flipped it open, I discovered disappointedly that it was empty. I turned to throw it in the trash and almost hit Lucas with it. I had not realized he had been standing at the door watching me the entire time.

"Don't throw that away!" Bending down to pick the empty box up off the ground, I watched Lucas's warm brown locks to fall across his forehead. I had to swallow hard for already missing that little unruly detail of him. "Something very special goes in here." He brushed the hair away, revealing his beautiful eyes sparkling with his every word. As he walked towards me, he pulled from his pocket the most delicate diamond ring I had ever seen. I confusingly looked at the beautiful diamond set in white gold and then at Lucas. He was grinning ear to ear as he had been doing the entire week. All he said as he slipped the hopeful ring on my finger was, "You didn't actually think I was going to leave without you, did you?"

And that was all it took. It was the most perfect proposal to me. That was the only future plan I needed. Lucas wanted to keep me, and I was content with whatever else happened.

I believe I floated through the graduation ceremony later that day. I had a permanent grin on my face, and I couldn't stop looking at the magnificent ring on my finger. Lucas's family members were the only familiar faces in the crowd. They cheered me on just as they did Lucas, and that made me feel a little less disappointed in my family for not being there.

Afterwards, Lucas's mom put together a surprise combination graduation and engagement party for Lucas and me at one of the hotel banquet halls near the campus. His entire family knew of him planning to propose to me on the day of graduation. I guess they were pretty confident that I would say yes because there was even a mini wedding cake presented for Lucas and me to cut just as we would on our wedding day. Kathleen always went above and beyond for her children. She spoiled each one of them. I do believe she spoiled me just as well, if not better. It was a wonderful night of celebration. A great memory that I like to revisit often.

~ ~ ~

I'm getting right lonely, so I rinse my glass and head to my place of refuge. I pull up in Miss May's yard a few minutes later and find her on the porch, slumped down in a rocking chair and snoring as loud as any grown man can.

"So this is what old, retired women do with their free time," I say loudly as I shake her awake in a less than polite way. She loves me anyway.

"Why, I wouldn't know," Miss May snaps groggily and sits up a bit straighter. "This is what this old, *employed* woman does until her idiot boss decides to open the restaurant back up. If you don't do it soon, I'm gonna die right here in this chair of pure boredom."

"You still don't work at the restaurant, do you?" I ask in amazement.

"Why not? The only thing wrong with me is that I'm old."

I occupy the rocking chair beside her. "Well. You shouldn't have to be bored much longer. John Paul will probably reopen by the weekend."

Miss May cuts me a look I can't decipher. "I think

it's time you get your butt back home. Girl, you standing on the doorsteps of thirty years old. You need to get on with life and grow up."

Yep. I knew she would tell me whether I liked it or not. Maybe I should have just let her have that nap...

"Miss May, I just don't think I can ever come home again. It's just too—"

"Home ain't that big white house that prissy heifer lives in. Home ain't no haunted house." She places her wrinkly hand over her heart. "Home is where yo' heart leads you and I think it's past time for yo' stubborn butt to listen to yours. You ain't gettin' any younger."

There goes that blame age thing again. I just roll my eyes at this. There's no use arguing with this here lady. But of course, I head on down that path anyways.

"Julia left way before I decided to. Why is it okay for her and not me?" I question rebelliously as I slap away a few aggravating flies that won't leave me be.

"'Cause that child's heart ain't here. It never was." We rock in silence for a stretch before she continues. "Them demons still won't leave you alone?"

"Me? Oh I'm *so* cured. You'd be real proud of me. I've gone through counseling and all that junk," I say sarcastically. I wave the demons off with my hand dismissively and slap at another blame bug.

Now she rolls her eyes. "And how'd that work out for you?"

"What do you think?" I take a deep breath of the hot, humid air. "Just too many demons chasing me around here," I whisper as I stare out at her tidy lawn. I focus on a rose bush by the driveway, full of white blooms. Julia flickers through my mind, regret washing over me. "I don't know if I can call Bay Creek home, again."

"Bay Creek ain't done a thing to you. People and life did. Stop blamin' this here town. Face the mess of it and get on with your life," she rebukes as she scoots out of her rocking chair, leaving me on the porch alone. A nice breeze finally bristles through and takes the flies with it, thank you!

I sit, rocking and contemplating what she said, until she returns with two iced tea glasses. We sit in more silence, rocking and sipping our tea until I completely drain my glass. My eyes are starting to float with tea, but it's so good. You don't find this tea up north.

"Miss May, you know I can't make a decision like this without Lucas." There's no bone in my body wanting to live anywhere besides Rhode Island with Lucas.

"That boy loves you more than his teeth. I bet Lucas would follow you to the end of this here earth, if that's what would make you happy."

"Let's leave this for another day, okay?" When her head nods in understanding, I place my empty glass on the small table and stand. "Thank you," I say as I give her a kiss on the cheek and get up to leave.

She says nothing, just pulls my hand in hers and stares up at me for a spell as if she is relaying a wordless message to me. And she is, because I get it loud and clear that she loves and misses me. I also find the hurt in her dark eyes that has been caused by my absence. I place a quick kiss on the back of her hand to let her know that I'm sorry for causing that pain before heading back to Jean's house.

I'm pretty wiped out and really hope to arrive to a quiet house so that I can rest for a little while. As I pull up the driveway, I find the opposite of what I had hoped for. My mood plummets. People are already buzzing in and out.

I enter the foyer, and a wave of aggravation sweeps over me. Someone has placed my blame flowers back in the original spot. I scoop up the massive arrangement and stomp upstairs to return it to my room. People give me a questioning look as I pass, but none dare ask what I'm doing. And the look I give a few is *I dare you.* They obviously decide to hold their tongues. One of them hussies is probably the one who hauled them back downstairs. As I set the flowers back on the dresser, I assess my room. The bed has been made, the dirty coffee cup removed, and my very small stack of dirty clothes has been washed and neatly folded and are now resting on the foot of the bed. *Well…someone has made themselves overly useful.*

I ease back downstairs and notice that the entire house has been cleaned once again, and the kitchen counters are restocked with delicious-smelling home cooking. I realize that there will definitely be no resting, so I decide to help myself to the large spread. I fill my plate with tangy barbeque, rice, slaw, and a slice of white bread. This is another southern treat that I have missed. Back home with Lucas, we eat mostly health-conscience food. We never indulge in strawberry shortcake with fresh whipped cream. That is exactly what I treat myself to after devouring almost my entire plate of barbeque.

Instead of feeling more energized from the food, I feel as though I can barely hold my eyes open. I must look pretty rough too. People keep coming up to me and insisting that I go lay down for a while. It doesn't take much convincing for me to go for a quick nap. I'm so tired that I barely recall climbing into bed.

Chapter Twelve

Dancing another violent dance with the devil on a demonic beach, I cannot escape. Dancing in sheer terror as icy sweat trickles down my neck. Nausea and dizziness seems to keep everything in an odd tilt. The beast yanks me close until I'm firmly against his vile body. Every point where our bodies meet stings as though bees are attacking me. A growl erupts from his body before he clamps his chapped, brittle lips to mine. His taste is bitterly sour, causing me to gag against his mouth. Panic ricochets violently over me as I push away, but I find myself trapped in his callous grasp. I feel the bite of his nails as they begin to penetrate the delicate skin of my exposed back. I try to cry out in discomfort and terror, but I am being suffocated by his lips overwhelming my own. My lungs burn and squeeze with fighting against the attack until he abruptly relents the torture. Confusion blurs my understanding. I try to blink it away unsuccessfully. I can see nothing clearly—the now, the future. I'm suspended in a world of hurt, disgust, and shame.

His tarnished skin repulses me with sickly, rough, brown patches and is scored with unhealed scars oozing grotesquely. His hands… no hands. Claws! Scaly talons strike out and tear my beautiful gown savagely into shreds. I am frozen with fear in the sand and cannot escape. Violent tremors are the only movement I can evoke from my body.

Suddenly he begins pushing and pulling at me in some type of horrendous dance and I have no clue as to how I'm staying upright. Every touch riddles my body with searing burns and throbbing blisters. A muted sob vibrates from my throat as I take in the thick blood slowly seeping down my bare thighs in wet streams. More confusion riddles me at the sight of my long, brown curls scattering over the sand. Panicking, my hand flies to my head and I can only feel scaly bald patches. *Hated… I am hated.*

I scream out in anguish, but no sound arises from my mouth. I have no voice.

I try fruitlessly again to escape this monster's grasp. Defeated awareness cinches my stomach, causing rancorous acid to scorch my throat, as I realize dancing with this beast will have a deadly consequence. His crystal clear eyes have turned a vicious red, and now he watches me in a revolting way—making me feel dirty and repulsive. He is growling out with laughter and piercing the night in an echoing abuse.

I tear my gaze away from his revolting form to search for help but only discover a scornful moon bleeding a harsh shade of red and the inky-black ocean crashing against the shore in a bitter attack with continuous abuse, wave after wave. I even find the powdery sand has turned on me and is now pricking and tearing my bare feet. I study it in bafflement and find it to be shards of glass. *Angry… Everything is angry.*

Lightening slashes hatefully through the sky and thunder screams in aggravation as I mutely beg for help. *Please someone. Please save me. Please…*

I'm trying to pull my arm out of his grasp when I realize it has withered to resemble a dead vine. *More screaming. Still no voice.* I'm in agony and my heart is beating in an erratic pattern so intense it pounds harshly in my ears. Surely I will die in this beast's arms. I've danced a dance with death, yet only excruciating pain claims me. I can find no relief.

Finally the volume of my voice breaks through, and I am suddenly awake. I bolt up to a sitting position in my bed as the bedroom door opens swiftly. A tall man emerges from the dark and is now filling the doorframe. Sheer terror abruptly paralyzes me. One nightmare appears to give way to another. *No…Please no… Please don't rape me…*

Short gasps of air escape painfully as I begin to hyperventilate.

"Are you okay?" John Paul asks.

All I can do is sit there and continue to gasp for air. He begins to step into the room, so I protectively throw my hands out and bark out a *No*. He pauses and puts up his own hands in a surrendering fashion.

"Savannah. Are. You. Okay?" John Paul speaks in a stern yet cautious tone, emphasizing each word. I don't answer, so he begins to come forward again. I'm on the verge of completely freaking out.

"No! Go away!" My words come out in a wheeze, and my hands are still out in front of me. *"Please."* I feel like I will die if he enters my room. Confused understanding seems to pass through him as he steps back. We have a bit of a standoff as I continue shaking and wheezing.

Finally, John Paul, not seeming to have a choice, backs out of the room and quietly shuts the door. I vainly try to slow my breathing, but it feels like my chest has been crushed. The bed begins to quiver in protest from my violent tremors. Drenched in a cold sweat, my first priority is to get my constricting jeans and shirt off that I'm still wearing from earlier. The fabric feels as though it is glued to my skin and is choking me. The panic comes in crushing waves as I finally free my legs before collapsing onto the floor. As I lay here in a clammy state, I spot my suitcase and will myself to crawl over to it. I rummage along the bottom of it until I find my bottle of Xanax. I pop a whole pill and roll onto my side.

I lay on the floor for a while, waiting for the medicine to relieve the unbearable weight on my chest. I'm just staring under my bed, and an unexpected memory flashes of an eleven-year-old me hiding under there. She's quietly weeping and hoping not to be discovered. She is already over five feet tall and has trouble hiding under the cramped space. This image isn't helping my current state. So with great effort, I flip myself in the opposite direction and try to reassure myself that the memory can't hurt me.

"It's not the same bed, Savannah," I tell myself. But it's too late. The memory won't let me go. The pain of it is like a bitter friend who's showed up, refusing to let go of the grudge and just go away. It taunts me and I cower.

~ ~ ~

"Let's play hide and seek," Evan suggests. Julia giggles, and the boys whoop their agreements.

I inwardly groan, and my stomach starts hurting. I feel the vomit rise up and try hard to swallow it back down. Hide and seek with Evan is always a dirty game. I could refuse to play the game, but I know from experience that he will simply take what he wants from me while the others hide. It's a game I can't figure out how to win. The devil always wins.

I rush off in a mad dash as everyone scatters. I run straight to my room and push open the window. I have escaped him this way before. The garage roof is right under my window, so it's a pretty easy getaway—when it ain't raining, that is. But this day it is pouring in thick sheets. I only hope he will think I am crazy enough to chance it.

The rain is coming in the window and forms a puddle on the wood floor, but I don't care. I scoot under the bed in panic and only have to wait a few minutes before I hear him slip in and flip the lock in what sounds like hurried motions.

His bare feet pass by on his way to the window and I hold my breath until my chest burns—afraid he'll hear me. He stands there for a few moments, quietly chuckling. That wicked sound tells me he knows I'm underneath the bed.

Please no, I silently beg. My heart pounds painfully,

and I'm sweating profusely as I see he is moving closer to the bed. I silently plead for him to leave. Instead, he has a seat. The bedframe quietly groans from his weight.

His feet are mere inches from my face and I'm confused when they disappear. The bed shifts above me. Is he lying on my bed? Why?

Keeping my eyes wide open so I can keep guard, I clamp my hand over my mouth to hold in my whimpers of fear. Please go away. Please don't touch me today. I beg these words in my mind on repeat.

"You could come up here and join me on the bed." He says this quietly, too intimately, letting me know I'm at his mercy.

I remain frozen under the bed, almost to the point of not breathing. I knew he was toying with me, but I had no clue what his next move would be in this sick game.

A scream of terror rips from my lips when all of a sudden he drops to his knees and stares me dead in the eyes. I swear I am staring back at the devil himself. I start scooting in the opposite direction, but before I can get out of his grasp, Evan grabs ahold of my hand with his and yanks me near him until our lips crash together. I feel my heart hammering in my throat, as he takes what's not his to take.

Evan finally leans away, a grin sneered on his red lips. "Happy birthday, little miss." He pulls my hand to his mouth and places a kiss on it before leaving my room.

After the fear finally releases me from its snare, I scoot out and sit on my rug until my heart slows to a calmer beat. I look around the room, wishing it would come alive and protect me. To tell me it's just a bad dream. But I'm alone in this, and what Evan is doing to me is just another one of those hushed secrets trapped in the walls of the Thorton house.

I stay put on that rug, watching the rain pour mournfully into my window and cry a little bit more of myself away. Bit by bit, I am becoming more and more lost.

~ ~ ~

I can't take it anymore, so I crawl across the hall to the bathroom and pull myself up at the sink. I glance in the mirror and quickly look away from the mess of myself; knowing that will only make this worse. I set my bleary focus on getting the shower turned on to the hottest setting tolerable. Tossing my clothes to the floor, I carefully climb in and stand under the hot stream for a second, but my legs keep buckling. Not being able to stand upright any longer, I ease down and rest my head on my knees and allow the scorching water to pelt my back, hoping it will wash away the debilitating anxiety. I stay in this position, breathing in the steamy air and breathing it back out until the water begins to cool. I stay put until it becomes frigid cold, begging it to shock my out of this attack. I'm so sick of these things. They are incredibly crippling. I just don't know how to rid myself of them.

By the time I dress in a fresh T-shirt and comfy yoga pants, my blurry vision begins to clear up and my jumbled thoughts straighten out a good bit. Relief washes over me that I have dodged an emergency room visit. And I hate beyond *hate* resorting to that. Feeling somewhat settled, I decide to go find John Paul to set his mind at ease. I find him sitting on the front porch swing, a beer in hand and the weight of life pressing his shoulders down. I slump down beside him and let out a long, pensive sigh. The pill is doing its magic, and my body is feeling nice and numb.

"Sorry," John Paul says shamefully, as though he has done something wrong.

"Not your fault. You just interrupted one of my critically acclaimed nightmares," I say in a slow, sarcastic manner. The medicine has my tongue nice and relaxed. I feel his eyes on me, but decide to keep staring at the old rocking chair on the opposite end of the porch. The light breeze has it swaying gently. *Focus on that, Savannah. Focus…*

We rock in the quiet until he asks, "Do you have nightmares often?"

"Yeah, but they're just repeats of the same old

crap over and over. I'm quite used to them. They're starting to get right boring, actually." I try to joke the awkwardness away.

"Whatever nightmare that was playing tonight definitely didn't seem boring to me. Downright scary is more like it," John Paul says dryly, not buying a word of my joking.

"Oh. Don't pay me any mind. I'm a drama queen. Just ask your mother." I laugh it off.

"Enough, Savannah!" My brother's gruff voice echoes out across the porch. Even the crickets shut up and take notice at my seething brother. I pitch forward a bit when he suddenly stops the swing. The next thing I know, John Paul's hands have grasped my shoulders and turn me completely to face him. I'm not inclined to look him in the eye, but have no choice. "I am so sorry for not taking better care of you. I let you and Julia down." John Paul runs his hand through his hair with aggravation. "I wasn't stupid as to what was going on with Evan. All I cared about was my dang self. I liked having the freedom to come and go as I pleased. I figured as long as things stayed the way they were, I would have that freedom. Then that weekend happened and I wish I could have taken it all back… I *swear* I didn't know how bad things were until after that weekend." His voice goes hoarse with this statement.

I sit here staring back at him, stunned. We have never had a conversation about what had happened. I'm not sure why we are now. "John Paul—"

"You girls weren't ever right after that. Neither one of you would even sleep in your own bed." He shakes his head, and I can see his frustration building. "You on that rug and when Julia came back, she slept every night in Bradley's bed in my room. Man, we are a f—, I mean, um, messed up bunch."

"I didn't know that about Julia. I don't know much of anything about her now." This fact slices into me. I hate most of all that our relationship suffered. All of our relationships took a beating, I guess.

"Yeah. That girl cried herself to sleep most nights. Unlike you. You put so many blame walls up and closed yourself off. Both of you ran away as soon as you could, and I did nothing to stop you. I did nothing…"

"John Paul. It wasn't your place to fix what was going on. No one was paying attention. You couldn't have stopped it. You were just a kid too." I watch as tears spill from his miserable blue eyes. And oh how I wish I could cry right along with him. Watching this tough guy break like this is too much.

"I could have fixed things if I tried, but I didn't. I just sat back and watched both you and Julia fade away." He shakes his head in what must be his own disbelief and takes a long drink from his beer before he continues. "I carelessly watched my family disappear. First my two sisters and then my brother. I was *careless* with Bradley, and I was *careless* with you girls. I have paid every day of my life since." He rests his face in his hands, still clutching the beer bottle, and openly weeps. The swing vibrates with his sobs. I rub his back and wish I could take the pain away for him. I know better though. Nightmares don't go away so easily.

"Everything that happened, happened. We can't change it in any way. All we can do is try to live a better life than we've already lived." I pause to shake my head at my own words. I lick my numb lips and let out a half-laugh, half-sigh. "Shoot, what do I know? I'm so dang lost that I don't know whether to host my next dinner party or to get the wording right in my suicide letter."

My offhanded remark causes the swing to pitch forward again as John Paul sits straight up abruptly. The steely glare he shoots my way makes me flinch. Maybe I should have just kept that tidbit to myself.

"What in the heck is that supposed to mean?" John Paul asks before peppering the air with colorful expletives.

"It means exactly how it sounds. I'm lost as I can be. I have a college education, the man of my dreams, and still cannot find my place in this world. I don't think I want to keep this up anymore. And... I figured Lucas deserves better anyway." I shrug my shoulders and stare out over the dark lawn. Every so often I catch a firefly winking its spark at me, and I try to put my focus on that. I've had enough of this talk.

"You can't be serious?" John Paul asks, forcing my attention back to a conversation I wish I had not started.

"Yeah. Well you opened up to me so I thought I owed it to you to open up right back," I counter and it feels a bit like a lie. I accidently let the suicide notion slip out and wish I could suck it back in. That's one side effect I have with that tiny little pill—it loosens my tongue. I take a deep breath and continue down this conversation path since I can't find my way off of it now. "Your phone call interrupted me composing my suicide note the other day," I confess. I fiddle with my hands, too ashamed to meet his disbelieving glower. He's so mad I can feel it vibrating off him. I hear him take in a harsh breath. I sure do hope it calms him some.

"That's just stupid," John Paul snaps. Nope. He's furious.

"Yeah!" I snap right back at him. "Just as stupid as you thinking what happened to Julia and me or the accident with Bradley is your fault." I grab his face so he can't look away. It's flushed with his anger and feels fevered under my palms. "Bradley's accident was not your fault. It was life's fault. You two were just being boys. It's time you stop blaming yourself." Touching him becomes too much. I let go and try to push the rocking back to the swing, but John Paul is stronger and won't allow any motion to the swing. I huff out in my own frustration and cross my arms over my chest as we sit still, seething.

I can't take the intense silence threatening to choke me with guilt, so I glance in my brother's direction. "And don't worry about the whole stupid suicide thing. I've obviously been procrastinating over that decision. You know I don't follow through with most things, so I think I'm safe." I laugh bitterly.

John Paul shakes his head with a deep frown furrowing his blond brows. "It ain't funny." I couldn't agree with him more, but don't admit this.

He sits sulking while he stares at his beer as though he wished it could heal his wounds, but I know it won't. I grab the almost empty bottle out of his hand and begin heading inside the house. "I've got something much better than this nasty thing. I'll be right back."

I only hear him grunt in disapproval before shutting the door.

I grab two glasses from the cabinet, fill them full

of milk, and place them in the freezer to chill while I head towards the covered dessert plates to search out something yummy. The kitchen smells of chocolate, sugar, and gooey goodness, so I know there is a bounty of treats to be had. I walk past the famous cookie cabinet and stop in my tracks. I feel the wicked grin tug at my lips and crinkle my eyes as a wonderful mischievous idea whispers to me. I turn back to retrieve my mother's precious box of cookies. Luck has it that a new box is tucked on the shelf with a note from the baker sending his condolences. I spot a stack of sympathy cards at the end of the counter. I stuff this little note in the midst of the rest for Jean to discover after I'm long gone. Feeling quite impressed by my own self, I grab the two icy glasses of milk from the freezer along with the cookies and head back out. John Paul sits unimpressed on the swing until he gets a glimpse of the cookies and balks at me.

"Are you absolutely crazy?" he blurts out, looking like a kid about to get caught with his hand in the cookie jar. I have to laugh because this is close to the truth of the situation.

"They're just cookies and milk, John Paul," I say innocently as I hand him his frosty glass of milk. I take my place back beside him on the swing and, after tucking my glass between my legs, begin to open the box.

As I slip my finger under the edge of the seal, John Paul says, "You wouldn't." He eyes the box as though it's going to detonate when I break the seal and blow up.

"Oh, but I did," I sing full of silliness. I laugh as the seal comes free. I lift the first cookie out and give it a good long sniff. My mouth instantly waters from the nutty luscious aroma. I give my brother a big grin before shoving the entire cookie in my mouth. "So good," I mumble with my cheeks poking out full of cookie, feeling like a chipmunk. I dramatically chew and moan as the chocolaty treat melts deliciously. The longer I chew, the more hints of goodness show up—first and foremost deep chocolate, then smoky toffee, and then nuttiness from the almonds and surprising notes of coffee.

"You are gonna be in *trouble*." My brother croons in a whiny voice and I know he's about ready to play along. We've had too much heavy tonight, and I think some silliness will do us both some good.

I wash it down with a big gulp of milk and let some trickle out the sides of my mouth for full effect. This sends him over the edge, and he begins laughing so hard the swing vibrates. I feel the tension finally relent in that laugh and it warms me.

"All right now. Keep it up and you're gonna get us both caught." I laugh and I cram another cookie in as he stares at me. Cookie crumbs fall from my over-stuffed mouth as I try to speak. "Wook." I pause to chew and swallow so I can form the words clearer. "I'm not getting up off this swing until this here box is empty. So you can either grab yourself one, or just sit there and keep drooling as I enjoy."

"What the *he…ck*?" He corrects mid-word as he grabs up a cookie then hesitates. "You didn't monkey around with these did you?" he asks, eyebrow raised.

"You just witnessed me breaking the seal." I roll my eyes.

"I believe I witnessed your mother do the same that night." He smirks knowingly.

I snatch the cookie out of his hand and cram it in my mouth.

He chuckles before grabbing up another one and following suit by shoving an entire cookie in at once. And these babies are as big as my hand, just so you know. Before swallowing, he gives me a full chocolate teeth grin, and I know we might just be okay—for now anyway. We sit out on the swing until the sun hesitates around the edges of the new day and all the cookies and milk have been devoured.

Before heading back upstairs with a slight bellyache, I give him a big hug and tell him how much I love him. I have missed too many opportunities with my big brother. I'm beginning to see this, and I know I have really slighted myself. That stinking past sure has robbed me.

I ease down on the edge of the bed in a dazed exhaustion. Oddly, I'm wired at the same time. I know all of these sporadic bouts of sleep are going to catch up soon and will wreak havoc on me. I dismiss this thought for now and scoop up the photos I swiped from John Paul's room. As I flip through the images that have caused so much pain, I am compelled to go for a visit.

I ease back outside and begin my trek down the road. It's a gray hue outside in this dim, dawn light and the sounds of the new day sing through the breeze. Birds chirp a morning greeting while a few groggy frogs croak out their sleepy grumbles. I agree with them but my feet continue to propel me forward until the pavement transitions to dirt and I find myself at the edge of Bradley's field. It's already lighter now with more of a pink shade filtering through the sky. The field's wheat crop welcomes me as it lethargically sways with its heavy dew in the light breeze, perfuming the air in its earthly sweetness. A soft fog flickers and flows in a hovering manner around the area as I spot few deer helping themselves to a quiet nibble near the right back corner. We barely pay each other any attention as I weave through the rows until I reach the spot. I kneel down on the damp soil and am almost engulfed in the crop as I relive the horrible accident. Flashes of that day slash through my mind, and I find myself clutching my stomach from the waves of pain. The deep rut has been smoothed and the ground has hidden all the evidence of the spilled blood and broken hearts of that day, but I'm not fooled. I know those secrets are still here and are whispering their repeated devastating confession. It admits it all with brutal honesty. My eyes sting and my nose throbs with all the right signs, but my tears continue their refusal to come forward and grant me relief.

I continue kneeling with my hands buried on the tainted soil. I'm lost in my memories until I hear a faint clicking sound. I look up in the direction of the sound to discover John Paul standing by the edge of the field with his fancy camera trained on me. I say nothing. I just continue to stare vacantly in his direction. He doesn't acknowledge me either. The faint shuttering of the camera is rapid and I know he has at least taken a hundred photos by this point. I don't know why I permit this, but I do. I turn my back away from him, sending my long, loose, hair cascading over my face protectively and sit in this spot while I allow him to medicate his wounds through his creative outlet. If this helps to soothe his demons, I feel obligated to grant it to him.

The camera continues to capture me and the field as John Paul circles around. We mourn silently together in this eerie moment—him trying to capture something with me trying to release it.

The clicking fades with my brother departing just as quietly as he arrived. I mourn a while longer before going back to the house and falling into bed. I fade into a peculiar, calming sleep. My mind hovers on a thought before the morning disappears—*calm before the storm*.

~ ~ ~

A nagging knocking at the door summons me awake. Hoping whoever it is will go the heck away, I bury my head under the pillow and don't acknowledge it.

"Are you okay in there?" The muffled nag of my mother's voice yells on the other side of the door. I don't move nor make an effort to answer her. *Go away*. I should have known better than that. I hear the door open and slam forcefully. Great. My pillow shield is snatched out of my hand, causing me to flinch in surprise. I'm about to peep an eye open, but decide against it when Jean snaps, "I've been knocking for ten minutes now. Are you going to hide in here your entire visit?"

I cannot muster up enough strength to deal with her, so I roll over away from her and stay silent. A low rumbling echoes of a nearby storm outside. I can't help but recognize the symbolism here. *A storm's a comin'...*

"Don't you think it's time to get yourself cleaned up and come out and greet some of our company?" She is clearly becoming more agitated by the minute, which is evident in her sharp tone. I sure don't feel like dealing with this right now.

I finally drag my exhausted butt out of the bed and, without a word, begin gathering things for a shower once I realize she has no intentions of leaving me be. I feel like a zombie, I'm so tired.

"You don't know how to answer when spoken to?" Jean sounds like she is ready to explode.

I turn towards her to finally give a response, but meet the fiery back of her hand across my face. I blink away the shock as my vision tinges red. *No one is allowed to touch me without my permission,* I remind myself.

"Why are you such a disrespectful—" Before she can spit another word out, my hand strikes out to return the favor. I call forth all of the pent-up hurt I have towards this woman and slam her cheek with all my might. I have never struck my mother before and can barely believe my actions now. Neither can Jean, she just stands here totally stunned. Tears spill out her eyes almost instantly as she rubs her red cheek. Mine stings its familiar sting, and I'm satisfied that she is finally getting a taste of it herself. I don't try to rub the throb of mine away. I know from experience it only makes the mark shine brighter, but I don't share this with her. I want her to wear that angry mark in remembrance of this moment. It's the moment that this mess comes to a stop. *I've had enough.*

"You have struck me for your last time," I say through clinched teeth. It is all I can do to stay calm and speak evenly. "I'm a grown woman, and I will no longer allow you to abuse me."

"Abuse?" she asks as if confused. "What the heck do you know about abuse?"

"Oh, I do believe I know too much about the subject of abuse. Between your vile words and twitchy palm and Evan Grey's wandering hands, I do believe I've been taught a good bit about it." My body begins to quake all over and the tingling seeps into my fingertips. I storm over to my suitcase and haphazardly down three Xanax with a bottle of water I brought up with me last night. My insides are screaming, and I feel close to coming undone.

"What on earth are you talking about with Evan?" Jean asks.

My eyes cut over at her and watch as she wrings

her hands in what looks to be guilt at her lie of omission. "I'm talking about the man you left us with while you were out living your precious life. I'm talking about all that time that should have been spent making lasting memories with my mother. Instead, I had a sick man teaching me all I needed to know about sex." It is all I can do not to scream, but I feel my control slipping. Jean flinches at this as though I've just struck her again. Good. She needs to feel the vile sting of the truth. I hurl the water bottle across the room, causing the remaining water to scatter along its trek. I'm coming undone and feel the demons fighting against my determination to not allow them victory. But it's too late. I'm defeated. I take in a rugged breath and deliver another blow with my words. "Oh yes, he taught sweet Julia Rose all she would ever need to know about sex as well."

"I have no idea what you're talking about." Her voice falters with another lie, and we both know it. My mother has always been an awful liar. Her lies come out in stutters. I'm so ready to slap the stutter out of her. I take a step away from her to try to control this urge. She's scooting dangerously close in my direction.

"How could you not possibly know?" I'm irate at this point with my body jerking with uncontrollable tremors. "I know you remember coming home from your vacation that summer and noticing that Julia and I could hardly get out of bed. It definitely wasn't the flu, *Mother*." I have to sit back down on the bed because I'm trembling so badly. I run my hands aggressively through my knotted hair several times, trying to relieve some tension. I focus on the pain of my scalp from pulling my hair, hoping to gain some control. But it's not working. Jean says nothing. And really, what can she say? "It was from being raped over and over again by that devil. And you allowed it to happen." I whisper this because it hurts too bad to say loudly. The admission that my family allowed such a thing to go unpunished cuts just as deep as the act of the abuse itself for me.

"How dare you talk like this to me now. My *husband* has just died, and you expect me to be able to deal with this?" She gestures towards me like I'm a distasteful chore and begins pacing back and forth across the bedroom floor. It hurts that she sees me as something to deal with and not her damaged daughter.

"Yes, it's nearly twenty years past due. Because I'm sick of your constant disappointment in me when you're the one who should be ashamed. You were the one who allowed some man to play porn star with your daughters while you were out enjoying your *free* time. I'm disappointed in *you*!"

"How can you talk to me this way?" Jean heads for the door, but I grab her arm.

"Why have you always hated me so badly?" I beg for an answer. "Why?" I feel like a confused, helpless child. I shouldn't yearn for this woman's love and approval, but I desperately do anyway.

"How could I hate you? You're my child, Savannah. Of course I love you." She looks at me as if I am completely stupid.

"What you have for me is nowhere close to love. I want an answer on why you never did anything about what Evan did to Julia and me?" I'm adamant on making her admit to not doing right by us. She keeps tiptoeing around admitting her wrong.

"I did what I thought was best." She juts out her chin and crosses her arms in defense.

"What kind of crap for an excuse is that?" I yell and sling myself back down on the edge of the bed.

"It's the truth. I was afraid if it got out what Evan did to you girls, authorities would take you away. I thought the best thing for us to do was to try to forget it happened." She nods her head rapidly as if she is agreeing with herself on this convoluted idea. "I had no idea anything was going on until your father and I returned from that summer vacation. So I told Evan that if he came anywhere near my family again, I would kill him." Jean collapses on the bed beside me.

She lays her head in her hands and continues to cry. The emotions of everything are too overwhelming. I hardly have the energy to continue, but this is my chance to get things off my chest. I can't leave things the way they are. It's time to set things straight with my mother, whether we like it or not.

"Do you actually think my sister and I could simply forget something so horrible?" I ask. "It near 'bout killed Julia Rose."

"I didn't say I handled it right. I said I handled it the best way I knew how."

"Then explain to me why you have always been so awful to me." I need answers.

"I wouldn't call it that. I've always been stern with you to make you stronger. It worked, didn't it?" She sounds so convincing.

"Oh no, you don't get credit for my strength. Only I do." I continue. There's more to get out, and I have all intentions of unloading it all on her. "I know I was a mistake. You've always made sure I knew it too!" I yell.

"Is that what you actually think?" Jean looks at me in disbelief.

"I know I've not dreamt the whole thing up. You've always been so much harder on me than Julia or John Paul. Why?" I come unglued and begin screaming. I'm pretty sure the guests think our world is falling apart up here. Thunder pounds through the yelling in agreement.

"Because you've always had so much potential, but you've chosen to waste it." Jean gets up and walks toward the door then turns back around. "You'll never be able to make anything of yourself until you let the past go. Your past doesn't have to define you, Savannah. I may not have been the mother you wanted, but there's nothing we can do about that now. I am who I am."

I can't believe what my ears are hearing. How dare Jean actually think she can give me motherly advice, even if it makes some sense. No, I have not decided a career path yet. I'm still settling into married life with Lucas. I haven't had time to figure everything out and I'm still young. What was the hurry? It doesn't seem to bother Lucas. His opinion is the only one I care about.

"Your dad always knew what potential you were capable of. He made that clear in his will." Jean is now staring out of the window towards the storm brewing just outside.

"What in the world are you talking about?" I ask as I run my hands through my hair nervously.

She remains at the window silently, so I repeat myself. "What are you talking about, Mother?"

"He left you the restaurant and market," she

barely says over a whisper. This sends me into shock.

"Oh really? So I can take care of you the rest of my life. No thanks! John Paul should take over the businesses, not me."

Jean looks as disgusted as I feel. "Between my inheritance from my parents and what your dad left me, you'll never have to provide a dime for me. And as for John Paul, he couldn't handle the responsibility, nor does he want it. That boy's heart is in his photography. Your dad knew you would continue his legacy the proper way." Her tone lightens up a bit. "You've already shown your interest. You spent most of the day there yesterday, didn't you?"

My lungs tighten painfully as I start to hyperventilate. "I have to get out of here." I grab my bag, cram my feet into my shoes, and stumble out the door with the intention of running away from this life permanently. The dam I've willed to withstand the unrelenting years of hurt not only buckles under the pressure, it completely gives way, allowing all of the bitter memories to flood through me in a torturous taunt.

I surrender in defeat.

I have finally had enough.

I'm tired of being lost.

Chapter Thirteen

The storm is rolling in at an unforgivable rate as I pull up to the beach. I sit in my car for few moments in a daze and watch the rain meet the angry waves. The medicine is doing its job and everything is numb—from my lips to my mind to my soul—numb. It's a feeling I want to keep—to never feel the hurts and disappointments ever again. As this thought dances around my foggy mind, the idea materializes right in the midst of those swelling waves.

I stumble out of the car and become instantly drenched in the downpour, but I barely give it any notice. I stagger to the water's edge as lightening splits across the stormy sky. Mother Nature and I are on the same page with our restless moods. The roaring waves and thunder crashes all around me as the ocean beckons me even farther.

The demons whisper, *Come meet me. Let's dance our dance. Just give in. It's time.*

I am waist deep in the hostile water, swaying to the tempest. It's getting harder to focus on anything but the hazy whispers undulating in and out. My mouth feels like cotton, so I lean my head back to take in the tears of the sky when a wave crashes into me and knocks me under. I don't fight against it. I freely let the current beat me and pull me for a spell before deciding to reemerge.

I'm now chin-deep in the livid sea, and all I can think is to just go out a bit farther. I do, until I have no choice but to sink or swim. I tread the irritated waters for a while, trying to figure out what in the world I'm doing. But my mind is too disoriented from being overmedicated and cannot decipher the situation. I'm disoriented and feel as though I'm stuck in one of my dreams—maybe I am…

My eyes slip shut until a boom of thunder awakens me. I'm not sure how long I've been out here—seconds, minutes, a lifetime… My legs and arms are getting tired now and feel too heavy and so I decide to let go. I just let go…

Letting go, I allow the current to take me under. The ocean encapsulates me until everything is eerily quiet and peaceful. It's as if the deeper I sink, the less the storm can affect me. A peculiar thought flickers through my confused consciousness. Has peace been hiding under the waves of this ocean all along? My lungs begin to protest after allowing the ocean to claim me for a spell. No. The peace is not here either, I decide. Panic tries to push its way in and I think about propelling myself to the surface, but I rethink it. Instead, my mouth opens and breathes in the salty water. My physical body tries to protest, but I welcome the burning invasion. My ever-present demons sing joyfully, *just endure this for only a little longer and you can be freed. Let the tide take you away…*

I'm lost…I'm worthless…I'm confused…

In this moment, I let go completely. I stop fighting a fight I can never win. I suck more of the saltwater in with my body protesting, refusing to give it any relief.

Soon… It will all be over soon.

A hand snatches me up and I try fruitlessly to fight it off. The vice grip propels me to the surface and I can't wiggle free from it.

"Oh no you don't!" His voice breaks through in a gruff tone as he begins to pull me towards the shore. I'm so lethargic at this moment that I have no choice but to let him. In my next glimpse of consciousness, I'm being dragged onto the shore. My body expels the saltwater violently onto the wet sand as the rain slams into us in thick sheets.

"No you don't," Lucas says again through gritted teeth as he pulls me onto his lap. I weakly look up at him and notice his own tears mingling with the rain. I want to say I'm sorry for those tears, but more ocean makes its way out of my lungs at that moment. And then darkness pulls me under.

When I rouse back awake, I find myself shivering in Lucas's jeep. He is pulling up somewhere. I don't care where because, at this moment, the fire in my throat and lungs are overwhelming. I swallow and wince at the pain this causes. I begin to whimper and Lucas finds my hand.

"It's okay. You're okay. We're okay. It's going to be okay," he whispers in a continuous chant as he parks. He releases my hand, so I close my eyes. I open them almost immediately when he pulls my door open, swoops me in his arms, and carries me up the steps of an unfamiliar beach house. He pushes through the front door and carries me straight upstairs to what my jumbled mind guesses is the master bath. My eyes are so irritated that I don't even try to focus on anything particularly.

Lucas stands me up in front of a massive walk-in shower and turns on an assortment of nobs. The pelting water blends with the rain song in a melancholy chorus. I have to hold onto the wall while Lucas tries to peel my saturated clothes off. My yoga pants feel so sticky and I worry we will never get them past my shoes… That's when I notice I'm barefoot. I guess the ocean didn't get to claim my soul this day; I think and smirk at the stupid thought that it *did* get the soles of my shoes. I know, dumb notion. I blame it on my heavily medicated state.

Lucas gives me a curious, concerned look, but I just shake the idea and his question away. He bends down to work my panties past my feet and I have to hold onto his shoulders so I won't topple over. I really should not have taken three pills. My head doesn't feel like it is attached to my body.

He guides me gingerly into the warm streams of water as though I am the most fragile thing—maybe I am. All I know in this moment is the warm, vigorous water is delicious. I lean my head back and gulp the fresh water as though I have just been rescued from an extended stay in the desert. After shedding his own wet clothes, Lucas joins me in the shower.

He turns me towards him and begins to massage water through my tangled hair. His tearful eyes study me in an excruciating way. I see the pain etched across his beautiful features. I am a burden, and it stings me deeply for causing this. I try to speak an apology, but this produces a coughing fit freeing some more trapped saltwater from my lungs. I release it and follow up with a manly hacking spit, causing a boyish smirk to faintly appear on my Lucas's face as he rolls his eyes. In only a moment, the seriousness is back painfully in his features.

I gulp some more fresh water and watch as Lucas picks up a bottle of shampoo and begins to work it through my knotted hair. I give him a questioning look because the unmistakable aroma of eucalyptus and mint is none other than my own shampoo.

As he lathers and massages my head, he answers my unspoken questions. "I rented this beach house late last night. I was on my way to pick you up when I saw you peel out of your mother's driveway. I followed you to the beach..." His voice tightens at this. He gathers me up in his arms, and we both tremble while he sobs. I wish I could cry along with him. I hate myself for doing this to him. It's the first time I have witnessed Lucas cry, and it punches me deeply that I am the cause. Shame engulfs me.

I slur out an apology around a too-thick tongue. "I'm so sorry."

My speech pulls him back into focus as he eyes me. "How many did you take?" he asks.

"Too many." I lick my swollen licks. "But not enough." I bob my head to convey meaning.

"Savannah?" He's not content with my answer.

"Three. I only took three."

If this upsets Lucas more, he doesn't show it. He goes back to washing the ocean off of me. After rinsing my hair, he works a good amount of conditioner through my tangled tresses. He then moves onto washing my body in a tender, massaging manner. I'm not so far gone that I couldn't take care of this myself, but it feels too good not to indulge. His touch is so heavenly that I can barely keep standing. This man can pour so much love out with just his touch. He relays his heartache and compassion through the attention he gives me in this moment. Every so often he brushes a kiss on my shoulder or over my temple or where his hands have just washed. He is still slightly trembling, so I know this scare won't be leaving us so easily.

I have to get myself together. What I did was stupid and selfish. This man, who is practically worshiping me in angst at the moment, doesn't deserve this. And in this very moment, the realization slams into me so hard, my legs buckle, causing Lucas to have to hold me up. *I don't deserve this either.*

He holds me fiercely under the shower jets and begins to slowly rock us in a silent dance. He seems to always try to out dance my demons. I'm ready to finally let him too. It has taken me quite the journey to get to this point of intimacy with my husband, and now I feel like it is the only thing that keeps me going.

Love is giving. And love is accepting. Lucas's words echo through my mind as he continues to caress me. We stand under that water as I release more demons. I want to lay them all down. I want to be able to be healthy enough to love this man back the way he and I both deserve.

He eventually eases away and places me on the tiled shower bench and sets out to washing the sea off of his own body. He moves through it fast. I watch as he places his hands on the wall opposite of me as if he needs it to balance himself. The water cascades down his taut shoulders and I can actually see the burden of this morning's monstrous event weighing on him. He sniffles a few times, but seems to pull himself together by the time he shuts the water off to face me.

He runs his hands roughly through his wet, curly locks as he gazes at me. Keeping his hands on top of his head, he whispers, "You are to never do that again." I nod in agreement.

Lucas pulls me out of the shower stall and begins to dry me with a soft thick towel. Once we are both dry, he gathers me in his strong arms as though I'm the most precious thing and carries me to bed, where he continues to pour out his love for me. His confidence seems to wane a bit and is replaced by urgent uncertainty and fear as he holds me tighter than normal. This is usually a trigger for an attack and I wait for it to creep up but it never does. Maybe it's because I focus on Lucas in this moment and not my fears or simply from being overmedicated. I know I'm the cause of this. His body trembles with the fear I placed there. I wish he had not witnessed my darkness, but he did and there's nothing I can do about it now. All I can do is relay my apology in this instant. I am so sorry, but I seem to have no control over the demons that are holding me captive. I want to be free of it just as much as Lucas does. He wants to fix me and I want him to, but we both know it's not in his power to. It's not fair to put such a burden on him. He's tried to carry it ever since we've met.

"I'm sorry," I confess as I burrow close to him and his warmth. "I'm so sorry." These words repeat every so often, but he seems to only be able to slightly nod his head in recognition to them.

As we comfort each other, both storms pass and finally give way to peace. At least it does until nearly dawn when the fuzz of Xanax seeps completely away and my stress level starts to rev back up again.

I lay in my Lucas's arms as I listen to the waves lap against the shore. I've been listening to this lulling song for hours now as I contemplate everything. My eyes have awakened it seems after yesterday's failed suicide attempt. I'm thankful that this is the end of that attempt instead of being buried on the beach hill with my dad tomorrow. I've been given another chance, and I need to figure out how to make it count.

I ease out of Lucas's arms and slip on a baggy pair of sweatpants and an oversized T-shirt I find in his suitcase. I swipe his keys and start to head out.

"Hey?" he asks in a groggy tone as I'm about to leave. I turn back to find that fear in his eyes.

I move back to the bed and climb in his lap for a few minutes before I whisper, "I need to go see Miss May. I'll be back shortly. I promise." I kiss the scruff on his cheek and head out.

The rain is coming down in only a whisper now as I pull into her driveway. I find Miss May standing on her porch in curlers as if she has been expecting me. Maybe she has. I'm beginning to think she has a direct line to God.

Before I can reach her front steps, my legs give way and I collapse in the muddy yard. Something significant shifts inside me. I don't know what overtakes me in this moment, but the next thing I know, I am screaming to the top of my lungs. I scream and I scream as Miss May kneels beside me. I fell her wrap her arms around me, sheltering me from the world as she's always done. Her body rocks alongside mine as my soul expels all of the toxins wave after wave.

"I can't carry it anymore! It's too much! How can I let it go? I have to!" I scream out in agony, raising my head towards the mournful sky. The cool mist mingles with a hot liquid that is trickling down my face. It scares me because I think I'm bleeding somehow. I reach up to wipe the warm liquid off my face and am confused when I inspect my hand and find no trace of blood.

I'm not bleeding...*I'm crying*! My body finally releases the flood of grief and bottled up pain. I pull on Miss May desperately and I know she sees a mad woman before her as the levy finally breaks free and I sob wholeheartedly with my body trembling violently.

"You gotta give it to God, child. He the only one that can take it away." She continues to hold me as my screaming escalates.

I'm fed up and scream out to God, "Why God? Why?" I scream this over and over until my voice tires. "I don't want this anymore!"

"He trying to hand you a better life. One with peace and love. He's already gave you Lucas. Take what God is begging to give you, child." She pulls back so I have to meet her gaze. We are both sopping wet and muddy, but it barely registers. "Give God all that bad stuff. You know you's sick of carrying it.

Give it to Him child and live!"

She rocks me as the rain lets up and the sun begins peeking out as if on cue. In this moment, I agree to give it up. I can actually feel the burdens leave me. I cry a long cry—the tears of hurt and abuse and of nightmares eventually wash away and I am renewed with tears of relief.

We eventually make our way to the porch. We sit in an understandable silence as the new day wakes up oblivious as to what has just transpired in this muddy front yard. Miss May and I don't share, we just keep rocking in our chairs.

"I need to get back to Lucas before he gets worried," I say as I rise from my chair. I kiss Miss May on her cheek and head to the jeep.

"No more of those stupid stunts you tried pulling yesterday, young lady," she says as I open the driver's door. I don't ask her how she knew about that. I'm guessing it's the same way she knew I was going to visit this morning—my other saving grace.

"Yes ma'am," I say before closing the door.

I pull up at the beach house and give it a quick inspection, taking it in for the first time. Lucas has rented us a Mediterranean-style bungalow with creamy stucco walls and a terra cotta roof. The man amazes me. He knows I'm not a fan of the cliché cookie-cutter beach structures that dot most of this shore. Leave it to him to seek out a unique one. I shake my head with a smile and head straight to that enormous shower to wash off the mud.

Once I emerge, I find my belongings have been gathered from Jean's and brought here. I pull on a sundress and pad out with wet hair to look for my Lucas. I find him on the balcony with two cups of steamy coffee along with a stack of papers on the table that has been dried. I stand behind him and wrap my arms around his bare shoulders. He is wearing only a pair of shorts, and his body is nicely warm, so I greedily soak it in. The day is heating up pretty fast, even with the beach breeze.

"I love you," I whisper against his wavy tousled hair. I begin to pull away, but he holds me there with a firm grasp.

"Then never try to leave me again." His voice is thick with emotion. He is still not over yesterday. I guess I wouldn't be either if I watched him do something so dangerous… So stupid.

"Promise," I say as I kiss my way along the side of his neck. He pulls me around and into his lap, holding me until I begin crying again. This seems to scare him just as bad as yesterday, because Lucas has *never* seen me cry.

"Savannah?" he asks cautiously as he sits me up so he can study me, sorrow scorching his green eyes.

I smile to reassure him, but he doesn't seem to buy it. He probably thinks I have just stepped off the cliff and plummeted to Looneyville. I try again by pulling him towards me and crush my lips against his. I have never allowed this intensity, but I feel I have finally let enough go that I can handle it. I kiss him with all my might, conveying to him how much I love him. He is guarded at first but seems to finally let go of his caution and meets my passion with his own urgency. Lucas deserves to feel as much love as he has always freely given me. I feel no tingling in my fingertips and the sudden rise of my heart rate feels invigorating instead of crippling. I'm swept away in the freedom of this moment and a fresh wave of tears release from me.

I kiss him fiercely and knot my hands in his hair roughly. We are both trembling with excitement over this bewildering new moment we are sharing. Lucas says nothing more. He releases a low fervent growl before he lifts me up in his strong arms and carries me back into the beach house—the coffee forgotten.

Chapter Fourteen

The afternoon opens up brilliantly and finds me and Lucas back on the balcony. We are munching away on shrimp burgers and onion rings he has grabbed up from the Beach Shack, which is conveniently located about a quarter of a mile down the beach. The sandy shore below us has become noisy with visitors soaking up the sun and surf. A few surfers are catching the last of the waves that have been kicked up during the storm. I itch to join them, but stay put and cram another delicious onion ring in my mouth instead.

I am blissfully content as I sit here, and it surprises me. I look over at my favorite guy and smile a toothy smile at him. He returns it with his boyish grin as he picks up the stacks of papers we left unattended earlier. I slurp up some of my soda before asking, "What are those?"

He looks over at me before going back to studying the papers. "They are the tax files and bank records for your dad's businesses from the past three years." He tries to hand over one of the papers, but I don't look at it. I continue to stare at him with my silent questions. He knows what I'm asking, so he answers. "I had John Paul bring them along with your belongings this morning. He told me on the phone yesterday about the will when I called to let you know I was on my way. I couldn't get ahold of you, so I ended up calling him." He doesn't seem a bit surprised at my dad's wishes. Why am I the only one to not see that one coming?

"Why are you reading over this?" I pick a stray shrimp off my plate and pop it into my mouth. The fried treat is delectable.

"I'd like to know what we are getting ourselves into." He answers while he makes a notation on the paper.

"Look Mr. Businessman, I haven't agreed on anything."

He gives me a look with his brow slightly raised before focusing back on the papers.

What was that look about?

We sit for a while, with Lucas studying the

paperwork and me munching through the rest of my lunch.

"Did you know that your dad left no debt on either business?" he asks eventually.

"No, but that doesn't surprise me," I say and finally begin my own investigation with the paperwork. I don't get very far before my phone alerts me to a new text message. I look over at the screen and sigh in relief. Julia. Finally.

It only says, *I'll be there,* but that's enough. I need her. I need her like yesterday, but am glad to get to have her tomorrow.

I've not seen her but very briefly over the years since what happened that year with Evan. Julia didn't even show up for Bradley's funeral and I'm still not sure she will for our dad's. We're not close as I wish we could be. It's as if Evan Grey and the devil planted an ugly, thorny vine between us, and we have never really been able to figure out how to get around the hurtfulness of it.

Chapter Fifteen

Too many long months passed before Julia finally returned home from the facility my grandparents had placed her in to nurse her back to health. Even though she no longer resembled a skeleton, my sister was still quite slim, but her beauty had been restored once again. A warm glow replaced her pale skin, and her hair had a golden shine present once more. Her big, blue eyes still had an emptiness about them though, but I figured that was a permanent feature. I could guess my eyes held that resemblance to her.

Julia formed quite an attitude while she was away from us. This did not go over very well with Jean, especially since she was the one to receive the brunt of it. Julia's reserved, well-mannered persona was replaced with a prissy arrogant attitude. She had this remarkable confidence about herself too that I envied.

She announced one day right in the middle of chores that she and I were going to the beach. She didn't wait for Jean's refusal. She grabbed our suits, the keys to the car, my hand, and dragged me out the door. Even though I knew there would be unpleasant consequences, it felt great. I'll never forget the dumbfounded look on Jean's face as we walked out of the house.

"This is fun, right?" Julia asked as we sunbathed on our towels after a swim.

"Yeah. This is great. I'll probably get a face-frying when we get back for going along with you." I couldn't help but feel uneasy about our return to home later that day.

"You are one brave chick. You don't fool me," she said.

I remember looking over at her. She looked flawless with her golden skin and white, flowing hair. No one would be privy to the scars riddling her from inside. It was my first notion that my sister would make one killer actress. She didn't fool me though. And I wasn't fooling myself. I felt nowhere close to being brave. "You're joking, right? I'm just a scaredy cat."

"Savannah? Were you not the one that called Grandma and Grandpa? Were you not the one to sneak them in the house to get me help?" Julia pulled her oversized sunglasses off and tried to look me dead in the eyes, but I couldn't meet her gaze.

"If I was brave, I would have stood up to Evan and not let him hurt you so much. Instead I just ran away." Shame washed over me while Julia stiffened at the mention of that devil's name. The guilt of me disappearing and leaving her to endure who-knows-what has always eaten at me. Especially after noticing those bruises on her that awful day. He had never hit me. Rape was enough, but I can only imagine how being secretly beaten could inflict more life-long damage.

She bolted up off her towel and snatched me up too. "I never want you to say his name again, Savannah," she whispered, trying to hush the conversation away. "I will never discuss this with you again. I can't and I won't. You are brave. You survived." She chanted this a few times. I think she was trying to convince both of us. With that, Julia released me to collect her things and announced our day together was over. She never invited me to another beach excursion or anything else with her again. Well, with the exception of two trips, that is. I'll get to that in a minute… Maybe…

It wasn't long after our beach day that Julia was discovered by a modeling agency at the mall. The agency had set out to scout some new fresh faces for the industry and Julia definitely fit the bill. That very same day, my sister came home, packed her bags, and headed for New York to begin her modeling career. I was shocked and completely crushed that my sister had so easily walked out of my life without any hesitation. She had finally found her way out and hastily took it. I guess I couldn't blame her—except for the fact that she left me behind. My eyes were opened to the fact that it is every man for himself. And I also came to the conclusion that I could only depend on myself. I know it sounds bitter and cold, but that was my life. That thin thread of hope that me and my sister could mend our relationship and overcome what we had endured severed completely after she left. It finished breaking us apart. I didn't want to give up on us, but I felt I had no choice.

My sister's demons followed her all the way to New York and took up residence with some newly discovered demons as well. Julia got so wrapped up in the lifestyle of drugs and partying that it landed her in rehab a few times. She barely visited and only called on holidays. In many ways she had begun to remind me of Jean. She was the most important person in her own world, and our mother had always acted the same way. Our rare conversations always revolved around her and the big adventure of the moment. If I did ever get a word in, Julia would just interrupt with "Oh, that's nice" and without hesitation go right back to talking about herself. She stopped hearing me all together. I was no longer significant in her world, and I would eventually become use to it.

I made the mistake of visiting Julia the summer after I graduated high school. Yes, here we go. It ain't pretty, just let me tell you. It was such a shock to actually be invited to come see her. I really missed her so I eagerly agreed to fly to New York—like an idiot. It was my first time on a plane, as well as to New York, and I had no idea what I was getting myself into. The flight went pretty smooth even though I was scared to death. I believe I stayed a nervous mess until my feet returned back to South Carolina soil later that week.

As soon as the plane landed in New York, I began wishing I had never agreed to the trip. For starters, Julia was too busy meeting with her agent to pick me up from the airport. This left me with the task of hailing a cab and figuring out how to get to Julia's apartment building all on my own. The cab driver could barely speak English and he had a hard time understanding my southern accent. We were definitely two very confused and very aggravated individuals. He finally pulled up at the correct building after forty-five minutes of "huh?" and "I not understand." More to my surprise was the fee for the cab ride. It cost me a good chunk of the spending money I had for the entire week's trip. I not-so-politely told him he was robbing me and the unfairness of it. He simply replied with another, "I not understand." "Bull" is what I called out to him before he abandoned me in the heart of New York.

Just when I thought the situation couldn't get any worse, Julia was not home yet. I was not allowed to enter the building without her, so I spent the first afternoon of my trip to New York waiting on a hot, busy sidewalk for my inconsiderate sister to show up. Fear of getting lost and heavy luggage prevented me from venturing too far from the building. I had enough sense to not leave my belongings unattended, so I just stood around waiting.

Luckily, there was a hot dog vendor only a block from the apartment building. It was the first morsel of food I had a chance to eat all day. I asked the vendor man to give me the New York Special, and I do believe it was the best hot dog I had ever eaten. Too bad it hit my stomach like a ton of bricks. Of course, Julia didn't make her way home for another two hours after I dined on that dang hot dog. By that time I was completely exhausted, my clothes were drenched in sweat and my stomach felt like a volcano ready to explode. I found some shade under the edge of the steps and spent the agonizing afternoon hunched atop my suitcase, praying for some relief. My sweaty shirt and jeans made my misery even more agonizing. The humidity in New York was just as relentless as it is in South Carolina. For some reason, I thought I would be getting a reprieve from that, at least. A few people actually tossed some spare change at my feet. I figured I probably looked pretty pathetic.

Just when I had made my mind up to try to journey back to the airport, Julia showed up. She looked so sleek and so thin. The heat didn't even seem to faze her. She exuded this cool, sexy demeanor, and I was instantly intimidated by her for the first time ever. There was no way I could ever pull off such a manner as that. I felt very lacking in her presence. Still do, if I ever see her.

"Hey chick," Julia sang as she breezed by me. She just seemed to float up the steps of the building. "Let's get out of this heat." She waved her prissy hand around as though to shoo away the humidity. It seemed to work for her. I mocked the same motion behind her back, but got no results.

With just a quick glance my way, Julia entered her apartment building. It took all the energy I could muster up to drag my things inside. I guessed all of her manners had to have wasted away with her figure. She never apologized for making me wait so long, nor did she ask to help me with my suitcase and bag. I was so close to calling Dad and begging him to come get me, but I didn't want to bother him.

Once we entered her apartment, I headed straight to the cramped bathroom and stayed for about an hour. My bag and I could barely fit in the small space, but I managed it somehow. I immediately peeled off my sweat-drenched outfit. The coolness hit my body and a wave of nausea and dizziness swept over me. After throwing up my first and last vendor hot dog, I sat on the edge of the tub and had myself a good pity party. The day had totally overwhelmed this ole southern girl.

After I pulled myself together, I began to check out my small surroundings. You could barely turn around in the tiny space. I caught sight of myself in the mirror and let out a little gasp at the sight of the knotted-haired, flush-faced train wreck that stared back. I quickly realized I was not ready to go face my sister being the mess that I was, so I began to snoop a little bit. I decided to check Julia's medicine cabinet out. It was filled with prescription pain relievers and sleeping pills. Sadly, that did not surprise me. In a small cabinet beside the tub were tons of makeup, perfume, bath oils, and face creams. It looked like the entire beauty counter from Macy's was crammed in there. I guess it took a lot to maintain that better-than-you look. Once my belly finally settled down, I helped myself to some of the pricier-looking body wash and used it generously during a much-needed shower.

After dressing in a cooler sundress, I reemerged from the bathroom feeling a good bit refreshed. Expensive perfume followed me around. I guess my sister had that indulgence right, because it did make me feel somewhat better. I looked around the apartment in pure amazement at how compact it was. The living room/kitchen wasn't much bigger than my bedroom back home. A beaded curtain served as the door to Julia's bedroom alcove, which was covered in clothing and accessories galore. The sitting area was not much tidier. Water bottles and cigarette packs were scattered on every table. I figured those were probably the two main staples in my sister's diet. I just couldn't get over how bony she was. She used to be so healthy looking with her long lean athletic built, but now she seemed frail in her rail-thin body. Like, if I bumped into her, she might break.

I had to maneuver around piles of magazines and the craziest-looking high-heeled shoes tossed all over the floor to get to the couch. Then I had to move things over just so I could have a seat on the bright violet-colored thing. The main colors in the room consisted of dark fuchsias, deep purples, and vibrant teals. I know that sounds crazy, but it worked. Minus the clutter, the apartment had an exotic appeal. Young and hip was the vibe—just like Julia.

"There you are," Julia said surprisingly. She popped out from her bedroom wearing a short silk robe. "I almost forgot you were here. It's my turn to get freshened up." Her speech was slightly off, and I wondered what might have been her drug of choice at the moment. I really didn't want to deal with a drugged-up version of my sister for the duration of my visit, but I guessed I wouldn't be given the choice on the matter.

Julia disappeared into the bathroom for what felt like eternity. She stayed in there for two and a half hours. Seriously! While she did who knows what, I looked through most of the magazines and even tried on some of her crazy shoes. Shoes were the only part of my sister's wardrobe I could wear anymore. I checked out some of the clothes that covered her entire bedroom floor. To my disbelief, they were all size zeroes. How on earth could someone be a size zero? What was next? Size negatives? I was actually *six* sizes bigger than her and that blew my mind. There went borrowing something hip and cool to wear right out the blame window. Talk about feeling self-conscious...

The emotionally and physically draining day hit me after a while, so I shoved the pile of stuff off onto the floor so I could stretch across my sister's couch. I easily dozed off. Julia finally emerged from the bathroom sometime later, waking me. The aromas of lavender and chamomile from her bath swept throughout the living room. She was still in her robe, but her hair and makeup were freshly done. I let out a long sigh of frustration at the thought of how long it might take for her to actually get dressed.

"I'll be right out." She then disappeared into the jungle of clothing for only thirty minutes. This surprised me.

It baffled me that I had been in her presence for about four hours, and the only words uttered was pretty much "hey" and "I'll be right out." No real conversation had taken place. I worried the entire week would consist of the same. Julia had become really wrapped into her own life, and she definitely made it clear that I wouldn't be getting in the way of it during my visit. I figured I should just try to make the best of it and not let everything bother me. I also kept reassuring myself that I would never have to visit her again.

It was nearing eight o'clock when Julia stood before me and twirled around to show me her next-to-nothing short, black skirt with a sleeveless, white blouse that was backless. The outfit was completed with lots of silver bangles and six-inch black stilettos. She looked absolutely glamorous and she knew it. Her wavy, platinum blonde hair was swept in a loose side ponytail that spilled over her right shoulder. I'm sure this was intentional as to show off her bare back.

"What do you think?" She acted as though she wanted my approval as she did her little prim show in front of me.

"I love those bracelets." I eyed them as I spoke. I really did.

"Thanks." She looked a bit disappointed at that being my only compliment. I had to put up with Jean's whiny needs too much. I refused to do it for Julia as well. I was sure she received plenty of attention without needing any from me.

"Are you ready?" She asked as she headed to the door.

I was still sitting on the couch with my crumpled sundress on and my hair a mess. "Ready for what?" I asked.

"For some fun." That was all the info she let me in on for the plans of the night.

"Well crap! I can't go out looking like this, Julia. I mean, really?" I motioned towards the length of my body, disapprovingly.

"Look, little sis, I've got plans for the evening, so get your butt in gear or stay here. It's up to you." Julia stared at her clock on the wall. "I'll give you fifteen minutes before I leave you." With her cell phone already plastered to her ear, she made her way to her room.

What the heck? I might as well live a little. I certainly didn't want to spend my first New York night alone in the cramped apartment while being smothered by overflowing size zero clothes. My size six self was a bit overwhelmed by that fact.

I went to the bathroom and tried to pull myself together, *once again*. I tried to copy the side ponytail look of my sister's, but just couldn't seem to pull it off, so I let it hang loose in its natural brown waves. I threw my well-worn jean jacket on with the white sundress, after trying and failing to smooth out some of the wrinkles. I rolled up the jacket sleeves before digging around in Julia's jewelry collection. I borrowed some chunky silver bracelets and hoop earrings to finish off my look. Staring into the mirror, I knew I wouldn't be able to hold a candle beside my sister but relented that it was as good as it was going to get. Within my allotted fifteen minutes, I grabbed a pair of Julia's western-style boots and headed out the door.

Julia hailed a cab like it was the simplest task to

do on earth. All she did was wave that prissy hand in the air and the street was at her command. I had a feeling that would not be the effect I would earn if I tried to mimic her. The girl seemed larger than life. I had to shake my head at her abundant glamour. We began the night at a little bistro, where I ordered a grilled chicken salad. I thought it would be best to play it safe after my incident with the hot dog. Julia only ordered a glass of wine.

"Aren't you going to eat something?" I asked the rail-thin Barbie doll. I felt awkward eating in front of her.

"Not tonight. I'm saving my calories for beverages," she said in a so matter-of-fact tone and a prissy wave of her hand. Yes, I keep saying prissy, because that is the best way to describe her. Really.

While I sat there trying not to feel self-conscious about eating, a *very* tall and very striking man walked in. He had to be closer to seven feet than not. He was probably Julia's age, but he was way too pretty to merely call him a guy. I about choked on my lettuce when he strolled right up to our table. Julia barely acknowledged the chiseled piece of art that was standing beside her. I felt my skin flush all the way down to my toes. Why did God need to make such a beauty as that? It only led to indecent thoughts. You know I'm telling the truth, and the truth is always welcome, right?

Then he spoke one word, and I thought I would completely melt on the soft velvetiness of it. "Thorton." That was all he said, and she still kept studying her wine as though she didn't care to notice him. But boy oh boy, how could she not?

The world refers to her as Julia Rose. They may not even know that Thorton is her last name. I was intrigued that this guy knew.

"Stone," she said eventually, causing him to chuckle.

He offered his hand for me to shake, but all I could do was just keep silently staring. "She doesn't like to be touched," Julia blurted out, making me want to touch her with my fists. *So embarrassing*. He cut her an amused look before placing his hand back to his side.

I rolled my eyes at him to relay my aggravation with my sister. He seemed to get it, because he gave me an eye roll and grin in return. This man had perfectly styled dark blond hair that fell lusciously just below his ears. He looked like he just stepped out of a men's apparel ad. He was clean shaven with a flawless complexion. A dark-blue perfectly tailored suit shrouded his long, lean body and the color accentuated his striking green eyes. They were such a vibrant hue that I seemed to not be able to look away.

Julia kicked me under the table to make me do just that. I cut my eyes at her as I leaned down to rub my sore shin and heard him cover a laugh with a cough. Great. He was *amused…*

"This is my sister, Savannah." She waved daintily in my direction and then she waved towards the gorgeous man. "Greyson is a model, if you can't tell." And I could. Oh yeah. He was well put together. It was obvious he was professionally styled.

"It's nice to meet you," he said towards me before directing his attention to my sister. "I'll see you next week, Julia. You ladies take it easy tonight." He gently placed his hand on Julia's shoulder. "Call me, if you need me." He then nodded his lovely head at me and strolled over to a group near the back of the restaurant.

As I watched him walk away, I finally found my tongue. "Great day in the morning. What was that and why don't you *like* it?" I had to fan myself with my napkin. *Wow* is all I can say. I wanted to ask her if she was she absolutely crazy. He not only oozed cool confidence, he was dripping with kindness. It shocked me that he wasn't cocky at all. Men that looked like that seem to think they had all the right in the world to be so.

Julia rolled her eyes. "He's just a friend. I met him the first year I was here. We do photo shoots together sometimes when they need couples in ads."

"Well, that man sure is *purty*." I wagged my eyebrows at Julia, causing her to let out a sigh of exasperation.

"He's not my type," she snapped, seeming to not want to continue the conversation. She started rummaging through her purse as though she wanted to find another topic to entice me with, but I wasn't close to being done with the Greyson Stone topic. Oh no.

I had no plans on letting her off that easy. I leaned close to her and whispered, "Is he gay?" That's the only type I could think of that wouldn't be hers.

"No." She glanced at him as he was laughing about something his company had shared. "He's too nice."

Oh. I forgot she didn't like nice either. Dirt bags were her type. It's like Evan had set the standards on how she thought men should treat her, which was morbidly low and cruel. Good grief. My sister needed to open her eyes to the complete package that all the other women in that restaurant had their eyes trained on. He had every female's attention in the place except for the one he seemed to have wanted—Julia.

I laughed at the absurdity of her statement. "Heaven forbid you find one that treats you nice." I looked over at Greyson and he caught me. I smiled really big and waved. He returned the favor with a more subtle wave of his own. He's entire face lit up with life when he smiled. Julia was missing out on such a nice view, and I was about to point that out when she hissed at me.

Julia grabbed my hand and placed it firmly on the table. "Don't encourage him, Savannah."

Well that's exactly what I was trying to do and had no plans of stopping until she dragged me out of the place. "Why don't you like him?"

"I do. He's one of my closest friends, but he won't leave me alone about my...*lifestyle*. We sort of aren't talking right now." Julia downed the rest of her wine and beckoned the waiter for another. After he refilled it and she took another hardy sip, she continued, "He's the one that dumped me off at that *facility* last year."

Oh, I had thought to myself. He was the one who checked her into rehab, so I had guessed he was trying to fix her and she didn't have any desire to be fixed. How she was reacting towards him was making much better sense. "Don't you have to agree to those visits?" I asked as I slid another curious glance towards Greyson. I was looking at him with a bit more appreciation at that point.

"I don't remember how that part transpired. The next thing I knew, I had a contract with my signature on it that stated I would visit a minimum of three weeks. The jerk somehow tricked me into it, and I lost four modeling contracts in that timeframe." She took another generous gulp of her drink and shook her head in frustration. This man had surely ruffled my sister's feathers not in the slightest good way.

I had lost my appetite at the idea of Julia being in such bad shape that she couldn't remember periods of time. I looked back over at Greyson, thankful she had someone in her world that actually cared. I watched him as he kept glancing at my sister protectively. Poor guy. There was no way my sister would ever give him the time of day. And poor Julia, because it looked like she was missing out on something exceptional.

I picked at my salad for not even five more minutes when Julia took the last sip of her wine and announced it was time to go. As we walked out, I gave Greyson another wave and smile.

"You ladies try to be careful tonight," Greyson instructed. "Savannah, it was a pleasure to meet you."

Before I could comment, Julia had dragged me out the door. I never got to speak one word to Greyson Stone, but have never stopped hoping that one day I will get that opportunity for Julia's sake. I guess from my eyes being opened so early in life by Evan, I've always seemed to have a good read on people. And I knew Greyson was a good man. I just hate that Julia wasn't into good men.

We spent the rest of the night and most of the early morning hours going from one club to another. I met what felt like was a million of her friends, who were mostly rail-thin models and gorgeous men. Julia slipped me a drink early in the night, which helped me loosen up quite a bit. I actually began to dance and enjoy myself a bit before the partying. I was still nervous being in such a new and strange place and the men were pretty darn different from the high school boys back home. I figured it was best to play it safe and keep my distance, but it was hard keeping distance in the crowded places. The fun didn't last long.

"Who's this little hot momma?" a guy asked as he kissed Julia square on the lips with such ease. She returned the kiss in the same manner, and that really bothered me. Of course he was gorgeous with brown hair and whiskey-colored eyes, and he knew it too. I knew first hand that beauty could be one nasty thing if you gave it a good look, and I didn't have a good feeling about that guy.

Thinking nothing of it Julia answered, "My little sis." Her eyes were trained on him as though he was the only thing she could see in the place.

"I have a name," I addressed him. "It's Savannah."

"What a southern drawl!" He sounded so delighted. "Say something else."

I dramatically closed my mouth tightly and crossed my arms defensively. I didn't feel like being someone's entertainment and was not about to be this arrogant jerk's. He roared with laughter at that.

"Ooh, that one's full of sass," Mr. Flirt said. "Sawyer Helms," he introduced himself, but I ignored him. He oozed cockiness and Julia liked him so that was all I needed to mark him off my list. That girl needed her head examined. She was all but groping him in public, and he was letting her. This guy only had *his* best interests in mind, unlike the Greyson dude.

I finally shook my concern off after a while for her relationship flaws. Really. Who was I to be trying to figure out such a thing for her, when I couldn't get past my own hiccups on the matter?

The clubs were loud, dark, and packed with all types of people. When we would leave one club to journey to the next, my ears would ring like crazy. I never knew where Julia was until she'd grab my hand to lead me to the door. Everyone just seemed to blend together. One minute I would be dancing with a tall, dark and incredibly handsome man. Then I would blink my eyes and be dancing with a hunky blond. It was too crazy for me. I always kept them a cautious arm's length away from me. They seemed to think I was teasing them, but there was no game I was playing. I knew I would freak out if they decided to get hands-on.

I believe I was a novelty compared to their normal type of company. The entire night I was referred to as a southern belle, southern peach, or cute cowgirl. This appeared to annoy my sister as much as it annoyed me. Neither one of us liked the attention I was receiving, but I'm sure for different reasons. I could tell she was used to being the one receiving all the devotion. Another phrase that was on repeat from most of her guy friends was that they hadn't seen natural beauty walking around them like me in quite a while. Maybe this was their polite way of calling me plain. Once again, neither Julia nor I cared for it.

As the night and early morning wore on, Julia became more and more wasted, and I became more and more annoyed. She could barely function by that point, and I was getting nervous about it.

My annoyance escalated and then completed exploded with some drunk dude. I ended up punching him square on his vulgar mouth after he had enough nerve to pat me on the butt and say some raunchy things he thought I would like for him to do to me and vice versa.

He patted his lip and checked for blood, but there

was none. "Look babe, that fine backside of yours was advertising," he slurred on a laugh.

I gave him a good shove, which only made him sway slightly. "The only thing I'm advertising is for you to keep your scummy hands to yourself, *babe*!" I spit the words out full of vinegar.

Julia stepped between us before I had a chance to land another punch. "Good grief, Savannah. Would you just chill?" she slurred. She was barely coherent.

"No! I want to go home!" I shouted over the loud music. I was trembling at the anxiety building up and was worried a full blown attack was about to hit.

She pretended to look at a wristwatch that was not there. "But it's still early," she said and pouted out her lip. I looked at my real wrist watch and found it to be into two in the morning. She still didn't relent, so I was stuck.

I had refused to go inside anymore clubs with my sister and spent the remaining time standing outside by a bouncer. Julia knew him, and he promised her he would keep an eye on me. Julia and I returned to her apartment around four that morning. I was so tired I could barely make it to the couch. Julia was still buzzing around like it was midday. She disappeared a few times while we were out. Each time she returned, she'd act pretty drugged up. I guessed the stint in rehab that previous year didn't help her much.

"Hey. Do you need something to help you sleep?" She came out of the bathroom carrying a medicine bottle.

Sleep? Really? How on earth a person could not be wiped out after all that dancing and chaos? I shook my head warily at her. "No thanks. Just a blanket and pillow will do the trick."

She returned to the bathroom without even acknowledging my request. I was beginning to think the girl lived in there. I grew impatient and went to find my own pillow and blanket. I wasn't about to wait around for who knows how long for some rest. I grabbed an extra pillow off her bed and a cover from the floor. They both smelled clean so I helped myself to them. I believe my eyes were closed before my head hit the pillow. I had no clue as to when Julia made it to bed.

I didn't wake up until noon the next day. I peeped in on Julia and she was still snoozing away, so I went to the fridge to find something to calm my growling belly. The only things in there were bottled water and wine. I rummaged through the cabinets and found not a morsel of food. I thought how absolutely crazy that was. I grabbed a bottle of water and headed for a soak in some of the bath oils I had spotted the night before. I hoped a long, relaxing bath would help me feel better and get my mind off my hunger. I was beginning to worry I would probably be starved to death by the time I made it back to South Carolina.

After the bath, I checked on Julia to only find her still sleeping away. I tried to wake her, but she wouldn't budge. I spent the next two hours reading magazines and looking over a city map I had purchased the day before at the airport. I began to feel nauseous, so I tried to wake Julia again. She rolled over and went right back to lightly snoring. I couldn't stand it any longer, so I located a phonebook and started searching the delivery section of the restaurant listings. I settled for the first Chinese delivery place I found with cheap prices. I called and ordered more than enough food, hoping that I didn't have a repeat experience with food as I did yesterday. I was a little embarrassed at the thought of how Julia would react to the large quantity of food. I helped myself to a twenty-dollar bill that was lying on the table to pay the bill. After all, Julia was supposed to be hosting me. I would probably have felt guilty if I wasn't so darn annoyed with her. After quietly paying the delivery guy, I took my spread straight to the coffee table and began devouring it. There was no way I could live an anorexic life style. I had to have my food regularly or I wasn't able to function.

Julia still did not wake up until about five that afternoon. She didn't ask about the leftover food on the table. She just picked a few pieces of broccoli out of the stir-fry veggies and made her way to the bathroom for the rest of the afternoon.

The entire week was pretty much the same. Party all night, sleep all day, and barely eat. I had really looked forward to Julia showing me around the city. I hoped she would bring me to a Broadway show or take a ferry out to see the Statue of Liberty as she promised. I had really looked forward to seeing a true New York fashion show. That didn't even happen due to Julia taking the entire week off to spend *quality* time with me. I guess she decided that the most-happening nightclubs were the only sightseeing I needed to check out.

By midweek, I absolutely had all I could take. I grabbed my map, an extra key Julia left near the door, some of her spending money, and headed out to discover what the city looked like in the daylight. I explored some artsy shops at leisure. I toured a local museum and bought some name brand knockoffs at sidewalks vendors. I even bought myself a cheesy "I Love New York" T-shirt with the big red heart on it from a souvenir shop. Of course, I ate as well. I really enjoyed this part of my trip. I even skipped out on the rest of the nightly partying once I found the courage to venture out on my own. I was delighted at discovering the unique charisma the city possessed.

I concluded on my visit that my sister and I had nothing more in common than our history. I most definitely had no desire to visit her again.

On my last day, I had to leave Julia a thanks and goodbye note due to not being able to wake her up. Whatever she took to go to sleep really scared me. It was like she was dead, yet still breathing. I remember sitting on the edge of the bed after shaking her vigorously to wake her, only to have her continue in her coma-like state. I scanned over her frame, and that scared me as well. Only wearing a light tank top and bikini panties, Julia was almost completely exposed. She lay on her side with her hipbone and shoulder blades protruding. It was like her skin could barely keep the bones covered. I sat there puzzled as to why society painted women who looked emaciated as the portrait of beauty. Did beauty equate to unhealthy?

I felt so uneasy and wanted to just pretend she was okay, so I sat there long enough to resolve that maybe my sister had everything figured out. As she lay there motionless, no nightmares seemed to be haunting her. Nightmares chased me too often for my likings. I looked down at my thicker frame and looked healthier, but that was just the outside. I was the one who couldn't tolerate people touching me, while Julia let them hang all over her. She always seemed cool, collected, and carefree albeit by a pill or alcohol. I was the one plagued by severe panic attacks. Maybe… I shook off that notion and left my sister to her life. Who was I to try to figure her out? I was only eighteen and quite a mess myself.

Feeling unsettled and hopeless, I headed out for one last stroll around the small part of town I had become familiar with. I visited a bakery, which was highly recommended by some locals I met in a coffee shop earlier, and placed an overnight order for a New York style cheesecake to be sent to Miss May. I wanted to surprise her with it. Her sweet tooth was bigger than anyone else's I knew. I grabbed a single slice of cake for myself and sat at a patio table to enjoy it as I watched the city bustle by one last time. The cake was so rich and creamy. With each luscious bite, my thoughts drifted back to Julia. The realization that she would never be able to experience such a simple pleasure as eating a slice of cheesecake hit me in the pit of my stomach. I sat there staring at my half-eaten treat, not being able to take another bite. I was stunned at the pain I felt. Evan had robbed her of any simple joy this life offered. Everything revolved around complicated and dangerous—effortless was not a part of her world. I silently and tearlessly wept as I pondered all that had been robbed from my older sister. She was hiding under a drug-induced persona of having it all together.

I made my way back to Julia's apartment. I just had to check on her one more time. I left my sister another note, begging her to get some help and telling her how much I loved her. I sat on the edge of the bed, watching her sleep and trying to figure out a way to fix her. Not being able to come up with a solution, I reluctantly headed to the airport. I had wished I could gather my sister up and bring her back home with me, but New York was her life, not Bay Creek, and certainly not me. It was one of the few times I could remember actually wanting to go home.

Chapter Sixteen

Morning arrives with a mournful realization that today I will have to say a final goodbye to my dad. There is already a small crowd gathered, all dressed in black, when we pull into Jean's driveway. The mood is more somber than the past few days. Jean actually speaks to us as we enter the living room. She takes Lucas's arm and introduces him to her company, and I'm totally floored by her kindness. That is my mother. She always knows how to treat others better than me. I'm relieved to see her be so welcoming to my husband though.

Jean, John Paul, Lucas and I quietly ride in a black stretch limo to the chapel. No one speaks a word on the short drive. As we pull up in front of the chapel, another limo pulls in as well. Julia Rose exits the back, wearing a pair of oversized sunshades and a black slip dress that drapes over her frame. Her six-inch stilettos and a large brimmed hat rub me wrong. She's in full-blown starlet mode. She definitely does not fit in with the small beach town anymore, and her ensemble screams it. Jean seems so relieved to see my sister has finally made it. Julia joins us before we enter the chapel, and Jean embraces her in a hug that obviously lasted too long for Julia's liking. After giving John Paul and me a quick peck on the cheek, Julia takes John Paul's arm and we walk in together as a family. We share the front pew, and Julia keeps her glasses and gawky hat in place the entire time. It is the first time we gather in almost a decade. Regret and shame is how I feel at this sad fact.

The service is heart wrenching as most funerals are, but more so for me today. It's my turn to remember my loved one and to let him go. The large auditorium is overflowing with mourners. Many of my dad's employees have put together a touching tribute to him, filled with sayings my dad was popular for sharing. They also recount many memorable stories and pictures that represent my Dad's remarkable life. There is one picture where he and I are behind the counter at the market together. It captures me as a teenager with fluffy bangs, and my dad seems so young. Tears sting my eyes as I look through memories.

John Paul shares a short eulogy for the family. As he stands stoically in front of the congregation in his dark-grey suit, my heart swells with respect for him. I can only imagine the strength it is taking for him to stand there in front of us all and speak.

John Paul scans over his company and stands a bit straighter when he glances at my dad's casket before he begins. "Our father was a passionate man who loved our mother with every inch of his heart. He is the love of my mother's life and has always been a man that his children could look up to. Dad always put his all into anything he did. He was a good provider and a wonderful boss. His two businesses are landmarks to his dedication. He has set a good example that I know I should live my life by. We love him and we will truly miss him. We appreciate all of you for taking part in our father's life. I'm proud to say that his legacy will live on with my sister Savannah's help. She will see to it by taking over ownership of the restaurant as well as the market. This was our father's wish. He knew she would take care of them just as he would. I hope that very soon, we will all be able to gather back at the two establishments that our father dedicated his life to. This will be the best way that we can all honor him. Thank you." John Paul concludes in a shaky voice and eases back to the pew beside me, but he won't look at me.

People give me knowing glances the rest of the service as if they knew all along that I would take over the businesses. It is all I can do not to knock John Paul over the head for announcing my dad's wishes. I've not even decided if I want to take over them yet. Now what am I going to do? Lucas keeps giving my hand a slight squeeze as if letting me know it will all be okay. Julia is the only one that actually looks shocked by the news. She was always the favorite and maybe she thought she would inherit the family businesses one day. The child in me wants to stick my tongue out at her when she gives me her look of disbelief. I don't recall anything else shared during the service that follows my brother's announcement.

We somberly move to the graveyard and lay my dad to rest beside Bradley. During the finalization of the service, I keep my focus on my cousin's tombstone. The blue pearl granite headstone with intricate carvings of ocean waves is most fitting for him. My dad saw to that detail. The inscription states: *Whispering through the ocean's waves and the song of the mighty surf, I am with you always.*

The mourners eventually depart to give the family some time alone. We arrange some of the plants around both gravesites and stare numbly for a while. It's over too quickly, yet dragged out long enough.

To my mother's disappointment, Julia says her goodbyes to us at the gravesite. "I know you're not already leaving, sweetheart. You just got here." You can hear the hurt in Jean's voice.

"I know, but I'm in the middle of shooting extra scenes for my next movie. There's no way I can cancel. My plane leaves in an hour." She gives everyone a quick hug and climbs into the back of the waiting limo. Before she closes the door, she flashes our mother a big smile and says, "Maybe I can get back this way soon." Everyone knows that won't be happening.

Sensing something is up with my sister, I hurry towards the limo. "I'm going to make Julia give me a ride back to the house," I shout over my shoulder before climbing in. As I close the door, I turn to confirm my suspicions. My sister sits here shaking and big patches of hives are popping up all over her. "What's wrong, Julia?"

"I guess I'm still allergic to the South," she mutters as she pulls her oversized hat and sunglasses off, revealing herself as a hot mess.

"Excuse me sir, please head two blocks to the right. We need to make a stop at Bay Creek Pharmacy," I say to the limo driver. He gives his head a quick nod and gets us there in a flash. I run in, grab Benadryl and instant ice packs, and hurry back to the limo. I give Julia two pills with a bottle of water and then work on placing ice packs on the nastier whelps.

"Is your flight really about to leave?" Julia shakes her head no to my question. "Sir, could you just drive us around the beach for a while?" I ask as I work on removing my sister's shoes. Once I get her more comfortable, I undo the straps on my own shoes and slip them off. I grab myself a bottle of water, stretch out beside her, and try to relax too. We ride in silence for a while. Every now and then, I move the ice packs to another location. Eventually, her skin begins to resemble her normal complexion, so I decide to give her a hard time.

"You know you stole my line of being allergic to the South. I have copyrights and everything. I think I should sue you, Miss Hotshot Actress. I mean, shouldn't you have sent me a check by now, compensating me for leading you down the path of fame and fortune?" We both giggle at my ridiculousness, which is exactly what I'm going for. After this difficult day, a laugh is much needed.

"I thought I could handle this." She pauses to give her head a disappointed shake. "Dad deserved better than this from me." She motions to the mess of herself. "I've been trying to get up enough courage to come here for the past three days." We sit in silence for a while before she continues. She is staring out the window vacantly. "I see ghosts all over this place."

"Me too," I quietly agree. I push the button to raise the partition between us and the driver, feeling the need for some privacy. "The demons just won't stop dancing," I murmur as I gaze out of the heavily tinted window too.

"I am absolutely shocked that you are moving back," Julia declares. "I thought you were out for good too."

"I haven't agreed to take the businesses, yet. Our brother got a little ahead of himself today. I have Lucas and his career to consider. It ain't just all about me." I hesitate with self-doubt. I look over at Julia and ask, "Are you shocked that Dad would leave them to me?"

"No. Absolutely not. You can run them with your eyes closed. I just couldn't get over you being brave enough to move back." Julia shrugs her thin shoulder.

This is a relief to me to have my big sister's approval. Confidence is not my strong suit. We ride around for a while, when a groggy eyed Julia turns to me. The Benadryl is kicking in for sure.

"Dad and Jean came to New York for a visit about a month ago," she mutters in a fatigued voice.

Confusion and jealously hit me all at once.

"Really? Why?" I ask.

"They wanted a New York vacation—hitting some Broadway shows and shopping. Dad called to get some recommendations as to where to stay and I suggested my apartment. He was so excited that he immediately agreed without even consulting your mother." She grins at that thought. "They stayed for a week. You'll be proud that I made sure to feed them regularly. I also didn't involve them in any extracurricular crime." She snorts, causing us both to chuckle.

"I'm glad you and John Paul both have had some recent time with Dad. I just regret that I didn't." I slump back in the seat and tears wet my cheeks once again. I'm still not used to this emotion finally bubbling out.

"He told me he was planning to visit you next. He planned to beg you to move back and run the businesses. He didn't think John Paul could handle it all. He knew you were meant to do it and just needed to convince you of it." Julia pats me on my knee. I try to shake the regret off. I know there's nothing I can do about some things now.

Eventually the limo driver to heads back to Jean's house. I hold my sister's hand the rest of the ride. I'm proud that I am finally able to find comfort in someone's touch now. My Lucas has finally gotten that through to me. I wish my sister felt comfortable enough to stay a while, but I understand I cannot chase her demons away for her. I just hate the thought of letting her go again.

"You think it would be all right with you if I send John Paul up to visit you for a few weeks after the dust settles around here?" I ask.

Julia chews on the idea for a few minutes before answering. "You know, I think that's a great idea. I think it would do him some good," she says with a lazy grin. "I'll make all the arrangements and let you know when to haul him to the airport."

"Just make sure I get him back to me in one piece."

"Sure. We'll behave—"

I interrupt her when my memory recalls a particular someone who wanted her to behave. I've not thought of him in years, but cannot help but ask her about him now. "So… Greyson Stone?"

She rolls her eyes and looks out the window. "No… Greyson Stone." She sounds somber on the subject. Maybe even remorseful for some reason.

"Why not?"

She looks back over me and shakes her head. "The guy just dropped off the side of the earth last year, and I can't get ahold of him. His phone number no longer works, and the modeling agency won't give out any personal information." She shrugs. "It's like he has disappeared in thin air."

"I hope he is okay," I say.

Julia's perfectly manicured brows pinch together with her own concern as she nods her head in agreement. "He's such a pain, but I really do miss him."

"I think you need to find him and hold on for dear life." I nudge her in the side.

"He's too good for me. Besides, I *can't* find him. Trust me. I've tried. I've lost contact with his parents, so I don't even know how to get in touch with them anymore, either." Julia gives me a sad smile before directing her gaze back out the window. She misses him, it's obvious.

Once we arrive back to the house, I slide my shoes back on and I give Julia a long hug before letting her escape. As I watch the long limo drive away, sadness seeps through me. Not knowing when I will see her again always leaves me feeling so empty. I want her back. I want that thorny bush severed at the roots.

I reluctantly make my way into the crowded house. The buzz spreads through the group of mourners that I will be reopening the restaurant and market soon.

"We're all so glad that you are going to continue

your dad's legacy." I hear this or something on the same lines of it for the rest of the day. I'm amazed at how many told me that they always knew I would one day be the owner. I myself never had a clue. I'm still not so sure what in the heck I'm supposed to do.

I find Lucas sitting on the porch swing with a plate mounded full of the southern specialty, chicken bog with a side of butterbeans. He is so handsome sitting there with his tie undone and his suit jacket draped behind him on the swing. He looks young and boyish with his curly hair dancing lightly in the breeze as he shovels large forkfuls of food into his mouth. I stand here for a leisurely spell to admire this treasure of a man I have been blessed with.

"Nice looking plate," I say as I eventually take a seat beside him.

"It's scrumptious," he says as he shoves another forkful of the bog conglomeration of chicken, smoked sausage, rice, and secret ingredients into his mouth. "So, when exactly are you reopening?" Lucas asks this with such ease that I don't know whether he is picking on me or being serious.

"I've not made my mind up if I'm going to or not. I could kill John Paul for announcing that today. Now everyone is expecting me to do it." I'm still fuming at my brother. I'm also very confused by it all.

"I think your mind is already made up. You just

don't want to admit it yet."

I shoot Lucas a puzzled look over his remark. "You've always talked fondly of the two places. It seems like the main highlights of your childhood. I think it would be a shame if you pass this up." He reaches over to tuck my long hair behind my ear so that he can get a good look at me. I meet his confident gaze with my uncertain one.

"I totally agree," says John Paul as he joins us on the porch. His plate is piled higher than Lucas's with chicken bog. It is the first time I have seen him with an actual meal since I've arrived, and I am glad to see it.

"Don't you think you've said enough today?" I'm still pretty upset with his announcement at the funeral. "Why on earth did you do that to me?"

"I'm not giving you a chance to run away from this. I figured if I announced it, then your stubborn butt would finally have to make a commitment on taking care of the restaurant and market. And before you start in with me, I had a long talk with Lucas. Dude said he could do most of his work right from here." John Paul is more serious about this than anything else I can remember.

"Since you're so passionate about Dad's businesses, why don't you get off your lazy butt and run them yourself?" I stand to walk back into the house and John Paul gently grabs my arm.

"Dad and I had talked a while back on how things should be taken care of, Savannah. He didn't offer the businesses to me. He explained why and I agreed. You are better suited to do it. But I promise you this, if he would have offered it to me, I would have gladly agreed. Not because I want them, but because I would want to honor his last wishes." He lets go of my arm and tosses his untouched plate of food in a garbage can next to the steps before jumping off the porch and stomping hastily down the road.

I storm off after my brother so I can choke out an apology to him. I'm stubborn. These things don't come easy to me.

I catch up to him as we round the corner of the dirt road just before Bradley's field. "Would you slow down? Good grief!" I yell at his back. "I have *heels* on!" I kick them off and continue towards him.

"Why should I?" He spits the question out, but stops anyway. He rubs his hands over his face and sighs before yanking off his tie in aggravation.

"Look. To be honest, I'm pretty ticked about that stunt you pulled today. John Paul, you didn't even take into consideration how I would feel." I stand my ground with my hands pressed firmly on my hips.

I know I told you I'm going to apologize to him. Geez. Just give me a minute. I'm getting to it.

John Paul circles around with his hands on his hips, as though he's deciding his next course of action. He quickly decides to keep going in the direction of the field, taking long strides, and me stumbling behind him. He stops at the edge and gazes towards the spot. I do the same in an amicable silence and wait for him.

"I want to *dream*…I want to *live*…I want to be *happy*…" he whispers out in hesitation. He glances in my direction before looking back over the field. "The only time since…" he pauses to clear his throat. I can detect the emotions thick in his words. "The only time since I lost him that I have had any amount of happiness is when I have a camera in my hands. Photography has become my dream, Savannah." He sniffs back tears as he turns towards me and shakes his head in despair. "My heart ain't in Dad's dream. Never has been. I can't do it the way he would have wanted it done."

I eye my big brother sternly. "There's no way I'm going to take this on…" With this declaration, John Paul throws his hands up in defeat, mumbles out a few choice words, and turns to leave. I grab his arm and turn him back towards me. "*Unless* you agree to sneak me down to Scully's Cove this very instant."

Confusion, then understanding, flickers over his face. He shakes his head vigorously in opposition.

"*He— um, Heck* no! There's a tropical storm brewing up off the coast. The waves are way too gnarly." He crosses his arm and pinches his brows together to emphasize his protest.

"Why else would I be making a stink about wanting to go *today*?"

"Your girly butt can't handle those big boys!"

"Fine then. Nice seeing you. I'm going back to Rhode Island." I turn around and head in the direction of the house.

"You sure about this? I can take you next week when the weather is safer." The reluctance oozes from his voice.

"It's either today or never. How bad you want your dream, big brother?" I know I have already won this battle so I rub it in a little bit more for good measure. I'm the little sister, and it's my job. Right?

"You sure?" he asks again, and I know he's hoping I change my mind. He should know better. I'm stubborn—remember?

"Shine yeah!" I say then let out a whoop with excitement. I've been itching for this chance since I arrived home again.

~ ~ ~

We obviously cannot go back for our gear from

the house. I mean, how can one successfully sneak a surfboard out without a house full of mourners not getting suspicious? We end up *borrowing* bikes from the neighbor kids and haul tail to Scully's Surf Shop. The surf shop is named after the famous cove we are about to seek out. We run up a considerable tab with the needed supplies for our excursion.

We swap our funeral clothes for bathing suits topped with wetsuits and hand over the tags to the cashier before selecting our boards. I find me a sweet seven-foot two-inch Surf Betty. She is iridescent white and decorated with brilliantly colored hibiscus flowers. She should be taming the waves off the coast of Hawaii, but I hope I do her justice against the tropical storm waves off this South Carolina coast.

I go with a fun board but John Paul is all business with his selection. He rolls out with a manly six-foot-two-inch Perfection Fish. It's gorgeous with flames of fire and ice licking up and down the deck. The edges are accented with intense black patterns—it's tough.

We slow down long enough on the beach to prep the boards with wax before running full force towards the awaiting ocean. Now this is the one place where I truly feel free and at home at the same time. I'm nearly breathless with anticipation.

John Paul is faster at slicing through the water and I get caught inside, so he backpedals to help pull me out. We both duck dive under an unexpected wave and finally make it past the break.

Adrenaline is coursing rapidly through my veins as I search out my first wave. Before I can advance, John Paul grabs my ankle and pulls my board around until I'm facing him.

"You understand that nothing, and I do mean *nothing,* can happen to you on my watch," he says sternly. I see the apprehension skirt along his face.

I totally get why he says this. I will never understand the burden of guilt he carries for Bradley's accident. "Look, the only thing that's going to happen on your watch is me catching more waves than you, old man." I laugh wickedly before pulling away from him and towards pure bliss. "Now let's do this!" I squeal like an overexcited girl. Well, I guess that's exactly what I am.

I begin paddling towards a promise of a wave. With my hips firmly pressed to the deck, it's only me and the ocean, and it's hypnotizing. I leave all of the hurt and stress of the last several days on the shore and am ready to let the waves carry me away for a while.

We spend the afternoon competing for the best wave, with me only wiping out a minimal amount of times, but my brother rides the water like it's second nature to him. He is so fluid and graceful with this magnetic balance that I envy. I'm a bit rusty with my technique at first but eventually pick it back up just as you would with riding a bike.

By the time we make it onto the shore, my legs are trembling with exhaustion. "This has been the most fun I have had in ages." I giggle as I plop down on the beach. John Paul sits beside me, laughing. I'm pretty sure he's laughing at me and not *with* me. I am acting rather silly, but I don't care.

We sit and admire the majestic beast of the sea for a bit before he asks, "You seriously staying?" He's still not sure if he can be allowed to hope, I see. My brother deserves the freedom of hope.

I lean my head on his shoulder. "Yes, I'm seriously staying. I think maybe it's finally time to come home." I smile at the idea for the first time ever. I look out over the waves as the sun glistens off them, and I swear to you that big ole ocean smiles right back at me.

"Tell me a Bradley and John Paul tall-tale," I command as we sit on the beach to dry out some.

John Paul seems to be deciding which one, so I patiently wait. A wicked grin slowly creeps on his face, and when he starts speaking; boy does he serve up a doozy!

"Me and my man went fishing down at the Lewis Pond early one morning. You know that place should be called a mini lake, it's so massive. It hides all kinds of creatures, and you ain't wanting to tangle with 'em. We had just been there the day before and came close to finally snagging the king of that pond. That ole catfish had eluded fishermen for close to a decade. Mr. Lewis was pretty sure the monster was at least up to a hundred and fifty pounds and close to five feet long. Me and Bradley were eatin' up to wrangle that sucker in. Problem was, that catfish kept snapping our blame lines. We threw in the towel and pedaled straight over to the docks and talked Mr. Doyle out of some of his highest tension fishing line. He swore it could haul in at least a five hundred pound shark, so we felt pretty confident we finally had what we needed. So we were back down to the pond early that morning. We went to the same shallow area we had played tag with the beast the day before and got down to business. We filled the big hook full of rotten chicken livers and went to it. That bait stunk so bad, we thought the flies were gonna haul us away." John Paul mimics casting a fishing line and swatting at flies all at once.

"We hadn't been out there not even ten minutes when Bradley's pole came to life like a demon-possessed something." John Paul jerks about as he fights with his invisible pole. "Before I knew it, the pole was being dragged into the pond with Bradley right along with it. That's when I saw what he was playing tug-of-war with. And just let me tell you, it sure wasn't no catfish. It was a blame gator, and that thing had no intentions of losing to a ginger dude. But that gator didn't know that the ginger dude could get hot under the collar. It was Bradley's lucky fishing pole and my boy had no plans on losing it to a greedy gator." John Paul pauses to look at me. He shudders as though he's recalling this memory, but I know him better than that. He's really pausing so he can think up the rest of the story. I wait eagerly for him to continue to spin his tale.

"So the next thing I know that gator is bucking around like a wild bull with that boy riding it for dear life while punching it. He was swearing like a furious sailor and looked like he had gone pure crazy! I'm a southern gentleman, so I ain't repeating it to your delicate ears." He winks at me as he continues, causing me to laugh. My brother and the word gentleman do not go in the same sentence and we both know it. "It all happened so fast that I don't even think the boy knew what he was actually doing." John Paul is animating the story with his arms slinging around lively. He punches the sand to mimic Bradley beating on the gator.

I'm laughing hysterically at the farfetched story. "What happened?"

"I tossed a bag of the rotten chicken livers out in front of the ugly monster to distract it and it worked. The gator tired of playing tug of war and dropped the pole and slithered over to the livers. Bradley didn't lose his pole nor did the gator take a chunk of him, so we figured we won the battle. We gave that thing plenty of elbow room and went right back to fishing like nothing had happened."

I push my shoulder into his. "You know… If the whole photography thing doesn't work out, you can always make it as a professional storyteller." We both chuckle.

Do I believe a word of this story? No. The reality was probably closer to them boys going fishing and saw a gator swim by during their trip. The picture John Paul painted of Bradley is crazy in itself. He was mocking how people paint redheads as such fireballs. Our cousin was no such thing. He was the mildest, most considerate person I had known. And unlike my brother, he didn't use foul language. If this could have even remotely been close to a true story, John Paul would have played the lead role and not Bradley. I just know Bradley would have gotten such a kick out of the tale as much as I just did. We laugh until it turns into crying, and John Paul wraps his arm around me and we grieve for a spell. It's something past due and feels cleansing to be doing it now after all of these years.

With the sun setting, we eventually pedal our wet sticky selves back towards the house. We are loaded down with our funeral clothes hanging from the handlebars in plastic sacks from the surf shop. I hold on to my Betty for dear life in one hand while I to steer my borrowed bike with the other.

We have a hard time explaining to a group of eyebrow-raised mourners back at the house how we ended up on surfboards for the entire afternoon—especially since we had just buried our dad earlier this morning. We don't get past the porch before we are caught. We try to explain it away, but just end up looking like two guilty kids. I keep glancing at a smirking Lucas. He is having a hard time keeping his composure and has to hide a laugh behind a cough a few times during our confession.

Jean steps on the porch to scold us. "Just what do you have to say for yourselves?" she asks. Her face is in a snarl.

At this moment, John Paul's stomach lets out a loud gurgle. "I'm starving," is the only thing he has to say before he grabs my hand and leads me into the kitchen. We are still damp and sandy, but pay it no mind as we load our plates full of country cuisine. I even grab an extra plate and scoop up anything chocolate to accompany my meal. After we both chug our first glass of tea and refill it, we file back outside to the porch to enjoy our bounty of food. The porch seems like the only place where we both feel comfortable, so we sit in the swing and gorge while we explain the fundamentals of surfing to a curious Lucas. We promise a trip to the surf shop and ocean soon.

Lucas shakes his head as he leads me to his Jeep soon after we finish eating. "I can't believe I have a surfer chick for a wife," he says as he chuckles quietly. He pulls me close for a kiss and whispers, "A sexy one at that."

The sun has long gone for the day, and a beautiful full moon has taken over for the night. The clouds have decided to take a hike too, and so a crystal clear night sky glows softly.

I sigh as we head up the wide, tiled steps of the beach house. It's really a lovely bungalow and I have to admit I love it.

"What?" Lucas asks as we push through the front door and into the impressive foyer. An intricate wrought iron chandelier cascades from the ceiling and greets us as we head into the kitchen.

"I'm gonna really hate to leave this place," I say as I run my hand over the blue Spanish tile on the kitchen counter.

Lucas grabs a bottle of water from the fridge. He

takes a sip and offers me some. I take a big gulp before handing it back.

"We sign the paperwork on it tomorrow, milady," Lucas says as he slightly bows and gives me a wink.

"What?"

He places the bottle on the counter and pulls me towards him. "The realtor is swinging by in the morning before I have to head back to Rhode Island. I've got some loose ends to work out there before we set out on this new venture."

My brows pucker because I have not considered this life change for my husband. He soothes the pucker with his thumb and answers my unspoken concerns. "Don't worry about it. As long as I have my beautiful wife by my side I'm content with whatever life puts before me." He looks around. "This place isn't so bad."

I'm still not so sure, so he pulls me closer and places a kiss on my forehead. "Mmm…salty." He chuckles as he licks his lips before continuing. "Savannah, I can do most of what I need to do for Monroe Enterprise from here." He has a point. He does most of his work from our condo, so I let it go.

"Fine," I say as I release him and peel off the wetsuit. He eyes the turquoise bikini that was hidden underneath.

"Nice," he says before pulling me back towards him. I take this opportunity to rid him of his tie and undo the buttons of his shirt. I run my hands along the smooth expanse of his chest. "You're a bit overdressed," I whisper as I slide the shirt completely off. I glance back outside and turn to lead Lucas there.

He abandons his socks and shoes on the deck as we pass by. Once we make it onto the sand, I circle my hands around his neck. "I've danced many a dances with demons on this beach in my dreams," I say as I meet his eyes. "I want to dance with my angel now. I want a better relationship with this beach. Think you can help me out with that, big boy?"

"Absolutely, love," he murmurs. With understanding, Lucas gathers me in his arms and we set out on a dance that is achingly sweet. As we dance, I shed what's left of my demons. I've carried them long enough. We circle and let the melody of the sea lull us into our own intimate world. In this moment, I think that maybe, *just maybe,* I'm going to be okay.

Chapter Seventeen

The sun is dancing in warm glowing tones so beautifully throughout the room this morning. I can hear the ocean waves kissing the shore good morning just outside. I feel so peaceful and content in this moment, and for the first time the picture of myself staying is crystal clear.

I roll over and watch Lucas sleep for a while. He is stretched out lying on his back and is as always hogging both sides of the bed, with one hand hanging off his side of the bed and the other holding onto my thigh. The man sprawls in his sleep as if he is always seeking me out. I'm confident that I can live anywhere and accomplish anything as long as I have him by my side. I quietly sneak out of the bed and let him catch up on some much-needed rest. My family and I can be pretty exhausting, and I feel bad for Lucas having to deal with it all.

I get dressed and head down the shore to the Beach Shack to pick up some local breakfast favorites for Lucas. It is just as I have remembered it. It still looks like an old shack about to fall over, and it is already packed at seven in the morning. Several fishermen, already adorned in their fishing bibs, are grabbing large cups of coffee and biscuits to go. I recognize a few of the older ones for they are direct sources for the restaurant. One of the men waves me over. He's a big, brawny man who looks like a lumberjack in fishing gear, with a red plaid shirt peeping under his bib. He sports a bushy, black beard that goes well with his bushy head of black hair. He looks rough and can act tough, but he is just a big teddy bear.

"Hey there, sweetheart. It's a pure shame 'bout your old man," Billy says as he pats my shoulder in a condoling manner.

"I agree," I say in a low voice. The realization that he is truly gone keeps creeping up on me unexpectedly. It just doesn't seem right at all.

"You call me up when you need the market restocked, okay?" he says as the rest of his group starts shuffling towards the door.

"Sure thing, Billy," I say and resume my people

watching.

There is a good-sized crowd of sun-worshiping tourists ready to get their day at the beach underway. You can pick up whiffs of sunblock floating faintly through the air as it mingles with the greasy aroma. The tourists are easy to spot. They are the ones that stand before the large menu board with their mouths gaped open and their eyes bouncing around at the choices. They seem at awe over the delectable breakfast options and are having a hard time trying to decide what they want. This is opposite from most locals, who never lift their gaze to the menu board. They normally have a set favorite and order it religiously every time – me included. I have not set eyes on the menu in almost a decade, but I know exactly what I want.

"Good morning, darlin'. What can I get ya?" the waitress at the counter asks.

"I know what that young lady wants. Don't worry her with ordering!" a familiar gruff voice pipes in at the kitchen opening. I look over to find a short, burly man grinning at me from underneath his thick, unruly, grey whiskers. He wipes his hands on his greasy apron as he approaches me. He is a good bit shorter than me, so I have to stoop at bit to receive his hug. I notice he is barefoot as always. Jarrette is the owner of this fine shack and cooks up the greasy yet scrumptious fare.

"There's no way you remember my order," I say.

"You want an order of the best biscuits and gravy with extra sausage, apple stuffed pancakes, and a large coffee," he answers proudly with a huge smile. He's confident he has it right. Of course, he does.

"Double the order and you've got it right, sir. And it's to go," I smile back.

"Comin' right up," he says as he heads back into the kitchen. I can't help but wonder what the food health inspectors think of his bare feet. I shake my head and laugh.

The waitress hands me a cup of coffee, as is the longstanding tradition of the Beach Shack to give customers with to-go orders a cup of coffee to enjoy while they wait on the food. As I sit at the counter waiting, I look around at the buzz of everyone coming and going. I watch the restaurant staff working in sync with one another and I begin to get excited about my opportunity of running not one but two businesses of my very own. I finally feel like this is what I'm supposed to be doing with my life.

I admit I love the laidback atmosphere of Bay Creek. That was never the issue. I will just have to stop looking in the past and keep my focus on the present and towards the future. Before I get too far out there daydreaming about my new life ahead, the waitress delivers my food. I pay and head back to the beach house to surprise Lucas with the delicious breakfast. It is all I can do to stay out of the bag until I get back. The aroma makes my mouth water in anticipation. I just know it's going to be good. The evidence is clearly on the white bag in the form of glorious grease stains.

I quietly creep upstairs and find Lucas still sprawled out, sleeping away. I wave the bag back and forth close to his nose until he opens one eye at me.

"Hmm. That smells wonderful." He stretches a long stretch and gives me a quick kiss before snatching the bag out of my hand. I love how playful he can be first thing in the morning. He is one of those obnoxious morning people. I am not, and this trait of his is annoying if he wakes before me. But since I have been up quite a while, I'm enjoying it. He sits up and begins pulling the food out. I sit here and admire the view of him in his rumpled boxer shorts. His light brown hair looks so boyish with the curls sticking up all over. Those bedroom eyes of his…

"I think this is for you," he says as he hands me a note that has been tucked in the bottom of the bag, which forces me out of my lustful thoughts. I pull my eyes away from Lucas and read the note. It states in scrawling handwriting that is none other than Jarrette's, *Good luck with the restaurant and market. I know you will do your dad proud.*

"Humph." It is inspiring to know that people have faith in me.

We munch on the delicious breakfast and joke about how we probably have gained a good ten pounds apiece in the past few days. *Not really, but still.* There are just too many good southern cooks living in Bay Creek. We laze around in the bed for a good part of the morning, enjoying the slower pace for a while.

"I can already tell you we have to replace this queen-sized bed with a king, Mr. Bed Hog." I laugh while playfully shoving him off my side of the bed. No matter what size bed we own, it will always be the same—as it should be.

We laugh my joke off before I start wrestling with some doubt. "Do you really want to give Bay Creek a shot?" I ask. I burrow close into his comforting chest and breathe in the warm, familiar smell of him.

"Only if you want to," Lucas says. He wraps his arms around me and pulls me even closer. He places a gentle kiss on my forehead. I love his strength and gentleness all at the same time. We lay in each other's arms for a while before I begin to try to talk us out of moving.

"But what about your job? What about our condo? What about your family? Won't you miss them?" I let out a long list of questions.

Lucas brushes a light kiss over my lips before looking me in the eyes and says, "We can make this work. Have a little faith."

"Easier said than done, Mr. Monroe." I sigh and give him a long kiss before I climb out of the bed. I need another opinion. *I'm not procrastinating, okay? I'm just making sure…*

"Not running away, are you?" he questions as he tries to grab a hold of me.

I squirm out his grasp, giggling. "No sir. I promise to return." I grab his Jeep keys and blow him a kiss as I skip out the door.

I head straight to the one who I know will give it to me straight, whether I want to hear it or not. I pull into her driveway and am about to climb out of the Jeep when the passenger door opens, surprising me. I have no idea where the little lady came from. She's quicker than I give her credit for.

"Take me for a ride in this Jeep Wrangler. That way I got plenty to talk about with my great-grandbaby the next time he visits," She grunts as she tries unsuccessfully to climb up into the tall Jeep. She may be fast, but she can't climb worth a lick.

I have to laugh as I walk to her side to give her a boost. "Up you go, old lady," I laugh some more as I plant her in the passenger seat.

"It comes in handy to have an unusually tall

Thorton child around," she chuckles herself.

"I ain't that tall. It's that you're unusually short," I say with a smile.

"Watch your mouth, young'un," she says, causing me to laugh some more.

I climb back in and pull out onto the highway, still laughing at the craziness of the situation.

"You know, you really shouldn't talk to old people like you do." Miss May says with a smirk.

"I really can't help I'm a smart-mouthed brat." I laugh.

"Good point." She laughs too. I love this woman more than my teeth, 'cause she gets me and loves me anyways.

I drive Miss May down to the pier and along the beach boulevard, while she wears a huge grin on her face. She waves at everyone, whether she knows them or not. I eventually park at a beach access and we gaze out over the crowd already gathered on the sandy shore. It's gonna be a beautiful day.

"When we reopening?" she asks as she looks over at me. She is quite a sight sitting there with her hair rollers tucked in neat rows over her silver head, wearing Lucas's Ray Bans. The sun was giving her eyes a fit, and they are the only shades I could find in the glove box. These are the Wayfarer style that my man can pull off charmingly. Miss May—not so much. She doesn't seem to mind, so I keep my smart-mouthed closed for a change.

"I just don't know," I say hesitantly.

"Well, we both know yo' procrastinatin' butt is gonna eventually do it, so just go ahead and decide already. I'm sick of sittin' home." She looks at me over the top of the sunglasses. She eyes me until I roll my eyes back her. "I ain't gettin' any younger, you know."

"Don't I know it, and that's one of my problems. I don't want to even think about doing any of this without you." I let the silent understanding of this statement pass between us. I know we don't know the number of our days, but Miss May's is clearly becoming limited. I banish this thought—it hurts too much to even think it.

"You ain't got to worry 'bout a thing, 'cept openin' back up. Them places runs themselves. Besides, I've been trainin' my granddaughter, Vanessa, for the past five years. Another five years and she should be able to handle it on her own." She slides me a wink over the rim of the sunglasses and smiles.

"Well, that sounds mighty appealing. Vanessa and I used to waitress together," I say as I pull on my ear in thought. We let the subject drop and I drive Miss May around the beach for a while longer.

Later in the afternoon, I drop Miss May back at her lovely little home.

"I sure have missed you, old lady," I say as I give her a long hug after scooping her out of the Jeep and depositing her in the yard. I walk her to the porch.

"Me too, girl. You 'bout to see a lot of me, don't worry. I sure am glad you finally decided to reappear. We've got a lot of catching up to do," she says as I turn to leave.

"I look forward to it. You have to promise to share your cheesecakes from Julia with me, though," I wag my finger at her.

"As long as you and your handsome husband drive me to church every Sunday in one of yo' fancy cars," she offers.

"You have yourself a deal," I agree.

I head over to the restaurant for a visit. I push through the door and inhale deeply. My throat catches over the absent aromas of fresh seafood being prepared. It's an injustice, I know. I walk over to my dad's and my favorite booth and have a seat. This is the booth we would normally take our late lunch breaks together. I sit and inspect the dining hall. It is crisp and fresh with newly painted white walls. There is no evident dust on the giant ocean and beach shore landscape paintings by a local artist, R.H. Ewol. There are three original paintings along the left wall. They have always been a favorite of mine. I scan over them slowly and then look around some more. This place has been so well cared for, I can only hope I'm able to do it justice.

Tears begin to slide down my cheeks as more forgotten memories pay me a visit. I scoot under the table to make absolutely certain that this is the exact same booth. I smile when I see the evidence that it is. Lucas carved our initials on the underside late one night after closing. It was the night he accompanied me back from college to ask my dad for his permission to marry me. I run my fingers along the carving as that memory dances happily.

Dad took a break long enough to share an appetizer and a glass of sweet tea with us before Lucas bravely asked him. My dad was so thrilled for us that he stood up on the booth bench and announced to the entire restaurant our good news.

"Ladies and gentlemen, I'd like to share with you all that my beautiful daughter has been blessed with finding her true love, and he has asked my permission to marry her," my dad announced proudly. The crowd broke out in applause, and I can still remember my face becoming bright red. "I guess I have no other choice but to agree!" He was crazy about Lucas, as anyone who meets him is. Dad seemed so proud and happy for me that grand day, it was one of my favorite days to spend with him.

The only way I could ensure my dad giving me away was to have the wedding in Bay Creek, which was perfect for a beach wedding at sunset. It was a breathtaking evening in late August. The warm breeze wasn't too overpowering, and the ocean was peacefully calm. The stunning landscape served as the wedding decorations. It was more exquisite than any floral bouquet or draped fabric could have ever offered. I'm not one of those frilly types of girls anyways. Out on that beach, I felt free and content without any pressure of putting on some show for the guests. It was a ceremony like one should be, in my opinion.

The men wore white linen shirts and soft khaki pants with bare feet. The women wore coral sundresses with their feet bare as well. I wore a simple white sundress with my long, dark, wavy hair adorned with a cream and coral–hued hibiscus flower tucked behind my ear. It was a simple service of Lucas and I pledging our love and commitment for one another before our close friends and family, and most importantly, God.

My parents took care of the reception, to my astonishment. It was held at the restaurant. Jean planned the entire mouthwatering menu. Best of all, Miss May helped to cook it. My mother also decorated the restaurant very elegantly. Candles served as the main lighting, and simple white floral arrangements with delicate pieces of driftwood tucked in various places cascaded on each table. A section of tables was removed and a portable dance floor was brought in. I'm smart enough to have recognized Jean's intentions to simply show off her talents, but it didn't bother me. It was the best day of my life, no matter her intentions. It was one of the very few times where it felt as though she and I waved temporary white flags. We kept our distance from each most of the day, sure, but I never saw her giving me that *you stink* look.

I scoot back into the booth and reminisce for a long while. The good memories are there, I'm beginning to realize. I've just buried them so far under the bad ones; it's a relief comfort to know they are there. All I have to do is hunt for them and stop letting the nightmares blind me. I resolve a few things in this moment and abruptly stand and make my way to my dad's office. I think I've put this off long enough, don't you?

Sitting in his chair behind the desk, I pick up the phone and record a new voice message. "On behalf of my family, I, Savannah Monroe, would like to thank you for your outpouring of support during this difficult time. In honor of my dad's wishes, I will be reopening the market as well as the restaurant within the next week. We will be planning a Patron Appreciation Celebration in memory of my dad. Details of the event will be posted on our website and will be in this Sunday's paper. Thank you again." I'm already thinking of some menu specials and maybe offering a free appetizer table for the event as I hang up the phone.

I eye an extra shirt hanging from a hook on the back of the office door. I smile, knowing that a complete changing of clothes is tucked in the bottom drawer of his desk. I slide the draw open for confirmation. And sure enough, the stack of clothing sits there folded neatly. Jean demanded this after me and Dad played in the inlet that afternoon. I smile at the memory and grab the shirt off the top of the pile. I bring it to my nose and inhale the faint scent of his cologne.

You know…If I allow it…I do believe I'm going to be just fine. The freedom of letting go of my demons has given me a better perspective. I know I have wasted too much time. It's amazing how a dreaded trip home again can assist in finally making peace with the nightmares spawned here.

Epilogue

A year has passed…And I'm still home!

Things were bumpy at first, but I'm happy to say that I have finally gotten into the swing of things. Both of the businesses practically run themselves. So well in fact, I get to spend lots of time with Miss May in the kitchen. She has made me play nice with the creek kids—that's what I call them most of the time. They call me Old Lady Monroe, so sometimes I still call them brats. Once a week, I am on hush baby and sweet tea duty. They all voted unanimously that I not share anymore lessons with them. Fine by me.

I work alongside Vanessa, and we have formed quite a bond. It hit me just a while back that she is my very first girlfriend. We even do the girlfriend things like shopping. I guess I have come a long way. Don't tell Miss May, but I think Vanessa can cook just as good as the old lady!

I'm also happy to tell you that my brother is famous now. Yep, and he blames it all on me. Don't worry. He's over being mad at me about this. In fact, that was short lived.

I went behind his back as only a little sister can get away with. John Paul opened The Thorton Photo Gallery a month after our dad's funeral. His most mesmerizing piece is this stunning mural collage that takes up the entire back wall of the studio. It is an array of his images intricately pieced together and is none other than Bradley's field. It spellbinds visitors who have no clue of the history behind it. It is a mirage of the field. The first time I saw it, I was left speechless.

To describe it to you is such an injustice to its magnificence. But I shall try anyway. A section of the mural is of various sunsets filtering together to create one, and all along the top depicts vast rainstorms with varying tempests. Foggy images lend a mystic quality as they undulate around the center of the piece. But the most haunting part of all is the very center. These images capture perfectly and eerily a mourning woman. Now I wasn't crazy with the idea of me being figuratively and physically the center focus of my brother's art piece, but you become so enveloped into the story being told and can easily see past me.

It is absolutely brilliant, so I had no other choice but to go behind his back and enter the mural in a prestigious national photography contest.

I had talked him into accompanying me on a quick trip to California. John Paul didn't find out the purpose of the trip until we walked through the door of the art museum. Blown-up versions of his mural hung on display throughout the exhibit.

I was the most hated and yet the most loved sister in the same moment. Hated because I totally caught him off guard. Plus I think there is some unsaid rule about not messing around with an artist's work without their permission. It would be like him posting this letter I've written to you on the internet for the entire world to read. That would totally suck because this is a pretty private conversation we've been having here.

But I was also the most loved in that instant as well, because he won every blame award given that night. It put his talented behind on the map as well. It opened bountiful doors for his career.

John Paul lives only a few beach houses down from mine and he helps me close a few nights a week. That is, unless some high-profile photo shoot whisks him away as it has done this week. He is in Fiji at the moment shooting surf images for a surf magazine.

Yes. I'm green with envy, also so proud of him.

Honestly, the loss of my dad still stings. But memories, those precious jewels, keep coming to the surface and oh, how I cherish them. One comes to mind now. I've decided that my family should be known as the Cookie Bandits—my dad included.

This past Christmas, Miss May roped me into helping her make cookies for our creek kids. That day while I was standing by the counter rolling out the sugar cookie dough, a special memory of my dad tapped me on the shoulder and brought a smile to my face.

It was of a past Christmas, and Jean had prided herself on these fancy cookies she had made for Santa. They were beautifully decorated and smelled heavenly. She dared us not to touch them, saying they were for Santa and Santa only. She had indulged a little too much on her holiday wine and had to retire early that night. Temptation was just too great, so when I snuck downstairs to swipe a cookie, I was horrified at what I saw. You can imagine how startled I was to find my dad scarfing down the cookies. He must have just gotten home, because I remember the savory aroma of cooked seafood clinging to his clothes.

"Daddy!" I scolded him.

"Shh…" He tried to hush me but ended up

spraying cookie crumbs everywhere.

My eight-year-old self was near tears when I noticed he had eaten every single cookie and Santa wouldn't be getting any.

"Don't cry. Shh…" he tried again unsuccessfully. His mouth was overfilled and his cheeks bulged out, causing him to look like a chipmunk. He raised his hands up in surrender as he tried to chew the treats quickly so he could swallow.

"What about Santa?" I sniffled.

He started pulling me towards the front door. "Come on. Slide some shoes on and I'll make this right. Just please don't cry."

And making it right, he did. He drove us straight to the restaurant where we mixed up a batch of sugar cookies. He said he had the recipe memorized from watching Miss May make them over the years. Once we baked them, he gathered the cookies and me and headed back home to set them out for Santa. He let me eat a few, and I went to bed happily afterwards.

Now just let me share what I find so funny about this memory with seeing it through my adult eyes. Santa did eat those fancy cookies and the poor man had to eat another plate full after his busy daughter went to bed. My dad had an unexplainable bellyache Christmas Day and declined any dessert.

I snicker now just thinking about it. It's a good

memory and reminds me how much he cared about me. Boy, do I appreciate it so much more now.

As for Jean…Well, I have to admit, that women blessed me with the grandest gift she has ever given me earlier this year. She moved to Florida.

She signed the house and its belongings over to John Paul as expected, packed her bags, and departed without so much as a glance back. I know it's for the best. Some things just aren't salvageable. We are simply at an impasse…

Now, I have to tell you, that house met its demise rather abruptly not even a month after our mother's departure. Luckily and *coincidentally,* all of John Paul's photos had been conveniently relocated to his gallery the week before the fire. (I clear my throat here and don't judge.) I only asked my brother once about this.

He simply replied, "Some demons need to be properly sent back to hell." And that is all he would say about that. I couldn't agree with him more. It's a relief and comfort for the sin-stained structure to be gone. It had held a tremendous weight with the secrets always crying out and now it is at peace, too.

I wish I could share something wonderful and positive about my sister, but I've only spoken to her one time since Dad's funeral. I hope in her time Julia can figure things out for herself. I worry and I pray and hope she is fine. But I have my doubts.

My Lucas is doing great. We spend most of our mornings at the home of Ocean and Waves. He has become quite the surfer. And let me just say, a tanned slightly rumpled Lucas in board shorts… yummy! He manages the two businesses and just lets me enjoy the social aspects of it really. He turned a majority of his responsibilities in Rhode Island over to his older brother, but he still does a good share of work for his family business as well via the Internet and occasional trips back home.

That hot man in question has just sauntered through the office door and—I kid you not—he is carrying a surfboard and only wearing slightly damp board shorts riding nicely on his lean hips. His curly hair is going in every direction, giving him the air of boyish mischief. My eyes take in the nice view of his bronze shoulders, speckled with the sexiest freckles. Channing Tatum has nothing on my man. I continue watching Lucas as he props the board on the wall and heads over to the closet where he keeps a change of clothes for work. The man is eye candy and I can't help but watch. He is about to free himself from those wet shorts and I'm about to not be able to form another cohesive thought, so I clear my throat to get his attention. He looks over at me as he pulls the shorts a bit farther down, exposing a delicious tan line on that well-formed backside of his.

I hold my finger up for him to pause and mutter, "Nuh-uh." If that man takes those shorts off I might as well forget all else. Don't focus your eyes at me disapprovingly. He's my husband, and I'm allowed.

Those luscious eyes hold a wicked glint as he heads back to the door to secure the lock. *Focus, Savannah. Focus.* Okay…Where was I? *I've got to wrap this story up quickly.*

I'm amazed that God can take a mess of a life and make something wonderful out of it. I no longer feel like a mistake, and I'm confident that I have found my way in this world. The demons don't dance so much anymore. As much as I hate to admit it, my mother was correct when she said that I am the only one that can decide who I am. My life is my own and I get to choose the direction of it. Past experiences and daily struggles do make an impact, but it is up to me whether I allow it to be a negative or positive impact.

That day face down in the mud in Miss May's yard was a day of reckoning between me and God. I gave Him all my hurts and disappointments, and asked Him to free me from it all. And He did! I had made such a simple freeing gesture into something so complicated. Why do we do that?

So this is my journey to come home again. Even though it's been a long, challenging course, I have persevered. Did I think it was possible? Absolutely not. I didn't make the journey unscathed, but I know now, that with God, all things are possible.

I found myself. I really did. I found myself. Right where I hid.

Coming Home Again Playlist

"Carry On" by Fun
"Demons" by Imagine Dragons
"Landslide" by Stevie Nicks
"Sail" by Awolnation
"Ghost" by Ella Henderson
"The Struggle" by Tenth Avenue North
"Time After Time" by Cyndi Lauper
"Glitter in The Air" by P!nk
"Pepper" by Butthole Surfers
"I'm Not Who I Was" by Brandon Heath
"Oceans" by Hillsong United

ABOUT THE AUTHOR

If T.I. isn't writing a book, she's reading one. She's proud to be a part of a tiny town in South Carolina where she is surrounded by loved ones and country fields.

For a complete list of Lowe's published books, biography, upcoming events, and other information, visit http://www.tilowe.com/ and be sure to check out her blog, COFFEE CUP, while you're there!

She loves to connect with her reading friends.

ti.lowe@yahoo.com

https://www.facebook.com/T.I.Lowe/

Made in the USA
Monee, IL
31 December 2023

50853542R00204